# HUNTING
# FOR HEMINGWAY

A DD McGIL LITERATI MYSTERY

# HUNTING
# FOR HEMINGWAY

DIANE GILBERT MADSEN

**THORNDIKE**
**CHIVERS**

This Large Print edition is published by Thorndike Press, Waterville, Maine, USA and by AudioGO Ltd, Bath, England.
Thorndike Press, a part of Gale, Cengage Learning.

LIBRARY OF CONGRESS CATALOGING-IN-PUBLICATION DATA

Madsen, Diane Gilbert.
    Hunting for Hemingway : a DD McGil literati mystery / by Diane Gilbert Madsen.
        p. cm. — (Thorndike Press large print mystery)
    ISBN-13: 978-1-4104-3218-6
    ISBN-10: 1-4104-3218-1
    1. Insurance investigators—Fiction. 2. Hemingway, Ernest, 1899–1961—Manuscripts—Fiction. 3. Large type books. I. Title.
PS3613.A289H86 2010b
813'.6—dc22                                      2010034512

BRITISH LIBRARY CATALOGUING-IN-PUBLICATION DATA AVAILABLE

Published in 2010 in the U.S. by arrangement with Midnight Ink, an imprint of Llewellyn Publications, Woodbury, MN 55125-2989 USA.
Published in 2011 in the U.K. by arrangement with Llewellyn Worldwide, Ltd.

U.K. Hardcover: 978 1 408 49347 2 (Chivers Large Print)
U.K. Softcover: 978 1 408 49348 9 (Camden Large Print)

Printed in the United States of America
1 2 3 4 5 6 7 14 13 12 11 10

This book is dedicated to my dad,
Albert N. Gilbert,
and best friend
Andrew Raymond Klosowski (Ray)

Both gone too soon

# ACKNOWLEDGMENTS

All my thanks to Christopher Andrew Schneider for crafting the Hemingway short story fragments. His writing talents are truly remarkable.

I will always appreciate talking "all things Hemingway" with my Oak Park neighbor, Morris Buske — a true gentleman and scholar who was a delight to have known.

There's only one Thomas J. Joyce of Joyce and Company Rare Books in Chicago, and I can't thank him enough for his expert advice on manuscripts and bibliophilia and for his friendship.

Many thanks also to Leslie Hindman of Leslie Hindman Auctioneers in Chicago for her kindness and invaluable insights into the complex world of auction houses.

Sincere appreciation to Gordon Drawer for again being the vigilant wingman on Chicago verisimilitude. His suggestions and humor are always right on.

Thanks to Grace Morgan, agent and friend; and to Bill Krause and the rest of the team at Midnight Ink for all their talent.

As always, ever to my husband, Tom Madsen.

All things truly wicked
start from innocence.
— ERNEST HEMINGWAY

# PROLOGUE

December 2, 1922 LAUSANNE, Switzerland: The Chateau Ouchy: The American was twenty-three, tall and muscular, a veteran of the First World War. He'd recently arrived from Paris to cover the Greek-Turk Peace Conference for the *Toronto Star* newspaper. He was newly married and cabled Feather Cat, his private name for his wife, to come join him in Lausanne.

December 2, 1922 PARIS, France: 74 rue de Cardinal Lemoine: The wife was also an American from the Midwest. They lived off her dwindling inheritance in a tiny loft apartment in Paris while her husband worked at becoming a writer. Feather Cat had a bad cold and had not accompanied her husband, whom she affectionately called Poo. Responding to his pleas, she packed and made arrangements to take the train to Switzerland. She loaded all her husband's writings into a separate small valise so that he could work on them, and maybe sell something.

December 2, 1922 PARIS: Gare de Lyon Train Station: The train, typical of the time, had compartments to provide passengers with privacy. Feather Cat handed her baggage to the porter, keeping the small valise. She went straight to her compartment. Before departure, she left to check on her luggage and purchase a newspaper. The valise was gone when she returned.

December 3, 1922 LAUSANNE: The train station: The husband met Feather Cat when the train arrived. She wept uncontrollably, unable to tell him what was wrong. Poo comforted her, saying that no matter what had happened, nothing could be that bad. She told him of the missing valise and his work.

December 3, 1922 LAUSANNE: The train station: Disbelieving, the husband immediately boarded the next express train for the twelve-hour journey back to Paris. Poo left Feather Cat in Switzerland.

December 4, 1922 PARIS: 74 RUE DE CARDINAL LEMOINE: The husband inquired at the Gare de Lyon train station. He searched the entire loft. He found only one story, "Up in Michigan," in the back of a drawer. Three years of writing, including the carbon copies, were gone. He was especially angry about the carbon copies.

# ONE:
## DAY 1: SUNDAY

Love is like a war — Easy to begin —
Hard to end.
— SCOTTISH PROVERB

My name is DD McGil, and please don't ask what the DD stands for. I'm female, blonde, a Scot, and in the insurance investigations business — all of which, I frequently remind people, doesn't necessarily make me a bad person. I make my living in and around the Windy City — quite a nice place, politics aside. Chicago strives to be an elegant city, but somehow it never gets too far from its name which, taken from the Ojibwa Indians, means "skunk."

Chicago, known as "the Second City" until L.A. went on steroids, is 579 feet above sea level. There was a time when my feet were firmly planted on terra Chicago — but not lately. I'd like to start at the beginning, but there wasn't really a beginning — only an ending. It all happened eight months ago — eight long months ago when I was in the midst of a great relationship with a terrific guy named Scotty Stuart. Eight long months ago when I didn't believe in curses. Then my doorbell rang, and I got the news. Since that day I've been fighting desperately to keep my head above water.

The problem was that things had been going too well, and I'd forgotten one of my Auntie Elizabeth's favorite maxims. She warned me at least a hundred times that we Scots must always pay attention to the cogs in the universe and keep watch over our shoulder — most especially when things are going well. I didn't. And that's when the universe ran me over.

It was a Tuesday, a frosty Chicago evening with the wind howling and the stars so bright and clear any sailor could have easily navigated his way to my third-floor walk-up apartment in Wrigleyville. I remember I wasn't at all upset when Scotty failed to appear for our *tête à tête* dinner. He was involved with the International Monetary Fund, doing all kinds of top-secret things with worldwide currency, and was often called away unexpectedly, especially in the wake of the current global economic crisis.

So I shrugged it off, sipped my pinot grigio and petted my cat, believing I was safe and secure, 579 feet above sea level. As I watched the clouds obscure the moon, I never saw the big wave headed right for me. I thought I knew everything there was to know about Scotty Stuart, but I didn't know what I really needed to know.

After two frantic days without any word from Scotty, the cops finally agreed to list him as a missing person. Then for the next four months, I investigated. I should say tried to investigate. There were no leads, no clues as to what had happened to him or where he'd gone. His car was gone. His cell phone and credit cards hadn't been used, and no one had heard from him. He hadn't bought an airline ticket, a train, or a bus ticket. I harassed the cops at the police station every day. I harassed Scotty's friend in the Treasury, Harry Marley, whom I'd met working on the HI Data counterfeiting case, and I constantly touched base with Jerry Frehling, Scotty's boss. For all my hotshot investigating, all I uncovered was a big zero. No one had seen him — nobody knew his whereabouts. Even my Aunt Elizabeth, who often has premonitions, was no help. All she could say was, " 'Tis a blank, DD. Try as I might, only darkness swirls. I ken nothing."

Her pronouncement and the fact that there wasn't one single clue made me even more frightened and more obsessed. I had to find out what happened. I dropped all my other jobs, made it my only case, and kept investigating, using every angle I could devise.

Then late one night, my doorbell rang. I was curled up with my cat on the sofa, and a sudden chill shook me. Scotty! I rushed to the peephole, hoping, wishing, praying. No luck. It was someone I'd never seen before — a big guy with broad shoulders and a good haircut wearing glasses with steel frames. He didn't look like a cop, but you never know. Sighing, I opened the door on the chain — wide enough for me to see him but not wide enough to let my Ragdoll cat, Cavalier, run into the corridor. How was I to know that even that little opening was enough to let the wave crash in on me.

"DD McGil?"

"Who wants to know?"

He flashed a Secret Service identity badge at me, but held his thumb over his name. My knees buckled. I grabbed the doorknob for support.

"Stop searching for Scotty Stuart," he whispered in a low voice.

"What?"

"Listen to me. I'm only going to say this once. He's in witness protection, and you're not doing him or yourself any good."

"But . . ."

"No buts. You're causing problems you can't even imagine," he hissed. "For God's sake stop looking for him if you want him to stay alive."

*He was alive! But could I believe him?*

"Where . . ."

Before I could say another word, he'd already turned and hurried along the hallway and down the stairs and was out the door before I reached the landing.

Now it's four months later. I did give up the investigation. I had to. There were no more leads, no more clues, and I couldn't — wouldn't — take the chance that I might put Scotty in more danger. I went through the worried stage, the anger stage, the horror stage and the grief stage. I'm past all that. I've even outgrown the "We'll always have Paris" stage. Now I'm in the anti-social stage. I generally spend evenings at home with Cavalier. We share TV dinners and watch the tube like an old married couple.

My father had a favorite saying, "Let your wants hurt you," and that's exactly what I was doing. I had walked down the same path after my fiancé Frank's death a few years ago. I was in a rut, and that was part of the trouble. I suppose that's why Tom Joyce, my erstwhile friend who runs the well-known Joyce and Company bookstore in Chicago, handed me a ticket to a Hemingway docudrama performance at Northwestern University.

"Something came up, and I can't use it," he said, pressing the ticket into my hand. "You go."

"I . . ."

"Go for my sake if nothing else," he pleaded. "You're getting positively moribund."

"Adjective, from the Latin, meaning in a dying state."

"Not exactly dying, DD, but I do think stale. You're in the same state you were after Frank died. You've lost your vitality. I know you've started working again, doing a few jobs for your attorney friends, but you hibernate in your apartment every night with your cat. And believe me, I like Cavalier, but you're stuck in time."

"It's not like that."

"I know you cared for Scotty. I liked — I like him too. But if Scotty is in witness protection like that Secret Service chap said, then you must realize you'll never see him again."

"I won't accept that."

"And that's exactly your problem. Look, if they had to whisk him away in the dark of night like they did, and he accepted it, knowing he was going to hurt you and Jerry and his business, it means something really big and bad is after him — right on his heels. And it means — whatever it is — it'll probably be after him for the rest of his life — and yours. The first step is to take this ticket and go to the play."

"I feel trapped, like the Great Wall of China is surrounding me. I can't see over it, under it, around, or through it."

"The Great Wall, you know, was constructed around 210 BC and is made of 3,873,000,000 individual bricks." He obviously wanted to change the subject.

"Are you making that up?"

"I never make up facts or figures. You know that. It's on the web, and they figured it out mathematically. Anyway, take the ticket."

I knew he was right about me, and the "moribund" stung me into promising him I'd go.

Nonetheless, I was having second thoughts. Lethargy is so easy. I kissed Cavalier good-bye, and his kitty meow sounded like he too was surprised I was actually leaving.

"It's not a date," I explained. "I'll be home early." I grabbed my purse and left before my mind changed again.

The stage production was entertaining and surprisingly historically accurate. It featured a Hemingway look-alike re-enacting scenes from the author's life. The theme was "A New Book for Every New Affair." It was based on the theory that Hemingway wrote his best four books to each of his new wives in turn — *The Sun Also Rises* in 1926 for Hadley, the first wife; *Farewell to Arms* in 1929 to his second, Pauline Pfeiffer; *For Whom the Bell Tolls* for Martha Gellhorn in 1940; and *The Old Man and the Sea* in 1952 to Mary Welsh, his last wife. It was an interesting presentation, but I abruptly stopped paying attention when my old college flame, David Barnes, appeared on the stage. I had no premonition he'd be back from Paris directing the production. He seemed to be staring right into my eyes during the rest of the docu-drama.

When the lights came back on, I sat contemplating the empty stage. My feet were being trampled on by the usual scramble of exiting patrons, but I was immobile, damning myself for breaking my own cardinal rule. Years ago, I'd vowed to keep out of the clutches of academia, and most especially from anything to do with Hemingway. I guess some people never learn.

I wasn't sure if he'd seen me or not, but I didn't want to be within twenty feet of David Barnes, damn him. I melded into the crowd heading for the nearest exit and kept my head down. Suddenly, in a flash of brown hair and blue eyes, there he was, saying in that unmistakable David voice,

"DD McGil. I thought that was you. Sometimes it's hard to see out from the stage through those lights."

There was no escape. Tom Joyce and his rotten ticket. I knew I should have stayed home with the cat.

I looked up at him. "Hello, David."

"Where the hell have you been, DD? I've been trying to find you for months. Nobody at the university knew where you'd gone."

"Guess I'm not the only one who's not so good at keeping in touch," I said, thinking about all the years he'd had to call or write.

"I know, DD. I'm sorry."

"Luckily I didn't hold my breath." I edged around him. We were nearly the only ones left in the rapidly emptying lobby. As I squeezed by, David put his hand on the back of my neck, under my hair.

"Wait a minute, DD. I really need to talk to you."

The intimate gesture stopped me. David hadn't changed much since I'd seen him last. He was still tall, handsome, trim, and boyish. And those piercing blue eyes hadn't changed either, except for a few small lines at the corners. He was more tan than I remembered, but that might have been from stage makeup.

I closed my eyes. Long-suppressed memories of graduate school flashed through my consciousness. David had been an up-and-coming Hemingway scholar and my first grand passion. I remembered the hard work, the cold cast of light on campus during those Chicago winters, and the delirium of falling in love very fast and very hard. As it turned out, I'd fallen much harder than he, and he'd dumped me for a fellowship in Paris to study twentieth-century American expatriate writers. "I'll write you every day," he'd promised at the airport. But that was well over a dozen years ago, and we hadn't seen each other since. It was David Barnes who first taught me how complicated life could be. Then I'd met Frank. And then Scotty. I like men, but statistically speaking, my luck with them was shitty.

"There's something I really need to talk to you about," he said. "I was looking for you because I've got big news. I finally made it. C'mon, have dinner with me. I need your advice."

The David I knew never needed anybody's advice, least of all mine.

I looked into his eyes, trying to read him, damning myself for a fool the entire while. This is always how I get into trouble.

"Just what do you have in mind?" I asked.

"You always could put things in perspective," he said, flashing that old David Barnes smile.

If I really were to put things into perspective, I'd run for the door. For some reason, I didn't.

"DD, right now everybody around me has an axe to grind, and I can't trust them," he said. "Will you help me?"

My little internal voice was shouting no — NO. But he had me. I was curious, and being an insurance investigator teaches you to listen. So instead of ducking out I said, "Okay, let's hear it."

# Two

Time . . . is all we have.
— ERNEST HEMINGWAY

I drove us back to the city in my Miata convertible. It was one of those beautiful summer evenings that stay with you for the rest of your life. The night air was hot and steamy, but a small breeze coming in off Lake Michigan made the trees sing. Nighthawks circled above, dining on clouds of bugs, their sharp calls punctuating the din of traffic.

It was strange to be talking to David, hearing his voice again after all the years and all the hurt. It wasn't romantic exactly, but I think you never get over your first true love.

After stopping for Chinese take-out, we went to David's apartment. It was a converted loft on the outskirts of the Loop that had once been a vacant factory. This trendy area had attracted all the upwardly mobiles from the Loop's financial district who paid more rent per month than I earned per year. But today many units were vacant, their former occupants victims of the economic meltdown. Redevelopment used to be a good thing, but my, how times were a-changing.

David flipped on the lights. His enormous living room was decorated with brown leather furniture and oriental carpets. I spotted a Wan Li clay horse that stood out among the antique Chinese pottery, and I wondered who'd done the interior decorating.

Floor-to-ceiling bookshelves lined the walls. Knowing David, they undoubtedly held a lot of first editions. And there were treasures, like the early typewriter with pride of place on the shelf among his extensive Hemingway collection. His artwork was an interesting, eclectic mix. I glanced around, wondering whether David had a roommate, but didn't see any evidence.

David's place far outshone my shabby-chic third-floor Uptown walk-up. Even in this crappy economy, David could have bought ten of me.

"That's very beautiful," I said, admiring a large bifold screen with hand-painted cranes reflecting the soft light.

David smiled. "It's Tang and very unique. Did you know that cranes in flight symbolize good luck?"

*Furtively, I touched the screen, hoping some of it might rub off on me.*

His cell rang. He answered, excused himself and drifted into another room. Meanwhile I enjoyed the panorama of the city from his windows, breathtaking even to a native Chicagoan like me.

"You've certainly done all right, David," I said as he returned. "English lit grads usually don't wind up in a place like this."

"All right? As usual, you're the master of understatement, DD." His eyes twinkled. "I'm a genius at winning those big-buck research grants."

"I thought money was getting really tight in this awful economy."

"Yes, but I do know how to get whatever's out there — and that's the trick."

*More likely who to get it from, I thought, remembering his mastery at manipulating our university professors.*

"There's something special I want you to try. It's an Australian wine." He left the room, saying, "The Chinese haven't figured out how to make a good red yet. Ha."

He returned with two glasses of deep red wine. "A Shiraz," he said, handing me one.

"You'll like it. Full bodied, like the Aussies."

We clinked glasses as he toasted, "To old times."

The wine was lively and satisfying. "Mmm," I said appreciatively. "No hint of the outback."

"I knew you'd approve." He took another sip. "DD, I heard about Frank. I'm sorry."

*I wondered how many times he was going to say he was sorry.*

"I heard you two were about to be married. He was a good man. But why didn't anybody at the university know where to find you?"

"It was a long time ago. I'm not in the academic rat race anymore. I do claims investigations for insurance companies."

"Insurance? That doesn't sound like you. What happened to that ground-breaking research you were doing in the seventeenth century?"

"It's over, that's all." I didn't want to talk about the whole lousy deal with Frank, with his death and with what happened afterward. We were about to be married and had been so happy. But after he died, his colleagues at the university needed to blame someone for what happened, and they blamed me. Not only did they insinuate I was responsible for his death, they also refused to publish my book, *Restoration Scandals*. They suggested it wasn't scholarly enough to merit publication by the University Press and debunked it as too risqué. The research, they'd conceded, was flawless. But the content, they decided, appealed more to the prurient interest of the common man instead of to the rigorous requisites of a scholastic treatise. Never mind that's exactly what I'd aimed for. I understood why they were against me. With Frank dead, I didn't care any more what they thought, and I walked out. In a few weeks' time, I'd lost not only my husband-to-be but also my career. That's how I ended up doing what I do now, insurance investigations, and that's how I met Scotty Stuart. But I wasn't about to go into any of this with David, so I just stayed silent, hoping he'd drop the questions. He took the hint and said, "Well, face it DD, you were never a typical academic anyway. You always rubbed those people the wrong way."

"Remember Dr. Bailey?" I asked.

"She had the vapors over that genealogical research you did on the word 'fly.' "

"Yeah. The verb was fine. So was the insect. But the nominative 'gentlemen's apparel' was too much for her."

"You know damn well that wasn't the phrase you used to describe that particular piece of clothing, DD." We both laughed, our shared past reforging an old bond.

Debating with myself to go or stay, I took another sip of the Shiraz and asked, "So what kind of help do you need from me?"

His eyes narrowed, and after a drawn-out pause he said, "Remember how I always wanted to unearth those lost Hemingway manuscripts?"

"You mean the ones stolen from his first wife, Hadley, at the Paris train station?"

"You remember. A-plus."

"You used to say they might provide key elements to Hemingway's personality and writing style."

"Ready for a surprise? I've got them."

# THREE

The Corona #3 is the only psychiatrist I would ever submit to.
— ERNEST HEMINGWAY

I stared at him. Here we were, sitting over Chinese take-out, discussing what, if true, would be the literary find of the twenty-first century. The incident at the Paris train station in December 1922, where Hemingway's first wife, Hadley Richardson, lost a valise filled with everything he'd written for the last year was well known. Scholars and Hemingway buffs have speculated for years about whether the stolen manuscripts survived and their possible whereabouts. But no clue has ever been unearthed. I wondered if this was a con — some sick ploy to attract my attention after all these years. But that didn't make sense.

I put my wine glass on the coffee table and sat down on his leather sofa, stunned.

"I'm having trouble taking this in, David. Where did you find them? Are you sure they're genuine? My God, if this is true, everyone from the *New York Times* to the *National Enquirer* will be after you."

He sat down too. "It's true, believe me. Eleven stories, the beginning of a novel, and twenty poems, to be exact."

"This is incredible. After all these years . . ."

He swirled his right hand in the air. "Bring on Oprah, Ba-ba Walters, and the three-ring media circus."

I got up and paced the room. "David, at the risk of dumping cold water on your antics, how can you be so sure the stuff is really Hemingway?"

"Modern technology. The easiest part was having the paper authenticated. Then I verified that the pages were typed on a typewriter similar to the one he used at the time — a Corona No. 3."

"But that typewriter was from the early 1920s. How can they . . . ?"

"DD, ours is a truly marvelous world. There were two — not one but two original Corona Number 3 typewriters on eBay when I searched. And *voila* —" he pointed to the typewriter I'd noticed on the bookshelf, "there it is in all its glory."

I crossed the room to examine it more closely. "It's still in fairly good condition. I thought it was just a prop."

"It's no prop. It's vintage early 1920s — exactly like the one Hadley gave Hemingway on his twenty-second birthday in 1921 before they left for Paris. I even have the case for it."

"Does this one still type?"

"Technically, DD, the typist types, not the machine."

"Ha ha. Very cute. Well, can you use it to type something?"

"Absolutely. They were made to last. Remember Hemingway lugged his all over the world in war zones when he was working as a correspondent. On this one, some of the keys were sticking, but I cleaned it and oiled it and now everything works fine. I had to get a ribbon for it — that was the hard part." He inserted a piece of paper, moved it into position with the carriage, and pecked out "Hello DD McGil. It's about time I found you."

"Amazing."

"Amazing you're here right now, DD."

There was a sudden pause. I kept silent and carefully avoided making eye contact.

"Well," he finally continued, "what's also amazing is the highly sophisticated software

34

program I used to prove it was written by Hemingway. It categorizes word, sentence, and punctuation usage patterns. Believe me, the results indicated positively that the material is all one hundred percent pure Hemingway."

"Unbelievable," I said, sinking back into his sofa and ignoring the odors of the untouched Moo shu pork and Mongolian beef take-out. "Tell me everything."

"Years ago when I arrived in Paris on that fellowship, I started looking for them."

"That part I remember," I said wryly.

"I really am sorry, DD. I meant to keep in touch, but . . ."

"Forget it."

"Anyway, I went everywhere Hemingway lived or visited in Paris, even traveled to Spain, but all I ran into were brick walls. When I came back to the states, I investigated every place that had any connection to Hemingway, no matter how remote. I went to Michigan, Oak Park, Wisconsin, Kansas. Even Toronto. Nothing. Until three months ago. That's when someone sent them to me."

Now I knew David was conning me. I got up from the sofa and headed toward my purse, next to the untouched food.

"Wait. Seriously, DD, I know it sounds

crazy, but it's true. Please stay." The words tumbled from his mouth. "I really need your help. Please."

I stopped, clutching my purse to my chest, and looked at him. "Who sent them to you?"

"I have no idea. I wish I did."

"This whole thing sounds like something out of the supermarket tabloids," I told him.

"You know how much work I did for years trying to unearth these manuscripts, DD. But the honest truth is, the package arrived at City College simply addressed to Professor David Barnes. I'll show you."

"This sounds preposterous. Was there anything on the package? Any clues you could follow?"

"Nothing. I tried, but it's a complete mystery. Inside the package was an old valise, the manuscripts and poems, and a cryptic note in a purple, hard-to-read script listing the titles of the stories and poems along with the dates they were written. The note was signed, 'Regacs Ma Fily.' "

"Do you still have the note? Did you try to trace the shipper? Let me see the manuscripts."

"The manuscripts aren't here, and the note is with the manuscripts."

"That's it," I said, heading for the door. "I know bullshit when I hear it."

"DD, please. This is all true. After the way I left you, I know it's hard to trust me. But I'll let you see everything. I did put a trace on the package, but the shipper was a blind alley. It was sent from a shipping company in Quakertown, Pennsylvania. They searched their records, but the receipt contained a phony company name and false address."

"I can look at everything?"

"Absolutely. The only reason the stuff isn't here right now is that my attorney is concerned that other interested parties could get a warrant and seize the manuscripts when the news breaks. And it's going to break any day now. Probably tomorrow. I've got them in a safe place where they can't be taken."

"What are you going to do with the material?" I asked, still not convinced this wasn't some kind of con.

"Auction everything off. I've got a contract with a big auction house."

"You're not going to keep the manuscripts for research? You're already a big name in Hemingway scholarship, but this would put your name in the history books."

"My name will be in the history books even if I don't keep them. If I keep them, I'll be living in court and doing nothing but paying lawyers. The Hemingway estate, the Oak Park Hemingway Trust, the City College, they're like a school of hungry sharks. I need to sell everything as soon as possible. And it's important not to have any of the manuscripts published before the sale because of questions over public domain."

"Public domain? I don't see what that has to do with it."

"My lawyer says that if anything gets into print, that puts it into the public domain, which could mean that I'd have a harder time proving ownership."

"It sounds like your attorney's made it into a nice Catch-22. The sale of the stuff itself validates your ownership of it. I admire the mobius logic. He must think you've got a good claim if he's recommending you auction it all."

"He thinks it's air-tight because I've got possession. Nobody associated with the manuscripts is alive, so nobody can say what really happened to them."

"But won't the Hemingway Trust file an injunction to stop the sale?"

"The auction house tells me that generally only the government or a library challenges a sale. But because Hemingway is so hot and the time to sell is now, they didn't want to take any chances. They've already contacted the law firm for the Hemingway Trust and managed to get a signed release from them to allow the auction to take place."

"So you're free and clear?"

"Not exactly. I had to sign it too, agreeing that we'd fight out the proceeds from the sale in court."

"Does that mean you could be left with zero?"

"*Au contraire.* They had to acknowledge in the agreement that I have the manuscripts, possession being nine-tenths of the law and all that. So I've negotiated a guaranteed minimum percentage of the sale price. A percentage I'm happy with, even if the court awards me nothing additional."

"Clever," I agreed. "This agreement establishes provenance, and whoever buys the manuscripts at the auction will be the new legal owner."

"My lawyer thinks so. So does the auction house. Whoever buys stands to make a bundle if they want to get them published. And my court case with the Hemingway Trust over the proceeds will be fodder for even more publicity and drive up the value for the new buyer."

"I see." I was becoming convinced now in spite of myself that David was telling the truth. "This reminds me of the Marjorie Kinnan Rawlings manuscript of *Blood of My Blood* that was lost for seventy-four years and finally turned up in a box in somebody's house. Her second husband fought for ownership, but lost."

"The head of the auction house cited that case, too. They felt it strengthened my claim."

"So what do you need me for?"

"The manuscripts are insured, and the insurance company wants a look at all the material. So far I've dealt only with the top guy at the insurance company, and I gave him a few sample pages — nothing he could publish. Now they want to see it all or they won't insure. I don't seem to have a choice. I've got to show them everything."

"Okay, but you still haven't answered my question."

"I told you when we first met in the theatre that I had been looking for you. I was. I know you, DD. I can trust you. I still can't believe how lucky it was to just bump into you tonight."

*Yeah, I thought. Luck with a healthy dose of Tom Joyce. I was going to get even with Tom for giving me that ticket.*

"You realize what a colossal find this is, DD. I can't have the manuscripts in my possession. Think about it. It's way too easy for someone to serve me with a warrant and walk away with them. I'd loose everything. But you could take them in for verification. No one knows who you are, so they'll be safe. And I know you'll keep an eye on them to make sure no duplicates are made."

I sat down again, stunned.

# FOUR:
# DAY 2: MONDAY

About morals,
I know only that what is moral is what you
feel good after and what is immoral is
what you feel bad after.
— ERNEST HEMINGWAY

I woke up the next morning in David's bed.
It was still early, and it had been a long
night. David was still asleep. I needed to get
out and think.

I pulled on yesterday's outfit and drove to
my apartment to make up with my cat. All
the way back, I tried not to think about David. I knew I would have to deal with it, but
like Scarlett, not right now.

I live in a third-floor walk-up and continually remind myself that climbing stairs is
cheaper than a Thighmaster for staying in
shape. My apartment's the size of a matchbox compared to David's spacious loft, but
it has the advantage of being only two

blocks from Wrigley Field where the Cubs play. I try not to miss many home games, and being able to walk to the ballpark has saved me a ton of money in parking fees.

They were predicting a heat wave for Chicago — ninety-five degrees for today. It hadn't cooled off overnight, and my window air-conditioner unit buzzed loudly, clearly not up to the task set by Mother Nature. I silently cursed myself for not moving into a building with central air or, better yet, to Alaska. In Chicago, it's hard to decide if you're for or against global warming.

Cavalier greeted me by twitching every one of the thirty-two muscles in each ear. I wasn't sure if he was mad at me, or if he had another case of ear mites. I grabbed him and applied a few drops of medicine in both ears for good measure. Afterwards, I no longer doubted he was mad at me.

I tuned in CNN and listened to chatter about the massive heat wave hitting the Midwest. All the other channels were focused on the heat wave, too, so I checked my black book for today's appointments. An eight a.m. meeting with Phil Richy meant I would have to hurry. Phil's one of the attorneys who sends me claims investigation work. He'd told me next to nothing about this job, a sure sign I wasn't going to like it. He knew I'd take it though. I needed the work.

At ten-thirty, I had a meeting with Mr. Poussant, the IRS agent auditing my tax return from three years ago. He'd been hassling me over minor points and had phoned me last Friday in a royal snit. "Be at my office Monday morning at ten-thirty sharp, Mzz. McGil," he'd demanded. "And this is your last chance to bring in those receipts and the paperwork we discussed. Let's clear up this return once and for all."

Every time I saw him, my blood pressure exploded. I'm not somebody like Bernie Madoff that the IRS should maybe take a second look at. Doing insurance investigations is so low on the food chain that some paramecium make more money than I do. Even if I wanted to cheat, the difference on my tax return wouldn't amount to much. I'd uncovered only a few receipts, so I knew this meeting wouldn't be fruitful — at least for me.

I turned on the shower and jumped in. The cold, sharp water poured life back into me. I needed time to think about things before I saw David again. As I toweled dry, Mister Cat went through his grooming ritual. I couldn't tell if the heat bothered him. Cats are so hard to read.

"Stay there. I'll be right back," I ordered, as if he would dream of obeying. The kitchen tile was delightfully cool on my toes as I yanked open the freezer-door and pulled out my bra. It was just the right temperature after spending yesterday with the ice cubes. It had worked for Marilyn Monroe in *The Seven Year Itch* on late night TV last week, so I was hoping it would work for me, too. I slammed the freezer-door shut with satisfaction as Cavalier pranced in, too curious after all not to follow.

"See this?" I dangled the frozen bra like a treat. "I told you it would work."

I rummaged in my closet, deciding on a pale yellow jacket and skirt, no pantyhose. I slipped into a pair of Nine West heels and tried to avoid looking in the mirror. It's not that I'm bad to look at — a fact directly attributable to my Grandmother Mason on my mother's side. I'm not ungrateful for her long legs, blonde hair, and blue eyes that give me more than my share of attention from men. But I've got a generous dose of my father's Scottish Buchanan genes, which makes me a natural-born pessimist. I tend to focus on the downside of things, like here I am at thirty-nine with no millions in the bank, no Nobel Prize, and no handsome prince in my bed chamber. After

Frank's death, I left the academic world behind, and I left most of my friends and my social life behind, too. "A fallen academic" is what my best friend, Lauren, calls me. She complains that my insurance work takes up too much of my time. But truth to tell, I wasn't socially acceptable after the whole bloody episode with Frank. And now with Scotty gone, I prefer it that way. I've given up on the idea that my fairy godmother will wave her starry wand and put everything back together, *a la* Humpty Dumpty. I like what I do now, and I'm good at it. I'm my own boss, and it's as far away as possible from academia. True, the money's not great, but it's sufficient to buy food for Cavalier.

I scooped some Mighty Cat into his bowl and was in the middle of gulping down my own breakfast of vitamin pills when I heard the TV reporter mention Hemingway.

The story got six minutes of airtime. Network anchors interviewed an owner of the auction house, a Northwestern University professor who authenticated the manuscripts, and another professor who claimed they were frauds. I recognized the last one as the guy who'd played Hemingway in last night's production.

A rather pompous anchor then segued

into an armchair analysis with another Hemingway scholar on how the author had blamed his first wife, Hadley Richardson, for losing the manuscripts. He suggested Hadley had intentionally packed both the originals and the carbons, and, jealous of Hemingway's success, she'd lost everything on purpose. The loss of the manuscripts, the pundit continued, had caused a deep rift in their marriage that ultimately led to their subsequent divorce. The segment ended with speculation that the bidding for the manuscripts could top fifteen to twenty million dollars — even in this bad economy — due to strong international interest involving anything to do with Hemingway.

As I flipped off the TV, the phone rang.

"DD, are you sitting down?" It was my best friend, Lauren. "You're not gonna believe this. It's all over the tube. Somebody finally found those lost Hemingway manuscripts."

"I know."

"I was afraid you might not catch it."

"Better than that. I saw David Barnes yesterday."

"You're kidding. It's been . . . how many years since that super-rat left you standing there? Damn him. Wait a minute, DD. Are you telling me he's the one who found those manuscripts after all?"

"He's got them, but he didn't exactly find them. He told me somebody sent them to him."

"He got 'em in the mail? Jesus, DD, if that was the plot of a novel, no publisher would touch it. It's totally unbelievable."

"But apparently true."

"So why didn't they mention him on the news?"

"David specifically wants his name kept out of it." *I knew I could trust Lauren.*

"My God, DD . . ."

"Look, I really have to run."

"Wait. What's he look like? Is he still so handsome? I hope you shoot him. He deserves it for what he did to you."

"I've got to go, or I'll be late for a meeting. Catch up with you later today."

"I won't be here later. Nick has a backgammon tournament in Wisconsin, and we're flying up there this afternoon. Tell me now."

"In that small plane of his?"

"Yeah, but the alternative's five hours in a car." She sighed audibly. "Okay, I'm hanging up, but don't go and kill the bounder till we talk. This is some turn of events."

I hung up, glad that she'd stopped asking if there'd been any news about Scotty. Lauren and I have been gal-pals since high school. She grew up the center of a tug of war between her doting Japanese father, who named her after Lauren Bacall and encouraged her to be Western, and a beautiful Japanese mother, Iko, who firmly insisted she carry on the feudal traditions. It's a miracle she turned out so bravehearted, and over the years we've shared all our secrets.

I grabbed my briefcase, waived good-bye to Cavalier, and locked my door. Down the corridor, I knocked at 3-A, Glendy and Lucille's apartment. They're my elderly twin-sister neighbors who act like my surrogate mothers, as if I needed more than one.

Glendy, the older by two minutes, opened the door and peered out. "It's DD," she informed Lucille and pulled me in. "Got time for a cuppa and some biscuits?"

"It smells soo good, I'd love to, but I'm on the run."

"You're always on the run," they said in tandem.

"I wondered if you two would look in on Mister Cat after the Cubs game. I won't make the game today, and I'll be late coming home."

The girls, spry Southern chicks in their eighties, eat homemade biscuits every morn-

49

ing and go to Cubs games instead of "doctoring." They live on their small pensions and can't afford season tickets. So every few weeks, I anonymously send them some. They're having a ball trying to guess the identity of their secret admirer. Currently, it's narrowed down to any of seven gentlemen friends at the Salvation Army and bingo at St. Michael's.

"Does this mean you're finally going on a date tonight?" Glendy asked, smiling. "You need to get out again, DD. We liked Scotty, too, you know. And we miss him. But he's gone for good. You've got to start living again."

"And don't be so picky with men," Lucille chimed in from the kitchen.

"And don't worry about us taking care of Cavvy," Glendy assured me. "We're happy to. You know we're crazy about him."

"Oh, here's that special seed for the cardinals I told you about," I said, pulling a bag of dark seeds from my briefcase and handing it to Glendy. "Are you writing down the descriptions of any unusual birds?"

"You mean other than pigeons?" Glendy laughed as she placed the bag in a cupboard drawer. They're both members of the Audubon Society and each has her own pair of binoculars. Since I helped put a feeder on their back porch, they bird-watch from the kitchen window. Mr. Cavalier is allowed to watch, too. I wonder if they know he dreams of eating the birds, not identifying them. I never mention it.

I bade them good-bye and walked four blocks to where I'd parked my car, a little green Miata convertible of which I'm overly fond. I hurriedly crawled behind the wheel, put the top down and headed south to the Loop on Lake Shore Drive, trying desperately to suppress memories of Scotty sitting next to me. First I lost Frank, now I've lost Scotty. I winced at all the bittersweet memories and wondered how long it would take to start forgetting. Then I remembered David and last night. I didn't want to think about that yet.

All along Lake Shore Drive I caught bright glimpses of seagulls and colorful sailboats dipping and weaving across the waterfront. Despite the early morning heat, a parade of joggers strutted their stuff on Oak Street Beach.

Changing lanes, I turned onto Illinois Street and sped past Navy Pier and the Chicago River, then hung a right into Lower Wacker. I turned on my headlights as the road descended into the twists and turns of

Chicago's street below the streets. I love the surreal glow of the green lights that make Lower Wacker into an alternate universe. Navigating the Loop down here is always a few degrees cooler and much less congested. Most drivers can't find their way around the maze of Lower Wacker, and they can't rely on a GPS for help. A GPS can't do three dimensions.

I passed Trump Tower, formerly the site of the old *Sun-Times* building. I remembered watching shirtless crews hustle newspaper bundles into idling delivery trucks, and I rather missed the adventure of avoiding a crash as they squealed into traffic at outrageous speeds.

Lower Michigan also took me past the Billy Goat Tavern, a favorite subterranean haunt of Chicago journalists made famous on *Saturday Night Live* with "Cheezborger! Cheezborger!" It's also famous for the Curse of the Billy Goat. That dates back to October 5, 1945, during game four of the World Series, when the original owner, William "Billy Goat" Sianis, brought along his pet goat, Murphy, to cheer the team. When Cubs owner P. K. Wrigley refused the goat admission — even though he had a ticket — Sianis cursed the team saying they'd never win a World Series. Thus all true

Chicagoans — even non-Scots — firmly believe in curses.

Braking hard, I turned onto Upper Wacker and finally emerged back into the daylight. I had to blink repeatedly until my eyes finally adjusted from that green glow below to the sunlight here on Upper Wacker. Meanwhile I planned my day. After meeting Phil, I wanted to contact Tom Joyce, my antiquarian bookseller friend. Despite being mad at him for giving me that ticket, I intended to pick his brain on Hemingway. He might even know something about David Barnes that I didn't know.

I was still tired, but those vitamins were kicking in, and I had a feeling it was going to be a good day. I inserted a CD of Vivaldi's *Four Seasons,* turned up the volume, and let the music block out visions of David Barnes, Ernest Hemingway, and the IRS the rest of the way to Phil's office.

# FIVE

When people talk, listen completely.
Most people never listen.
— ERNEST HEMINGWAY

Phil and I go back a long way. It was through him I'd gotten into insurance investigations. After Frank's death, one of Phil's clients, a famous Chicago institution which must remain nameless, was unable to locate a priceless medieval manuscript. Phil, in his capacity as the attorney for the university's insurance company, begged me to find it. He insisted my academic background gave me an inside track. At the time I was so desperate for money to pay off Frank's bills, I agreed. Less than twenty-four hours later, I'd tracked down the precious item in the grungy Hyde Park apartment of a grad student who was planning to sell it over eBay. Phil was able to hush up the whole thing — no police, no publicity, and most importantly, no insurance claims leading to sky-high insurance rates for said nameless Chicago institution. He'd paid me well for that job, and he's been giving me work ever since.

Phil shared office space with three other lawyers in a modest building on the west side of the Loop. I got off on the fourteenth floor and pushed open the heavy double glass doors three minutes early, which for me was statistically outside the norm.

Gilda Fone, one of the two secretaries in the outer office, eyed the wall clock. "Is the world ending? Should I say a novena?"

I glared at her and reminded myself I'm not the only one with a license to smart-mouth. Gilda had a thing for Phil, and she'd cast me in the role of rival. She liked to scheme and dream and plant land mines for me wherever possible. I smiled thinly and moved away from her desk to escape the heavy perfume she always wore.

"Hello, Miss McGil." Mandy Morrison, the nice secretary, greeted me. "Sorry, but you'll have to wait. He's on the phone."

"This is the last time I'll be early," I quipped.

"This is the first time you've ever been early," Gilda snorted loudly, adjusting her oversized tortoise shell glasses.

Unable to refute the truth of her accusation, I headed for the drab waiting room. It smelled of plastic chairs and stale coffee, and the air conditioning here too was straining to beat the heat and humidity. The only reading material consisted of complimentary copies of *Law Digest.* I settled down to a good fidget, staring at the walls and thinking over last night with David.

Phil's office door popped open. "Gilda, is DD here yet?" Phil yelled.

Ignoring Gilda and Mandy, I got up and headed for Phil's inner sanctum. Like any good Scot, I always meet the charge head on.

Phil leaned across his untidy desk to shake hands, knocking a stack of file folders into the trash can in the process.

"Hiya, DD," he greeted me tight-lipped as he bent to reclaim his files from the garbage.

"I've been waiting. I'm not always late. What's the job? You didn't say much about it over the phone."

Phil settled into his squeaky brown leather chair. "Matt King flew in late last night from New York," he said, his eyes avoiding me. "He wants to meet with you."

"Matt's here? In Chicago?"

"Yeah," he said, twirling a pencil, another sure sign he was nervous.

*Shit,* I thought.

"What's he want to see me about?"

"I don't know, DD. You tell me. Matt King never comes to outposts like this. But he's here. And he specifically asked for you to be at this meeting." Phil finally made eye contact. "Is there something going on I don't know about?"

Matt was the grand poobah at American Insurance, and the last time I'd seen him was at a big International Security Training Seminar in Washington, D.C., where we'd been in his hotel suite, naked. I wasn't too keen on seeing him again.

"Well?" Phil prodded.

I've had trouble in the romance department ever since Frank died, damn him. And before I met Scotty, there was Matt. I thought Matt was the one. He'd made me so recklessly happy, I'd almost forgotten Frank. Then I heard, quite by chance, that he was ever so happily married to a former state beauty queen with two darling girls, ages two and three and a half. Matt and I hadn't exactly parted friends. But my great deductive powers told me this wasn't the time to tell Phil. Confession may be good for your soul, but it's bad for your career.

The silence lengthened. Finally Phil said, "DD. Please. What's going on? You know

I'm always on your side. But American Insurance is my biggest client, and I can't afford to lose them."

His phone buzzed. He reached out and grabbed the receiver. "Yeah, Gilda," he said, eyeing me. "Send him in."

He replaced the phone with a clunk. The door opened, and Matt King strode in, confident, sophisticated, and too damn handsome for his own good.

Phil stood up to introduce us. "Matt, this is . . ."

"No need for introductions, Phil," Matt said in that rich, persuasive voice of his, extending a muscular hand in my direction. "DD and I already know each other."

I found myself turning to him involuntarily, a heliotrope to the sun. Yeah, I thought, biting my lower lip as we shook hands, we know each other, but only in the Biblical sense.

Phil sat down, Matt sat down, and I held my breath, waiting for the shoe to drop. Life's all about falling down and getting up again, but I was afraid this time I might not be able to get up. Now he was probably out to get my job. To err is human. To forgive might be against company policy.

"Matt," Phil began, "if American Insurance has any problems with Ms. McGil, I can assure you that I've been more than satisfied with every job she's done for me. She's clever, reliable . . ."

"And honest, trustworthy, and good to her mother," Matt interrupted. "I already know all that."

"Then what's the problem?" Phil asked.

Matt leaned across Phil's messy desk to address him directly while ignoring the pants off me. "I've come here today because American Insurance has been asked to undertake a very special job, and we believe she can help us."

"What?" I asked a little too loudly.

Matt turned and flashed me one of his sexy smiles. There was no doubt the rat was handsome. His eyes were laughing, and his masculine scent very sexy. Charm like his, well, you know the adage.

"Have you seen the news today about the recovery of the lost Hemingway manuscripts?" he asked.

Phil's eyes opened wide, and he asked, "Is American thinking of providing coverage to the auction house?"

"Exactly," Matt replied. "We've just written a binder for fifteen million dollars on the manuscripts as artifacts. We believe that basing the insurance coverage on artifacts and not on genuine Hemingway manuscripts is sound risk management. But in fact the auction house is convinced the material is one hundred percent genuine, and we agree."

"How can you be so sure?" Phil countered, his lawyer-ness coming to the fore.

"They've contacted Hemingway experts, and we've done extensive computer checks on style and on word usage, proving definitively it was written by Hemingway."

*This whole conversation was extremely interesting, if not downright coincidental, considering last night. I silently chuckled. Was the universe finally handing me a boon?*

"Phil," I interjected, "I'm familiar with that computer software they probably used. I ran some of the programs myself to analyze various pieces of literature while I was at the university. It's amazingly accurate. If the tests are properly done, they can statistically analyze the number and sentence placement of nouns, verbs, adjectives, adverbs, and pronouns; choice of words; punctuation patterns; frequency of word usage, and so on. It's like verbal DNA. If they ran the stuff right, and they concluded the stuff is Hemingway, you can be 99.9 percent sure they're right."

"But," Matt held up his index finger, "there's one big problem. Nobody's seen more than a few assorted original pages of the manuscripts. We've had the available pages authenticated by the number one Hemingway expert in the country. Then the number one guy from the manuscript society certified that the paper was from the early 1920s, and that the typewriter was the same as the one Hemingway used. But we need to evaluate the rest of the material — all the original pages and all the carbon copies."

"Seems not just reasonable, but necessary that you examine the entire lot," Phil said. "Why won't the owner agree?"

*I bit my lip, wondering what was coming next.*

"Good question," Matt said. "The owner's giving us problems. He wants to keep the manuscripts under wraps until the sale. His lawyer told him that if the stuff had never been printed, it's not protected by copyright. And even if, by some remote chance, it had been printed, his lawyer told him that any copyright attributable to Hemingway would have long since expired. There's no copyright from the Hemingway family or anyone else on the material right now. This being the case, the owner is unwilling to reveal the full contents because everyone would be free to print it without payment."

*This discussion was exactly what I'd planned on having with Phil later today. It looked like I might be able to help David after all. Sometimes things work out nicely.*

"Is that right, Phil?" I interjected.

"It's a murky area of the law," he said, scratching his head. "And especially now with all the electronic media."

He paused, then went on. "A good argument could be made that if these are the long-lost Hemingway manuscripts, they would be in the public domain, meaning simply that the public has a right to produce any part of them at any time. But if the contents themselves are not available, and the material is kept secret until the sale, then, even without the specific copyright to protect it from publication, it's still not open to mass dissemination. The public may have a *de jure* right to publish it, but they don't have the knowledge to publish it."

"What do we know for sure?" I asked. *Knowing what I knew, this conversation was getting to be more and more fun.*

Phil said, "It's well documented that the manuscripts were known to be lost. And it's also documented that the manuscripts were never printed. Therefore there was no contract with any publisher." He turned to Matt and asked, "Do you know for sure that the manuscripts were found, not stolen, by the current possessor?"

"That's what he's certified," Matt confirmed. "And there's no reason to doubt him."

"Then, taken together, this definitely gives the current possessor some *de facto* finder's keeper's rights. I would say that if the material is sold at auction strictly as artifacts, the auction house has a good chance of avoiding any adverse legal consequences."

"That's what we at American Insurance believe," Matt said. "Hemingway's estate was settled a long time ago, and these manuscripts weren't a part of it. Our legal guys say that if the auction house sells them as artifacts, we're not going to get into any trouble. That's why the owner is trying to stay anonymous and auction the manuscripts as soon as possible. He can make a big splash and avoid a controversy that could hold up ownership for years in the courts."

"But," Phil interjected, "if the auction house represents they're selling the publication rights also, copyright problems with Hemingway's heirs could arise down the line."

"The Oak Park Hemingway Trust is already in there fighting for control," Matt explained. "They're claiming that the manuscripts have personal and historic significance and should be returned to them. We negotiated an agreement to allow the auction to proceed and to stop any injunctions. After the sale, the owner and the Trust can duke out the proceeds in court. Our legal department says that since the manuscripts have never been published and there's certainly been no copyright renewal, the current owner has every right to sell them."

"As I said, it's a murky area of the law," Phil repeated.

"Wasn't there a similar case with a handwritten Celine manuscript that had disappeared for fifty years or so?" I asked. *This was part of the discussion that David and I had had last night. This was definitely fun.*

"That's right, DD," Matt said, giving me his full attention. "The manuscript was *Journey to the End of the Night,* and it was missing for more than sixty years. I'm impressed you knew that." He nodded approval. "Our legal guys investigated it thoroughly. That manuscript, too, had been discovered by a private collector, and the French National Library tried to claim it."

"As I recall," Phil interjected, "there was a fierce bidding war. Didn't the library finally end up getting it at auction?"

"Yeah. They paid $1.7 million and got it only when they exercised their right to match the top offer of a private bidder," Matt explained.

"And wasn't the longest chapter of James Joyce's *Ulysses* auctioned off recently for $1.5 million?" I added.

"Also correct," Matt nodded. "And based on these and other similar cases like Rawlings' *Blood of My Blood,* our legal department assures me the chances are that whoever buys the manuscripts at the auction would prevail over any family challenger or the trust."

"So they're going to be sold with expectations for publication?" Phil asked.

"I'm putting myself and American Insurance on the line here," Matt said. "Sold as artifacts, the manuscripts would raise about fifteen million dollars and provide a nice, tidy premium for American Insurance."

Phil said, "But selling them as artifacts with future publication rights will more than double that figure, am I right?"

"Yes," Matt agreed. "And the nice fat premium will keep American Insurance in the black for quite some time, not to mention the hefty bonus coming my way. So I've personally convinced American that the risk versus gain factor is worth it."

"But you're at a stand-off," I said, "because you can't collect those big premiums unless you can verify everything's genuine and write the actual policy."

Matt nodded. "There's a lot of academics out there who wonder why only fragments have been authenticated. They're ready to denounce the find as the biggest hoax since the Kennedy-Monroe letters and the Jack the Ripper diaries. And let's face it, the media goes crazy over anything Hemingway related. These naysayers are hot to get the auction house, the owner, the buyer, the academics — you name it — on every talk show in the universe."

"What about that professor in the news who swears the stuff isn't Hemingway? Won't he create problems for the sale?" I asked.

Matt shook his head. "Don't be naïve. Just the opposite will happen. If the sale is surrounded in controversy, the price will shoot up significantly. The auction house has stopped just short of classifying these manuscripts as part of 'the realm of astonishing objects.' "

"So where does DD fit in?" Phil asked.

Matt smiled at me, then turned to Phil. "We need Ms. McGil to help us out. A background check on the owner has revealed she knows him, and we think she can help persuade him to let us fully examine all the originals and the carbons prior to the auction."

*For once, I thought, I wasn't going to have to earn my money the old-fashioned way. This assignment was turning into a breeze. Not to mention, I'd be there firsthand for the literary revelation of a lifetime.*

"Well, who's the owner?" I asked, trying not to smirk.

Matt's eyes narrowed. "Does the name David Barnes ring a bell?"

Matt had undoubtedly been hoping to catch me off guard and put me in the squeeze. My past wasn't any business of his, and suddenly I saw him with a brittle clarity.

"Well, DD," Phil asked. "What do you know about this Barnes guy?"

"It was a long, long time ago," I said, turning back to Matt. "What makes American Insurance think I'd have any influence over David Barnes now?"

Matt's lips formed a tight smile. I kicked myself for not having noticed these objectionable tendencies about him earlier, before I'd so eagerly jumped into his bed. He reached across a pile of file folders on Phil's desk and grabbed the telephone.

"Why don't we call him and find out?" Matt said, punching in David's number.

Smiling, I took the receiver from him, catching another whiff of his cologne.

The phone rang six times before a familiar voice said, "Yes, hello."

"Hello? David? It's DD McGil."

Matt reached over and brushed my arm. "Set up a meeting as soon as possible," he whispered.

"DD? Hi. Is it morning? I'm still in bed, and I . . ." A loud explosion ripped through the phone connection.

"David?"

A second explosion boomed.

"David," I screamed into the receiver. "David, what's happening?"

I heard a click, and the line went dead.

# SIX

Every man's life ends the same way.
It is only the details of how he lived
and how he died that distinguish
one man from another.
— ERNEST HEMINGWAY

"I think David's been shot," I yelled. "We need to call the police."

Matt grabbed the receiver, put it to his ear, then killed the connection. "There's something fishy here," he said. "Too much coincidence for me."

"Coincidence? What are you talking about? I tell you there were gun shots. David could be lying there, bleeding to death. We've got to call the cops."

Matt cradled the phone. "Your friend David Barnes is a real showman. Maybe this is another stunt of his to garner more publicity for the auction. Fifteen million isn't enough for him, it would seem. He wants more."

Matt punched in a phone number. I exhaled, relieved he was finally calling the cops and hoping David wasn't turning into part of the curse, too. "Tell them to hurry," I urged Matt. "It doesn't make any sense that he'd try to pull a publicity stunt on me."

"I'm calling David's number to see if he answers," Matt said.

*I should have known Matt wouldn't play by the rules.*

The three of us huddled around the phone, listening to the muted ringing on the other end. Matt let it ring a long time before he slammed down the receiver.

"I'm telling you, I smell an insurance scam."

"If you don't call the cops, I will. He's in trouble, and we could be accessories."

I reached for the phone, but Matt gripped it forcefully. Instead of wrestling him for it, I let go, grabbed my purse, and pulled out my cell. It didn't do any good. It was dead. I'd forgotten to recharge it last night.

"We've got a problem here," I told Phil, who was managing to look harassed and outraged at the same time.

Matt smiled at us both. "Exactly. We don't know what happened on the other end of this phone," he said smoothly. "Whether David's been shot or whether this is a publicity stunt, I can't afford to be involved. This won't do my career any good either way. And Phil, if you value our business relationship, neither you nor your 'investigator,' " he nodded in my direction, "will call the police or involve American Insurance in any way."

In big business, ethics-be-damned is the norm. But there was no reason for it now. Was there?

Matt stood up. "I'm heading back to New York immediately."

"Phil," I pleaded as Matt left the office.

"DD, we don't really know what happened, do we? So get over there right away and check it out."

"I know you're trying to postpone calling the cops to save your butt, . . ."

Phil peered out the door. "If David's been shot, what are the cops going to do except put up a crime scene tape?"

"Phil, dammit, he could be dying."

"Then get over there as quick as you can." He wrote something on a piece of paper.

"But . . ." I protested as he handed me the paper.

"That's David's address. It's not far from here. You can get there before the police would, if we did call," he said.

I didn't need David's address. I knew exactly where he lived. I rushed out the door, shouting, "Dammit, Phil. Call the cops."

It was less than a five-minute trip. I drove wildly, pushing hard to make time through the heavy morning Loop traffic. I had a sick feeling in the pit of my stomach and cursed Matt and Phil with every gear shift. Being in insurance investigations forces me to deal with probability statistics I don't really want to know. The odds were much more likely that David would die in a car accident — one in sixty, or a home accident — one in 130, than be murdered. But at the same time, the frightening statistics are that a murder is committed every twenty-one minutes, and there's a one in four chance of any of us becoming a crime victim. Maybe Matt's assessment was accurate about David being a showman. I hoped so, but something deep in my gut didn't agree.

I squealed into an illegal parking spot and ran into David's building, forcing awful images of finding David's corpse out of my mind.

His apartment number was 721. I frantically buzzed every other apartment but his for entry while I searched in my purse for my trusty Dyno Quick Lock Pick, a handy mail-order tool I'd given myself last Christmas. It lets me open almost anything, and in a pinch, doubles as a weapon if I run into an intruder, or worse yet, a murderer.

"Who is this?" a crackly voice asked via the intercom system.

"Who's there?" an elderly male voice demanded through a burst of heavy static.

Just then, a pretty young mom pushing a pink bundle in a stroller opened the door from inside. I yanked it wide to assist, then ducked in and rushed to the elevator, afraid of what I'd find once I got inside.

David's apartment was at the farthest end of the hall. My pulse raced when I saw the doorknob. I wasn't going to need my lock pick after all. One look at the marks and distortion told me it had been pipe wrenched. I recognized the damage easily because, although I'd never admit this to anyone, I'd had to do it myself a time or two in my work.

I grabbed what was left of the doorknob and swung open the door, peering through the crack at the hinges to be sure no one was hiding behind it. Then I stepped in, ignoring the little voice in my head saying, *No, don't.*

I paused to slip off my high heels. I

listened, but there was only a hollow, reverberating silence.

To my right was the living room. I didn't need to turn on any lights to see the chaos. The beautiful oriental screen with its golden cranes had been slashed and thrown onto a pile of overturned furniture, smashed Buddhas, shredded papers, rugs, paintings, broken lamps and ripped pillows. Strewn around the pile were needles of glass, all that was left of the wine glasses we'd toasted with last night.

I held my sharp Dyno tool tightly and stood very still in the midst of the mess, listening, afraid that whoever had done this might still be around. But all I heard was the sharp beat of my own heart.

Other rooms spilled off a long corridor, the kitchen at the farthest end. I tiptoed quietly, checking each room, terrified of what I might find. The spare bedroom office, the bathroom, all in disarray. If someone was still lurking, I'd have to rely on my Aikido training to defend myself, and Sensei would kill me if he knew I was on tiptoes.

As I entered David's bedroom I could see the unmade bed in the dimness. It was a jumble. A red jumble.

"David," I called. He was lying on the bed in almost the same position as when I'd left this morning. Only now one arm arched downward, nearly touching the beige carpet, where blood had dripped into a big red stain around his fingers.

My heart raced, and I prayed he was still alive. I started toward him when I felt a sharp pain in the back of my head. My eyes clouded, my ears rang, my knees buckled and I pitched forward onto the floor in a dark haze.

My family's always telling me I'm hard headed, and technically I guess they're right. I was dizzy and my stomach was topsy-turvy, but I never blacked out. Skirting the edges of consciousness was Sensei, scolding me for the fundamental error of getting caught from behind. Through the pounding in my ears, I clearly registered a soft sound of running footsteps, and I fervently hoped whoever had hit me was gone.

I tried to stand. My legs were rubber. Nausea welled up, and I dropped back to the floor. My head throbbed, and there was a warm liquid behind my right ear. Ignoring it, I took a few deep breaths and, despite the pain, slowly crawled to the bed.

David's blood had soaked everything. My knees were sticky with what had dripped onto the carpet. When I touched his arm, his skin had the cold, clammy feel of cement and his color was a dull gray. He was dead.

I looked at him closely. He'd been shot twice, once in the chest where blood coagulated around a gaping hole, and once in his head. Behind him, congealed blood matted the pillow along with other things that were probably brain matter. His blue eyes stared vacantly up at the ceiling. Faint traces of projectile gunpowder were embedded in his skin near the head wound, so I knew he'd been shot at close range.

I looked away and swallowed hard, trying to conquer my nausea and horror. I was not going to vomit on a crime scene. The phone on the bedside table jangled.

"Hello," I croaked into the mouthpiece, realizing immediately I shouldn't have touched it.

"DD. What's going on?"

"Thank God it's you, Phil. David's dead. He's been shot. The apartment's been ransacked, and I've been cracked on the head."

"Are you okay?"

"I think so. Just dizzy and a little cloudy. Look, I'm hanging up. I've got to call 911."

I got hold of a live operator and concisely relayed what I'd observed.

"Are you a doctor?" the operator asked.

"No," I said, watching the stain continue to expand on the carpet. "I'm in insurance." I knew this would shut her up, because nobody wants to carry on a conversation with somebody in insurance.

# SEVEN

Don't ask me a lot of fool questions if you
don't like the answers.
— ERNEST HEMINGWAY

The cops descended on David's apartment
like locusts over Utah. Murder in Chicago
isn't all that rare, and the cops performed
their awful tasks with the patina of gallows
humor they apply to keep sane.

After David's body was finally removed,
the photographers took more shots of the
empty, bloody bed. I was interviewed by a
series of faces, and as they shepherded me
out the door to district headquarters, other
cops continued to triangulate, measure, and
sketch throughout the apartment.

They took me through a rear door into an
inner-city police station that was clearly falling apart. Built in the 1940s, it had none of
the Officer Friendly feeling. It was painted
gritty gray and stank of urine, sweat, and

fear. I noted they had installed bullet-proof glass and cameras everywhere, their concession to modern times.

I soon lost track of time as well as the number of bad cups of coffee I'd drunk. My head hurt, and I was having trouble comprehending that David had been killed. Over and over they asked me to explain why my fingerprints were everywhere in the apartment and why strands of my hair had been found in David's bed and bathroom. They'd found my Dyno-tool and suspected I'd used it to break in the apartment. When they asked what I'd done with the weapon, it dawned on me how someone perfectly innocent might confess to a heinous crime just to be done with it all.

"So you're sticking by your story you were there the night before. Let's say I might believe you. Tell me again, when did you leave?"

"I left at six o'clock or thereabouts. I already told you that."

"So you stayed the night. You left at six. But you didn't kill him, and you didn't search his place?" Detective Brewer asked for the umpteenth time, his chair creaking loudly as he shifted position.

"You know," he said, "we can tell a lot from the way a room was searched."

"I told you before, I did not kill him, and I didn't search his apartment."

"Then why'd you take off your shoes? And what was that Dyno-tool for except to break in? And why'd you use that phone in the bedroom? If you're such a hot-shot insurance investigator, you oughta know a damn sight better," he admonished.

"I do. But I was in a fog. What did you find out from the way his place was searched?"

"Well, we're positive it was no professional job. And that makes it look bad for you, because it seems we got your prints . . . ," he rummaged through some papers I couldn't read upside down, "and the boys tell me only your prints, on the door to the apartment and on his phone. And we got your knee prints all over the blood on the bedroom carpet. So where does that leave us?"

Despite the horror of it all, I wondered how they could correlate knee prints. The coffee hadn't quenched my thirst, and I was thinking about a cold beer when the door banged open.

"Detective Brewer? They told me I'd find you here. I'm Phil Richy. Here's my card."

I looked up, the bump on my head giving me triple vision.

"Phil," I croaked. "Thanks for coming. Help me get sprung, will you?"

Brewer studied the card. "This says you're an attorney." He gave Phil the regulation once-over. "Are you representing — ?"

"Oh, no," Phil interrupted. "I'm not in criminal law. I'm in property law."

"Oh, yeah. Property law." Brewer nodded and smiled. "That's where, like Elvis dies and his estate is worth four million bucks, but today it's worth over four hundred million. Right?"

"Look, Detective, I'm here because she was in my office talking on the phone to David Barnes, the deceased, when the shots were fired."

"So you heard the shots, too, Mr. —" Brewer glanced down at the card. "Mr. Richy?"

"Well, not exactly. I mean she wasn't on the speaker phone. But Miss McGil got disconnected after she heard shots. When we tried to call again, there was no answer. And an important point is that somebody on David's end hung up the phone. Then she left, and later she picked up the phone when I called there to find out what had happened."

Detective Brewer cocked his big head to one side and looked at the ceiling. "Counselor," he told Phil, "there's a coupla alternative theories here to explain all that. Maybe Miss McGil here wasn't really speaking to Mr. Barnes at all over the phone in your office. Maybe she'd already killed him before she arrived at your office. We know she was there earlier."

Phil glared at me. I knew I was going to have hell to pay for not telling him I'd spent the night with David.

Brewer continued. "Maybe this was all a set up, and he was never on the other end of that phone call at all. Or maybe . . ."

"Look, Detective," Phil interrupted.

Brewer cut him off. "And maybe you're involved in this somehow, too."

Phil put his hands on his hips and shifted into Lawyer Mode. "First of all, have you got the murder weapon? Are her prints on it?"

"The gun wasn't found," Brewer said, smiling. "Yet. We know we're looking for a .32. We recovered both bullets — soft lead, 85 grains, all consistent with the small entrance wounds and the massive internal injuries. We're checking right now to see if she's registered, so it would be a lot better if she told us straight out."

"Oh, come on, Detective. There are millions of Saturday Night Specials in circulation. Has she been checked yet for particle residue? And what about the tool used to gain entry to the apartment?"

"That wasn't found yet either, Counselor," Brewer admitted. "But we'll get ahold of it."

"In fact, Detective, you found DD at the scene. She was the one who called you. How do you explain how she got rid of these things?"

"I don't have to explain that yet," Brewer said, rustling the papers in my file, then closing the file with a bang.

Phil turned to me, hands on hips. "Have they read you your rights yet, DD?"

"No."

"And, what about her head injury?" Phil continued full steam ahead on the Lawyer Express.

"Maybe we're thinking she did that to herself, mister property-law-attorney-that's-not-acting-as-her-criminal-attorney."

I shivered, convinced the cops had me pegged as their prime suspect. Phil was no defense attorney. And every minute they wasted on me meant the real killer was getting farther and farther away.

Phil glared at Brewer. "Has Miss McGil been given proper medical attention? And for my records, exactly what time did you bring her into the station?"

Brewer blinked, twice, and his slight smile twisted into a slight frown. "Now don't go filing a harassment suit against me. I'm only doing the job they pay me for. We need to find out exactly what happened. There's a lot of inconsistencies in what she's tellin' us. This isn't some risky high-speed chase where Miss McGil here is just an innocent bystander."

"You're wrong. That's exactly what she is — an innocent bystander." Phil turned to me. "DD, have you seen a doctor yet?"

"No," I shot back, sensing he'd found a critical spot. "And Phil, I'm dizzy. I've got double, no, triple vision. And look at my hair. It's matted with blood."

"All right," Brewer said. "I guess maybe somebody should look at her head."

# EIGHT

There are some things which cannot be
learned quickly.
— ERNEST HEMINGWAY

Phil agreed to take a taxi and retrieve my
car from outside David's apartment. Meanwhile a black police medic with graying hair
wearing thick glasses hurried in to examine
me.

"No stitches," he said after prodding the
sore spot. "But you probably got a concussion. An' you need a head scan," he said,
furrowing his brow as he hastily repacked
his medical bag. "We don't carry that kind
of equipment around with us," he said as he
left.

Brewer then led me to a different room
for trace metal and gunpowder residue tests.

"You got any objections, or you want an
attorney present?" he asked.

I said no, and he grinned like I'd just

confessed to killing President Kennedy.

A short, blocky female officer with bright red lipstick arrived to administer the test. Brewer leaned against the wall and never took his eyes off me.

The efficient red-haired officer sprayed both my palms with an aerosol chemical. I'd seen this test for trace metal done and knew it would show if I'd held a gun in the last twenty-four hours. But I wasn't up on the new chemical she was using because the technology changed faster than a two-month-old's diaper.

When she completed the drill, she picked up everything and left without a word. Then another field technician, this time a smiling young Hispanic with huge brown eyes and the remains of an acne problem, arrived to perform a residue test.

Brewer, interested, stood over the technician's shoulder. "What kind you gonna give her?" he asked.

"They tol' me to use the NAA test, Jack," the technician replied.

"That's good." Brewer nodded, making another note in the file with my name on it.

I raised my hands. "Wait a second. I want to know what the NAA test is and exactly why it's good."

"She wants to know," Brewer smiled at

the technician. "So I guess I'll give her the good news. See, Miss McGil, he's gonna administer the Neutron Activation Analysis test. It's a lot more expensive than the other powder residue test we generally do in the field. But we're gonna spend those extra bucks on you because it's gonna show up even the smallest traces of powder residue on your hands."

He paused, letting the ramifications sink in.

"Top quality weapons don't leave much residue," he said. "But this NAA test is capable of picking up anything that might be on your hands. See?"

"But if David was killed with a .32 and nothing in that caliber remotely approaches being a precision weapon, why are you bothering?" I was interested in spite of myself.

Brewer didn't answer, but nodded to the gangly technician who snapped on a pair of latex gloves and ordered me to hold out both hands.

The technician dipped a swab in a 5 percent solution of nitric acid and nervously wiped it over my hands. His breath smelled of barbecue potato chips. He did know enough to concentrate the solution on my palms and on the webbing between my thumb and forefinger where any gunpowder residue would tend to collect. If they found anything, they'd compare it with traces the lab boys probably had found on the floor and the base of the bullets. The minutest remnant would allow them to determine the type of propellant power, which would help identify the bullet manufacturer and the age of the ammunition. If David had indeed been shot with a .32, the boys in the lab had undoubtedly found powder residue on the bullet, because the .32 is a short barrel, and the explosion continues even after the bullet leaves the barrel and coats it with residue.

"There," the technician said. "That didn't take long." He put his kit away and asked Brewer, "You hear the latest about that axe murder?"

"Nah, I've been tied up with this case all day," Brewer complained.

"The rookie, Dolan, laid out the vic's bloody clothes to dry in the parkin' lot," the technician laughed. "He can't get used to the smell of blood, so he lays the wet stuff out to dry in the sun, an' they get to blowing all over the place. He's still out there somewheres looking for that effing shirt."

After putting away the equipment, he and Brewer left together, trading stories like high school buddies.

I was alone for the first time since the cops had arrived at David's apartment. I wiped my hands with the moist towelette they'd provided and tried to collect my thoughts. It was difficult enough to comprehend David's death, let alone the creeping certainty that the cops believed I had something to do with it. Innocent people do get caught up in the justice system, and some never come out in one piece. This was eerily reminiscent of the HI-Data killings I'd gotten involved in a year ago, and I wasn't eager for the cops to make that connection.

For an instant, I considered calling my Aunt Elizabeth for help. But I knew she'd arrive in Buchanan colors, treat the cops like so many expendable bryophytes and sporophytes in her unending quest to dominate all lifeforms, and land me in an even worse mess.

The door opened. Brewer entered, followed by a thin, older guy with pasty skin and eyes of no particular color.

They sat down on either side of me at the small table. "This is Lieutenant Healy," Brewer said. He then turned on a tape recorder while Healy invited me to make a statement for the record.

The harsh florescent bulbs cast the worst

possible light. Lieutenant Healy's bald spot reflected the bulbs in the overhead lights, and Detective Brewer's untidy eyebrows and graying shirt were highlighted in the glare. I wondered which of my faults was sticking out like a sore thumb.

"So Miss McGil," the lieutenant began as he slowly rifled through my file, opened before him on the table. "I see here your real name is Daphne December McGil. Funny name."

So what if my name was funny. It was a sore point with me, the unfortunate result of an unresolved feud between the two sides of my family. Peace was finally declared when they settled on calling me DD. I still saw red if anyone dared call me Daffy, and I prayed these two cops weren't going to stoop that low.

"Be sure you include every detail you can remember in your statement," the lieutenant warned, "no matter how small or insignificant it might seem."

Up to now, both Phil and I had scrupulously avoided mentioning Matt King, our employer. But if it was going to be Matt or me, I didn't have to think twice. I told them the whole story and listened as the desk sergeant was ordered to locate Matt and get him in to make a statement. For once, Matt

King was going to be the one inconvenienced.

The lieutenant shut off the recorder and told Brewer to get it transcribed for me to sign. They both left, taking my file with them.

Brewer returned alone. I signed the statement while he glared and said, "You're being let go for now. They weren't able to find any trace metal or particle residue on you. You're still a suspect though," he warned, "and you shouldn't leave the county. We'll be in touch." He left the room abruptly without wishing me a good day.

Phil came in as Brewer left. After making sure the door was tightly closed, he leaned close and whispered, "Why the hell did you tell them about Matt? You could have left him out of it."

I sat quietly, watching Phil pace around the table. "It wasn't like I asked you to lie," he said. "All you had to do was not mention him. We're in for it now."

"I tried not to bring him into it, Phil. Really. But they wanted every little detail. Sorry," I lied.

"And what did they mean, saying you were at David's earlier? Why didn't you tell us you'd been there?"

"Do you tell me everything, Phil?"

"This is different, DD. That Lieutenant Healy has his own theory. He told me he suspects Matt hired you to kill David."

"Oh my God."

"Keep it down, DD." Phil put his hands on my shoulders. "For all I know they're listening to us right now. I'm no criminal lawyer, but I know we can't legally anticipate privacy in a police station."

"I can't believe it. Matt's a suspect, too?"

"You two are it, DD, because they've got no one else."

"What am I supposed to do now?"

"Matt's on the way back here in the company jet," Phil replied, ignoring my peril and focusing on Matt's. "This isn't going to be pretty, and you're smack dab in the middle of it."

From this point on, Phil wasn't going to be able to help me, so I changed the subject. "Did you bring back my car?"

"Oh, yeah. The good news is she's here. The bad news is she had two parking tickets stuck under her wipers. Man, those things are up to eighty bucks a pop." He glanced at his watch as we left the office. "I better try to get in touch with Matt," he said and pulled out his cell. "Oh, by the way, I talked to that Medic. He said you needed a head scan. Maybe you shouldn't be driving."

"DD! DD McGil," a voice called as we were exiting. I turned. It was Lieutenant Morgan Fernandez.

"Morgan?"

"Word came down you were here for questioning in the Barnes case. I got here as soon as I could." He waved a hello to Phil, still on his cell.

Lt. Morgan Fernandez is on Chicago's cold case squad. We'd met through Phil, and he'd done me a big favor in connection with the HI-Data case. He helped me out then, but I doubted he could help me out now.

"I checked with Healy and Brewer. I vouched for you, but they're convinced you're involved. They think you haven't told them everything you know."

"And you're here to — what? Get it out of me somehow?"

"Hey, DD. You know me better than that."

"Yeah, I know. Sorry. It's been a rotten day. Look, I'm not involved."

"But your being there last night and finding his corpse this morning puts you squarely on the suspect list. You do see that?" He bent and whispered in my ear, "Dammit, DD, you never should have talked to those guys without a criminal lawyer. Have you got a good one?"

"It's that bad, huh?"

"It's not gonna be any picnic. Do you know Karl Patrick? He's one of the best. Want me to call him?"

"Thanks, Morgan. I know Karl. But I haven't got the bucks to pay a guy in his league."

"I'll front it for you."

"I may take you up on that, but I have some thinking to do first." Morgan was, I thought, a good guy. But I don't like to be beholden to anybody, even if we had dated in the past.

"Promise?"

"I promise."

"And promise you'll have dinner with me. I haven't seen you since that great lunch we had at Boston Blackie's."

"That wasn't my fault."

"I know, I know. They kept me up in Wisconsin and Michigan for months digging out stuff in that serial killer case. But things are looking up and we got local leads so I'm free — free-er anyway — and I'm gonna call you."

Phil finally emerged from the cool station onto the overheated parking lot where I'd been talking to Morgan. The asphalt stuck to my shoes. I stopped, suddenly remembering that ten-thirty appointment I had with the IRS. I looked at my watch. It was now after three.

"What am I going to do Phil? Poussant'll break me like an egg. Then he'll fry me. Maybe I should get a note from Lt. Fernandez? Or you could write a note for me. How about it?"

Phil swatted a mosquito on his cheek into a bloody blob. "For God's sake, DD, don't make such a big deal out of it. If I were you, I'd go get that head scan first."

I handed him a tissue from my purse.

"Thanks," he said, wiping away the bloody mess and handing it back to me. "You sure you can drive?"

# NINE

Never confuse movement with action.
— ERNEST HEMINGWAY

Today was turning into a nightmare. David was dead, I was a suspect, and any head scan would have to wait. I looked at the dried blood on my clothes. That would have to wait too until I cleared things up with the IRS.

I headed south on Lake Shore Drive, taking the quickest route to the IRS office and trying to think of anything but David's bloody corpse. In the middle of fighting the heavy traffic, my cell rang. I hate driving and being on the phone at the same time, but I picked it up in case it was Phil or Matt.

"Hello," I growled. "This better be good."

"DD. It's Barry. Barry Harris."

"How'd you get this number?" Barry runs a successful computer software company, and I'd met him while handling a case some time ago. His company is in competition with the company Scotty works — worked — for, so while I consider him a business acquaintance, I'd never given him this number. "I know you know a lot of stuff, but I'm unpublished."

"We have our ways, DD. You should know there's no database I can't crack. Anyway, the reason I called is I need you. I've got a red alert here."

"What's going on?"

"We just found out that somebody's dumping my hot new software onto the international banking market, and you need to find out who it is. Immediately. Can you get over here right away?"

"Barry, slow down. I'm driving and you're talking too fast. Actually I'm on my way to a meeting with the IRS."

I thought I heard him stifle a laugh. I was going to say I couldn't take the case, but then I thought of Scotty. Could this have any connection to Scotty's disappearance? I knew it was far-fetched, but the international banking market might be the thread of a connection, so I changed my mind.

"All right, I'll be there as soon as I can. And don't ask me about the rest of my day," I added sharply, hanging up so I could concentrate on driving.

I passed Buckingham Fountain, its cascading water glistening in the sun. At night when they flood it with colored lights, it's even prettier. No wonder out-of-towners still make it a Chicago tourist destination.

Just past the fountain, I turned into the old Grant Park parking lot under Millennium Park. After adjusting to the sickly greenish light umderground, I nosed into a space marked for compact cars only. The lot is still the cheapest thing going in the inner city, but the repairs they'd finally been making lessened the odds of my finding cement bits in my front seat when I returned. Naturally however, they'd still demand the full parking fee.

The IRS office was on the nineteenth floor of an older high-rise office building in the south end of the Loop. I elbowed my way through the pedestrians, pushed through the revolving door, then jumped into an already full elevator just as the door was closing. No wonder Carl Sandburg called Chicago the "City of the Big Shoulders." Usually it's stimulating, but today it was hard to deal with all that raw energy, especially when people gawked at my blood-stained skirt. Maybe I should have gone home first to change, but it was too late now.

I hurried down the long gray corridor to

the door marked IRS and announced my late arrival to the receptionist, Miss Wang. She looked up, scanning me with spectacular half-closed eyes. Her makeup was so perfect it might have been done on a movie lot, and her stunning figure was set off by a white suit that accented her dark hair and complexion. She seemed not to recognize me, though this was the seventh or eighth time I'd been here. I supposed that to her, all victims looked alike.

She flicked through a stack of papers on her desk, her long, brightly painted fingernails tapping as she shuffled. "You're very late, Miss McPill." She spoke not to me but to her papers.

"It's McGil," I corrected. "And I'm late due to unavoidable circumstances." I was reluctant to give any more details because the waiting room was crammed with other audit-ees.

She glanced at my bloodstained skirt. "Hmmm. Take a seat. I'll see if he can see you."

The government provides only hard, molded plastic chairs, because God forbid your ass should be comfortable while you waited to be raped and pillaged by your IRS in action.

My thoughts again turned to David. He'd

so wanted to discover those missing Hemingway manuscripts. I wondered where they were and what would happen to them now that he was dead. I'd ask Phil, if he was still speaking to me.

I flipped through a long-outdated issue of *Fortune,* hoping to pick up some hidden clue known only to the *cognoscenti* on amassing wealth. One by one, other victims got called. None of them came back. I hoped they were leaving by another door instead of being stacked up like cordwood.

An hour and a half later, I was still waiting. I suspected Mr. Poussant of using long waits as another IRS torture tool. When I reminded Miss Wang that I was still waiting, she announced, "Oh, he had to leave."

"What? When?"

"You'll have to make another appointment," she said, pulling out her appointment book and x-ing out my name with a red pen.

I put my hand across the book, preventing her from adding more x's. "Why didn't you tell me when he left? Were you going to make me sit here and wait all day?"

Miss Wang sighed audibly. She dropped her pen and yanked the appointment book from under my hand.

"You stood Mr. Poussant up today, Miss

McGil," she scolded, as if I'd done it deliberately. "Taxpayers can't just miss appointments. Where would we be if everybody did that?"

I exited with as much grace as I could muster, brushed a few cement chips off the hood, and paid a twenty buck parking fee.

The drive back to my apartment was a blur. I stopped to thank Glendy and Lucille for taking care of the cat. When they spotted the bloodstains, they started fussing. I explained I'd had a bad day, and thankfully they silently accepted the understatement.

Back in my own apartment, Cavvy and I had a long conversation about how much we hated death. Maybe I was hoping Cavvy would be able to keep me from hibernating and drinking too much, like I'd done when Frank died and like I'd been doing since Scotty's disappearance.

I couldn't face food. Instead, I poured a stiff Wild Turkey from the half empty bottle. One of Hemingway's characters, I couldn't remember which, said opening bottles is what makes drunkards. I'd try to remember that tonight.

The phone rang. I hesitated, then picked up.

"What's going on?" Lauren, demanded. "Are you all right? My dad called and told me about David."

Lauren's father, a Chicago police dispatcher, tells her all the news before the mayor even hears about it.

There was a lot of background noise on her end. "I can hardly hear you," I shouted. "Where are you?"

"In Madison, Wisconsin, at the tournament."

"Is Bob winning?"

"Never mind about that. Dad said you found the body, and you're the prime suspect. Did you do it?"

"Dammit, Lauren. Of course I didn't."

"Then who did?"

"I don't know."

"Why didn't you tell me about the sexual harassment case against David? What the hell's going on, DD? From what Dad says, you're in deeper trouble than you think. You better get a lawyer."

"I don't need a lawyer, and I can't afford . . ."

"Don't say another word. Just call Karl Patrick. Bob and I will pick up the tab," she insisted before she hung up.

Probably my mother and Aunt Elizabeth would call too the minute they heard the news, even though Auntie was in Scotland. Hopefully that wouldn't be till morning. I didn't want to talk to anyone else so when the phone rang again, I let the machine take messages.

I stripped and left my clothes in a heap, hoping the good fairy would visit and pick up after me. Standing directly in front of the air conditioner, I let its clean, impersonal air surround me like wind off a Canadian glacier. I could hear my father saying, "Let your wants hurt you a little." I knew he was right, but tonight it felt like my wants could fill a black hole in outer space.

I fed Cavalier and gave him fresh water. Then I took a cold shower, relathering again and again, thinking, as Hemingway said, "There is no reason why because it is dark you should look at things differently from when it is light. The hell there isn't!"

I dried off, refilled my Wild Turkey, then plunked naked into bed. The phone rang and rang again. I let the answer machine earn its keep and petted Cavvy until his purring drowned out the sound.

# Ten

A cat has absolute emotional honesty:
human beings, for one reason or
another, may hide their feelings,
but a cat does not.
— ERNEST HEMINGWAY

The ferocious pounding in my head wouldn't stop. I jolted out of a sound sleep, shaking away a fading dream. The pounding, I realized, was someone beating on my door.

Cavalier had been rudely awakened too. While I slipped on a robe, he leapt out of bed to investigate the ruckus. My head hurt, and the spinning reminded me of that concussion. Or maybe I'd had one too many Wild Turkeys on an empty stomach. One or the other, as usual I was behind the curve.

"What the hell's going on out there?" I demanded from my side of the double-locked door.

"Are you DD McGil?" a deep, male voice asked.

"Who wants to know?"

"I work with Barry Harris. My name is Mitch Sinclair, and I need to see you right away. Let me in, will you? It's difficult talking to a door."

"Got any ID?" I demanded, trying hard to focus. I wasn't inclined to open my door for anyone after what had happened at David's apartment, let alone for someone I didn't know.

"What?" he sputtered.

"You heard me. Slip your driver's license under the door."

I could hear him mutter under his breath, but eventually one plastic coated corner of a license appeared on my side of the door. I reached for it, but Cavalier got there first. His quick paw batted it out of my fingers, and, not even pausing to sniff, he picked it up in his mouth and ran toward his favorite hidey-hole under the sofa.

"Oh, nooo," I yelled, chasing unsteadily after him.

"What's going on in there? Miss McGil?"

I fell to my knees, coaxing Cavvy to obey, cursing between clenched teeth when he didn't. Finally I screamed, "Give me that thing, you brat." Of course it was all to no avail. Whenever you think you're in charge, just try ordering a cat to do something. I reached wildly under the couch as a last resort, hoping to grab a handful of his fur.

"What's happening in there?" The pounding on the door got louder. "I want my license back. Listen, it's hot out here. Let me in."

Cavalier was the stubbornest cat in the universe. "Okay, you win this round Mister Cat," I hissed, giving up the hunt.

I steadied myself and headed for the door. There was nothing I could do but let Mr. Mitch Sinclair in. I unlocked and wrenched open the door.

The man who stood lounging against the opposite wall looked for all intents and purposes like the Prince Charming my mother was always saying will come for me one day. He was over six feet tall and had a handsome, intelligent face. His thick, light brown hair had wispy wings of white at the temples. He had a trim, muscular figure with just the right proportions to make the clothes he was wearing look good.

Suddenly I was keenly aware that my hair was a mess and the rest of me probably looked like one of the lower life forms. My Aunt Elizabeth, the Scottish Dragon, is always telling me what to do and how to do it. She continually carps that I don't take advantage of my looks. I could hear her lecturing me for the thousandth time: "One day you'll regret it. You were lucky enough to get the Mason good looks, DD McGil. But what good does it do? You waste them, and that's a crying shame."

Mitch Sinclair's deep brown eyes took a long look at me in my rumpled bathrobe. He stood up straight, shook his head, and walked past me into the apartment, saying, "You sure got a lot of locks on that door."

I felt myself blush. "I'm security conscious," I said as I latched it behind us.

"You're close to Wrigley Field. You a Cubs fan?"

"Avid."

"Me, too. Lifelong," he said convivially.

A few years ago, *Cosmopolitan* did a study on what women look at first in a man. What I noticed from my vantage point was that he knew how to wear a pair of pants to his best advantage. He wore no jewelry except a discreet gold watch with a brown leather band, and I liked the look of his strong hands and wrists. He was certainly attractive, but I didn't want to think about that. David had just been murdered. Scotty was missing. I had enough grief to deal with for a long long time.

"It's hot in here," he said, looking around. "These old buildings are great, but they definitely need central air."

"So, you wanted to see me about something?" I asked, candidly, still studying the rest of his anatomy against my will.

"First things first," he said, staring at my dishevelment. "Can I have my driver's license back?"

"Oh, um, sure. Let's go sit down." I led him into the living room, admiring his broad shoulders and narrow waist, all the while wondering how the hell I was going to get his license out of the blasted cat's mouth.

As if on queue, His Majesty's head appeared from under the sofa, the elusive driver's license clearly visible jutting out from his sharp front teeth.

Mitch paused in front of one of my bookshelves. As he scanned titles, I plunked myself down on the sofa directly over the cat.

"I see you're a history buff. You've got a lot of seventeenth-century English. Interesting period. A person had to choose and be on one side or the other."

*Unless you were a traitor,* I thought as I rummaged under the sofa with my right hand trying to grab the license from Cavvy.

I had hopes Mitch Sinclair wouldn't notice.

Too late. As soon as he sat down, the contrary cat emerged into plain view and then leapt onto the cushion beside Mitch and offered him the abused license. Even from my vantage point, Cavvy's tooth marks were clearly visible on it.

Mitch took it, clenched his jaw and flipped it over, examining both sides. The silence between us stretched out long enough for Dr. Johnson to write his dictionary. Sighing heavily, he tucked the license securely back into his wallet.

"Look, I'm sorry about my cat," I said. "We're not used to receiving visitors so late at night."

At Mitch's perplexed glance, I checked the mantel clock. It was only eight-thirty p.m. Now I was totally embarrassed. "I thought it was after midnight." I sighed. "I've had one hell of a day."

I noticed him eyeing the open box of Godiva chocolates on my coffee table. "Go ahead," I pointed at the box. "Indulge."

"Thanks," he said, choosing a champagne truffle. "I haven't had a very good day myself. This'll be dinner."

"Sometimes I have one for breakfast. My mother says she craved chocolate when she was pregnant with me, so I blame it on her.

Want coffee?"

I came back with two cups of instant Taster's Choice to find Cavalier nestled in Mitch's lap, purring like a racecar engine. Somehow he'd gotten Mitch to tickle him in a favorite spot. They say cats can read a person's essence. I took this as a sign of approval.

"Thanks, this is good," Mitch said, sipping the coffee. "Anyway, I'm only here because of Barry. I don't like dropping in like this out of nowhere, but you might remember you promised to see him earlier today."

"Oh no. You're right. I forgot all about it. Sorry." Despite the awkward situation and despite my better judgment, I was having unclean thoughts about Mitch. He smelled good, and I wondered what he'd feel like, taste like.

"Barry's convinced you're the only one who can handle this urgent job," he continued, bringing me back to reality. "He waited all day, but you never showed."

"I already said I was sorry."

"Forget about that. The important thing is to get this settled. I asked a few people about you today."

*Whoa. Wait a minute. Who did he think he was? That's my job. I'm the investigator.*

110

"I found out quite a lot."

*I hated when somebody knew more about me than I knew about them. Especially on the first date.*

"So?"

"So your reputation's good. In fact, very good. But you're a one-man operation. Or I should say one-woman operation." He smiled and cleared his throat.

"All true, so far," I said, knowing I'd probably have done the same thing in his shoes.

"Unfortunately, being local means you've never handled anything this big, so I can't understand why Barry thinks you're right for this job," he said bluntly.

"I'd like you to call Barry right now and tell him you can't do anything for him. Once he realizes that, we can get on with the business of hiring somebody who can."

I watched him finish the coffee and set down the cup.

"Excuse me? Let me get this straight. You came to see me because you want me to call Barry and tell him I can't take the job?"

"Don't think of yourself here. Think of Barry. No offense. As I said, I hear you're good. But I don't believe you're capable of doing this job, Ms. McGil, and there's no telling how long it's going to take for him to realize you won't be able to come through."

"So you've already decided I can't per-form?"

"I'm sorry, Miss McGil. I'm not trying to insult you. Be realistic. It's just that highly sensitive technology is involved here. Technology far beyond your ken. And because of national security, the Feds have been hot on Barry's tail since the encryption technology started turning up in the international banking market. They're accusing him of being dishonest and illegally dumping the software for big bucks. You can see we can't afford to wait. I want to get the top guys at Gilcrest and Stratton on board immediately to clear this thing up. They have a track record and they know what they're doing."

My earlier embarrassment over my disheveled appearance faded like a wilted rose, showing only the thorns. *Who said I couldn't come through?*

"Oh, and by the way," he added, a thin smile on his lips. "Barry doesn't know I'm here, so don't say anything to him, okay? He's obsessed with you. Lord knows why. Thinks you're the only one to handle this, and he'll never agree to give this job to a big firm like Gilcrest and Stratton until you tell him straight out you're not gonna take it."

I bit my lip, quietly seething, and got my

112

cell phone from the recharger. When I returned, he and Cavalier seemed to be on best-buddy status.

"Beautiful cat you've got here. What's his name?"

"Cavalier."

"Like in cavaliers vs. roundheads?"

"Exactly."

"What kind of cat is he?"

"Male," I answered, making a face at Cavalier. "Barry still at his office?"

"Yeah, I think so," Mitch said, stroking Cavvy's head as he rattled off the phone number.

Barry picked up at once.

"Hi, Barry. DD McGil. I'm sorry I didn't get back to you earlier. Do you know a Mitch Sinclair?"

Mitch Sinclair glared at me and shifted, dropping Cavalier unceremoniously onto the floor.

"Well, he's here now. Yeah, right here on my living room couch. And he's telling me he thinks the big guns from Gilcrest and Stratton should be hired to handle that job for you."

Mitch Sinclair's eyes hardened.

"That's right," I told Barry. "He seems to think I'm not . . . adequate."

Mitch squared his shoulders and folded

his arms across his chest like Mr. Clean in that commercial. Except he wasn't smiling, and an almost imperceptible flush rose from his neck to his face, then disappeared.

"Oh, really?" I asked cheerily into the receiver. Mitch clenched his teeth and glared at me. If looks could kill, I'd be in cold storage at the morgue right now. Like my Aunt Elizabeth the Dragon always says, "There are no Scots diplomats."

"You say Harry Marley at the Treasury Department recommended me? Oh, that's okay with me, Barry. Yeah, I'll tell him. Bye."

I snapped my cell phone shut and smiled. "Barry says the three of us are having a meeting tomorrow morning at nine in his office. Think you can make it?"

Mitch Sinclair abruptly stood up and headed for the door. I followed, unlatched and opened it. He brushed by me in the doorway, and despite everything, his physical presence made my heart pound.

"Miss McGil," he said, facing me. "Thanks for the coffee and for your time. Believe me, I didn't mean to be rude. You're undoubtedly very capable in your field, and I'm sorry we had to meet like this. I don't know who Harry Marley is or why he recommended you, but we both know this job is way over your head. Sooner or later you're going to fail. I'll be there when you do. I just hope for Barry's sake it won't be too late."

The revised *Oxford English Dictionary* contains 615,000 words, but I was unable to think of one to say to him. I clutched my robe tighter against me. A breeze blew up my legs, making them tingle. I felt a delicious hot rush as his interesting brown eyes gave me one last glance before he pivoted on his heel and strode down the corridor.

He turned into the stairwell and disappeared out of sight. He was a good friend to Barry and now he'd cast me as the enemy. Tonight, I may have won a battle, but I suspected I could lose the war. Maybe he was right about the job being out of my league, but I'd never admit that, no matter how much I was going to regret watching him disappear into the sunset, taking my fantasy sex life along with him.

# Eleven:
## Day 3: Tuesday

I love sleep. My life has a tendency to fall
apart when awake . . .
— ERNEST HEMINGWAY

Exhausted, I fell back into bed, my mind
reeling. Toward morning, I dropped into a
deep sleep that kept me from thinking but
not from dreaming. I was in a shimmering
desert. A uniformed police officer jumped
off a camel and began to strip-search me. I
resisted. He pressed his hard body against
me. I could taste his insistent kisses, feel his
hands on my body. It was Mitch Sinclair,
telling me to yield the evidence. Somewhere
off in the background, I heard Miss Wang
ask if I was ready. Suddenly my flesh was
wet with David's blood, and I froze as his
cold, dead hand brushed my cheek.

I opened my eyes. Cavalier was licking my
face, bursting the bubble of my nightmare.

"So you're attempting to make up for being such a Quisling last night with Mitch Sinclair." He purred as loudly as he could, which I interpreted as agreement.

I had to agree with Hemingway this morning — things didn't seem any better in the light of day. David was still dead, I was still a suspect, and I had the same bad headache. My feelings about David were in a jumble. And I now regretted my foolish actions the night before in taking up the gauntlet against Mitch Sinclair. I was attracted to him against my will, and my own pride and stubbornness had simply set me up for a professional fight I would probably lose.

The weather channel confirmed there was no relief in sight for Chicago's heat wave. Even with my air conditioning, it was nearly as hot inside my apartment as out there. Mitch was right — I needed central air, but that was impossible in this old building. I promised myself to investigate a new window unit with more BTUs.

I fed Cavvy, and in spite of continual reminders that breakfast is the best meal of the day, all I could face was a strong cup of fresh-brewed chicory coffee. I retrieved the *Trib* from the lobby and saw that David's murder had made page one.

# HEMINGWAY EXPERT DAVID BARNES MURDERED

## — By Jonathan Hermann

Dr. David J. Barnes, 38, professor of English and internationally recognized Ernest Hemingway scholar, was found shot to death in his apartment Monday.

Scott Eider, a spokesman for the Cook County Coroner's Office, said Barnes had been shot twice and his apartment appeared to have been ransacked. No witnesses to the shooting have been found, and police are launching an intensive investigation.

Barnes, a professor of English at City College, was the subject of a bitter sexual harassment suit. A colleague, Beth Moyers, said he had hoped to have all charges dropped, but instead, a trial was pending.

According to reliable sources, Barnes claimed to have found newly discovered Hemingway stories and poems lost since 1922.

American Insurance confirms it has insured the manuscripts, soon to be auctioned by Bressmer Galleries.

City College officials are planning a memorial service next week.

The body was discovered early yesterday by Insurance Investigator, DD McGil.

Yesterday's anger, fear, shock, and sadness returned full measure. So now I knew what Lauren meant about sexual harassment. But the David I'd known surely didn't need to harass women to get attention. During the time we'd spent together, we hadn't always agreed on things. But he'd been so vital, so alive. I knew I'd been on the verge of falling hard for him a second time.

Who had killed him? And why? Was it related to the Hemingway find or to the harassment suit? Or to something else? Lauren was right. The cops were probably still considering me as the prime suspect, even though they'd let me go. The prudent thing, my Aunt Elizabeth would say, would be to look for some answers myself.

I flipped channels. Every station was covering David's murder. The heat wave was old news. And the media being what it is, the sexual harassment charges eclipsed the literary find. Because I was named as having found the body, I knew the whirlwind would engulf me, too. I listened awhile, then turned it off, sick at heart.

Cavalier dogged my footsteps, still trying

to make up for last night. I cringed when I thought of Mitch Sinclair, knowing deep down he was right about the job for Barry.

"I'm in way over my head," I commiserated with Cavalier, who for once seemed to be listening.

Needing to look more capable than I felt at today's meeting, I chose a mocha silk Ellen Tracy blouse and a creamy vanilla silk skirt. To appease the fashion gods, I added a wide belt and the way-too-expensive pin of a pouncing jaguar that Aunt Elizabeth had given me on my last birthday. As I'd undone the wrapping paper, *ma tante* had insisted I set some goals. "And one of them," she'd added, "ought to be to catch a good man. It's the twenty-first century, DD. Men today don't mind a woman who's sassy and lippy all the time." I'd smiled and said nothing. Auntie knew I'd relied all my life on being lippy — a habit I'd developed early on, thanks to my dad, who'd warned me never to allow myself to be victimized under any circumstances if there was a way to talk myself out of it. By now, Auntie knew that my being sassy was an old habit that kicked in automatically, just like riding a bicycle, driving a car, or making love.

To complete the outfit I found my favorite pair of Nine West pewter heels. The only thing wrong was that when I looked in the mirror, I saw two of myself. Even at that, I looked a lot better than I felt. Last night, the Wild Turkey had deadened the pain, but it wasn't doing me any good this morning.

The red light was blinking on my answering machine. I hit the play button and Phil's not-so-cheery voice said he hoped I was feeling better because I had to be in his office at two o'clock for an urgent meeting. "Matt's back," he said, "and he wants to go over some things with you."

*Great, Phil. Just what I need.*

I popped three aspirin and a multi-vitamin and listened to the rest of the messages. Aside from the six news reporters wanting interviews, I'd have to call Don, another attorney who gives me work, and my mother, and Tom Joyce. Apparently Aunt Elizabeth hadn't heard yet, thanks be to the gods.

I punched in Don's number.

"I heard what happened," he said without preamble. "Word is out you could be the scapegoat, so watch your butt."

"Thanks, Don. Don't worry. I'm doing fine."

"Good. If you do need anything, let me know. In the meantime, I need your help."

"I don't know, Don. I've already got a full plate."

"Look, all I want is for you to make one simple visit to Graue Mill in Oak Brook and evaluate their security system."

He paused, then sounding put-out, added: "I've hardly ever asked you for a favor, but I promised Anne you'd do this. She's on their Board of Directors, and it won't look good if you don't come through."

Anne was Don's wealthy, attractive, and very politically involved wife. She supports an array of charities, is extremely savvy, and knows exactly what buttons to press to get things done. On top of all that, I like her.

"You mean it won't look good if you don't come through, right, Don?" I laughed.

"C'mon, DD. Don't let me down. This is really important to us both. And doing something constructive during this murder investigation will get your mind off things."

"Okay, you earn points for that rationalization. So tell me what you need. I'll try to fit it in. That's the best I can do right now."

"I knew I could count on you. Here's what's happening. The Mill has had three break-ins in the last few months. Mid-States Casualty is about to cancel their ass if they don't modernize their security system. From what I've heard, it's antediluvian."

"Sounds like a big job to me."

"It's easy money, DD. All you have to do

is an evaluation and a recommendation. You've got to check out the existing system and then give me enough specific recommendations for substantial improvements to sway the insurance company over to our side. But you've got to get over there before the end of the week. If they get canceled, they won't get insured anywhere else without paying a fortune. Believe me, I'm doing you a favor."

Graue Mill, I'd read somewhere, was the oldest working mill in Illinois, famous for having been one of the northernmost stops on the Underground Railway for runaway slaves. Don was right. It probably wasn't a big job.

"Okay, I'll do it as a favor to you and Anne."

"Good. They're open until nine, and the job absolutely has to be done before the end of the week. E-mail your report to me here at my office. Okay? And did you hear about the crazy lawsuit Phil Richy has to handle?"

"Lately I can't tell what's crazy. Tell me."

"Get this. Some wife offed her husband. Got three to fifteen in the pen for voluntary manslaughter. Then she ups and sues her husband's former employer for denying her survivor benefits. God, I love the law. Don't forget, DD. Get that report in by the end of the week. Oh, Anne sends her best."

I hung up, entered it into my trusty black appointment book along with my two o'clock at Phil's with Matt. Then I returned mother's call.

"We're worried about you, DD," she said, broaching the subject in her usual crab-like fashion.

"You mean you're worried I might be arrested for murder, or you're worried I might have committed the murder?" *Did my mother as well as my best friend really believe I could be involved?*

"Now, DD, that's not fair. I know how badly that awful cad David Barnes hurt you. And I know what your temper is like when Buchanan obstinacy rears its head. You're so much like your Aunt Elizabeth."

You can't fool with kith and kin. Aunt Elizabeth and I were too akin as far as I was concerned. But there was nothing I could do about it.

"Listen, DD. This might help you," she went on. "I just finished reading the Second Law of Success, the Law of Giving. It says that every relationship is one of give and take. What goes up must come down. What goes out must come back. Receiving is the same as giving. Think about it, okay? If you accept these principles, he says you'll live longer."

I had to stop myself from blurting out that the difference in average life expectancy from 49 years in 1900 to 77.9 years today was due to improved diet and medicines, not to my mother's current hero, Deepak Chopra. But I'm not one to tell anybody what to believe. I just wish nobody would tell me, either. Lately, my mother, along with Glendy and Lucille, had been studying Deepak Chopra's *Seven Spiritual Laws of Success.* The ultimate goal of the little dears was to achieve success — not for themselves but for me. They worried about my love life, specifically the lack thereof, and they believed the Seven Laws would help "turn things around" for me. They took every opportunity to drop snippets of "the Laws" into the conversation. I'd already had it with Number One, the Law of Pure Potentiality, where I was supposed to align myself with the quantum soup and understand my true nature so I'd never feel guilty or fearful or insecure. And I was dreading Laws Three through Seven. But at least they'd stopped with the Feng Shui.

"Oh, and don't forget about my birthday, Sunday," she reminded me. "You will be here for dinner?"

*I'd completely forgotten.* "Of course I'll be there."

"Good. And bring along your mending. I know you hate to sew."

"Love you, Mom," I said, pleased she was handling the news about my involvement in David's murder so well.

I hung up, waved good-bye to Cavvy, and rushed out, reminding myself to pick up a nice birthday present for my mother.

"Pssst. DD. Come here a minute." Glendy and Lucille beckoned from their doorway. "Are you all right? Is there anything we can do?"

"Good morning ladies. You saw the *Trib,* I take it."

"Well, yes. And CNN, Fox News, and WGN," Glendy admitted.

"And we got texted by a bunch of the neighbors," Lucille added. "Oh, and your mother phoned, too. She's worried about you."

The girls, like most of their friends in the Seniors Club and the Salvation Army, have learned to use computers and they love to text on their Palm Pilots. They're like teenagers and never cease to amaze me.

"We promised to keep an eye on you." Glendy smiled sheepishly.

"Is it true what your mother said? You

used to date the one that got killed, David Barnes?" Lucille quizzed.

"Yes, I dated him, but that was a very long time ago."

"What were the ructions last night all about? Who was that handsome man banging on your door?" asked Glendy.

"The handsome man is strictly business. Sorry if he disturbed you. Really, everything's okay. I'm on my way to a meeting and have to hurry. See you both later."

# TWELVE

The best way to find out if you can trust
somebody is to trust them.
— ERNEST HEMINGWAY

Barry Harris' office was in the heart of the
Loop in one of the old, iconoclastic buildings. Parking around here was never easy
and they'd cranked up the heat on enforce-
ment so if you got a ticket, you actually had
to pay it. The good old days when any old
Chicago alderman or judge could get you
off the hook were gone. Now not even a
papal bull could save you.

I parked in an expensive lot two blocks
away and hiked to Barry's office. Normally
I enjoy a brisk walk downtown, but the past
few days of accumulated heat had turned
the streets oppressive and the crowds downright ornery. Fast-walking women in tennis
shoes shouldered the crowds with more
rough and tumble than the men. I fought

my way through the revolving door into Barry's building, and seriously contemplated Deepak Chopra's Laws of Success. Maybe it really was because I didn't understand my true self that my outfit was wrinkled, my hair was a mess, and I had absolutely no idea how I was going to help Barry solve his problem.

This vintage building hadn't changed much in fifty years, give or take the addition of a gazillion electrical upgrades. The old elevator still had its heavy accordion gate, and I checked the inspection ticket and uttered a silent prayer as I pressed the number for Barry's floor.

COMPUTER SOLUTIONS, INC. was painted in black letters on the frosted glass panel on the outer door, and when I entered, a very thin balding man with thick glasses approached.

"I'm Herman Marx, Barry's office manager." He offered his hand while glancing up at the wall clock.

"I'm on time, right?"

"Two minutes early even," he smiled.

The office air conditioning was on full blast, instantly reviving me. The aroma of freshly brewed coffee helped too.

"I just brewed a new mix called Jamoco Select," he said, recognizing my interest, and he filled a cup from an expensive cof-feepot.

As I took a sip, he removed his glasses, scratched his head and said, "They say you found some guy's body,"

"This is truly great coffee, Mr. Marx."

"Okay, I get the message. You don't want to talk about it. I know you're here about the piracy," he said, putting his glasses back on. "Follow me. I'll take you to the big guns."

He opened the door to Barry's office. Barry stood up and pulled out a chair for me.

"Glad you're here, DD. I see Herman got you coffee. Okay, then. Let's get down to it."

Barry was on perpetual overdrive, always doing at least two things at once. He talked almost as fast as he could think, and I knew he couldn't wait to get back to his work. His office had a vast array of electronics equipment, including some of the newest large screen portables as well as a lot of scanners and other equipment. Next to Barry's desk was a computer and video camera he used for international conferencing. He never had to leave his office to confer with a client.

"Sorry about yesterday," I apologized and

plunked my cup onto the table, spilling a few drops. I sat down, avoiding any eye contact with Mitch Sinclair. I was still thinking about David's murder, and my head was pounding. Nonetheless, I hated myself for noticing how handsome Mitch was up close and personal in the light of day. He was wearing a dark blue blazer with chinos and a white button-down shirt, open at the collar, and his physical presence was disturbing, despite the fact he hadn't yet said a word.

"You two already know each other," Barry said, a thin smile playing fleetingly on his lips as he briskly closed the door and sat down across the table from me.

"Yeah," I said, glancing directly at Mitch. Those attractive brown eyes seemed to look through me, not at me, sharply bursting my fantasy bubble of mutual attraction.

"Hello," he said icily.

"All right you two," Barry said abruptly. "Get into neutral corners and don't waste time sparring." He swiped away my coffee spills with his handkerchief and continued, "I heard this morning about what happened, DD." He leaned across the table and looked concerned. "So maybe this isn't a good time to ask for your help. I should be doing just the reverse."

"Thanks, Barry. I'm fine. They focused on me because I found the body, not because I had anything to do with the murder. Believe me, it'll all blow over soon."

*As I said the words, I wasn't sure if I was telling the truth or a lie. I just didn't know. But I did know I had to look into this problem if there was even the slightest chance of shedding light on what happened to Scotty.*

"So, I'd rather you just tell me exactly what's going on."

"Okay, DD. It's your call. To sum it up, I'm in a lot of trouble. I'm gonna lose the business, not to mention mega dollars, and maybe land in jail if we don't straighten this out immediately. The problem's exactly what Mitch told you. Some copyrighted software we developed for the International Monetary Fund has shown up on the open market, and we have no idea where it's coming from."

"Where'd it first turn up?" I asked, taking out my notebook.

"In this global economy," Barry said, "it's turned up all over — Europe, the Far East, the Caribbean. And the Feds think its being used to launder drug and arms money, but who knows?"

"Is that why the government's so uptight about this software?" I asked.

"Well, that and because it was especially designed to prevent theft, tampering, and monitoring. Explain it to her in layman's terms, Mitch."

"I'll try," Mitch shrugged uncomfortably, an Oxford Don being asked to teach the alphabet to a savage. "You see, this software allows money and information to be transferred securely from any computer to any other computer. The product is totally unique. Nothing like it is out there on the market. Two key elements make it special. First, the information is encrypted during transmission."

He paused. "You know what encryption is, I take it."

"Coded, right?"

"Correct, so as to ensure privacy in the transaction. Second, the highly sensitive software carries with it its own decryption key, thereby allowing it to appear in the receiving computer without that computer having any decryption software. In this program, only the computer which is being addressed can receive the encryption key and decrypt the message."

"What I don't understand," I said, "is if this program was developed under the IMF, why are the Feds hounding you now? They knew it wouldn't allow transactions to be monitored."

"We sold only to banks on U.S. soil, DD," Barry interjected. "Banks the Feds can examine anytime. They're hopping mad because the stuff is on the international market, and they regard some of this technology as vital to national security. They say all sorts of laws are being broken by its being disseminated overseas."

"How many copies are out there?"

"Legitimately, ten." Barry exchanged a glance with Mitch, who nodded agreement. "And they're all tucked away in vaults next to the gold bullion and diamonds in the big banks that bought the software from me."

"Well, somebody's copying one of them," I insisted.

"Brilliant deduction, Mrs. Sherlock," Mitch interjected. "See, Barry? She doesn't understand the technical problems involved. How do you expect her to tackle this?"

"Hey," Barry said softly. "This isn't the War of the Roses, you two. The software, DD, isn't something you can just sit down at a PC and copy. It takes some special equipment and some very special knowledge. People in the banks don't have that."

I glared indignantly at Mitch. "Well, somebody has it."

Mitch drummed his fingertips on the

table, frowning impatiently. "This is exactly why we need the top manpower over at Gilcrest and Stratton, Barry."

I decided not to take offense. This was strictly business. "Maybe he's right, Barry," I conceded. I glanced at Mitch who unclenched his teeth and relaxed.

"After all," I continued, keeping an eye on Mitch, "Gilcrest and Stratton and I could operate on parallel tracks." I smiled sweetly. "To the winner go the spoils."

"No," Barry insisted. "Forget it. They've got a bunch of used-up flat feet and donut-pushers over there. I'd be in jail for twenty years by the time they got their first break. Harry Marley over at the Treasury said you'd be the right one to tackle this for me, DD."

"Could anyone be pulling copies of this software over the Internet?"

"Impossible," Mitch answered. "First, our security doesn't allow anyone to hack into the computers. Also, none of the software is in any machine that's online."

"Well, some of the current computer hackers are doing some really amazing things."

"That's true. Some hackers have done almost everything possible with electronic equipment except maybe do the dishes,"

Barry said. "But that computer is off-line. Nobody would have access to it."

"Well, who in your office has access to the software and the equipment necessary to copy it?"

"Just me, Mitch, Peters, and Hilliard. Oh, and Herman, too. That's it. But I've known them all for a long time, and I trust them all with my life."

I glanced pointedly at Mitch. "What about clients?"

Barry and Mitch both smiled.

"Nobody comes here," Barry said.

"We always go to them," Mitch added.

"Most everything is done over the phone," Barry explained, pointing to the elaborate set-up next to his desk. "See, I use that Internet teleconferencing set with voice and video. And even if some CEO does visit when they hire me, they don't know a byte from a bit. None of 'em would know how to get their hands on anything."

"I'm going to need a complete rundown on your office security."

"Mitch can give you the details. We've got very tight security for the entire office. Everything's hooked up to the computer, even the fire alarm. I've asked Mitch to personally work with you on this. Here's his personal cell number. He'll be on hand 24-7 to answer any technical questions. I hope you two aren't going to have any problems working together."

Mitch glanced at me. He looked like he might throw up, and I wasn't jumping for joy.

"Something's bothering me, Barry," I said, deflecting the issue. "Even if I find the people who are doing this, those bootleg copies will still be out there. The damage is already done, so why bother?"

"Don't worry about that," Barry said enthusiastically, clasping his hands together. "I've got an upgraded version of the software, which isn't compatible with the previous one. When we distribute the new version, we'll distribute it only to the authorized banks. Once a terminal receives from it, it won't receive from the old one anymore."

"Ain't science wonderful?"

"Sure is," Barry agreed. "Once the new software starts being legitimately used, any other illegal receivers will be closed off, and the wounds will be sealed. The old terminals won't be able to depend on easy transference anymore."

Mitch chimed in: "Before we can release this new version, we've got to figure out where the leak is and plug it." He sighed loudly. "Otherwise we're just digging a deeper hole."

"You'll take the job, DD?" Barry asked.

I opened my notebook and jotted a few notes. "Before I decide, I need to look at your entire security set-up."

"Fine," Barry agreed. "Mitch, take her into your office and lay everything out for her, okay?"

"You're the boss." Mitch stood up and walked out the door as I continued scribbling on my notepad. When I finished, instead of leaving the office, I closed and locked the door behind Mitch.

"What the hell are you . . . ?" Barry stopped mid sentence as I turned to face him. I put my finger to my lips and shoved the piece of paper from my pad across the table under his nose: "Be Quiet. Office May Be Bugged."

Taking an electronic de-bugger from my purse, I checked Barry's office and all the equipment, floor to ceiling. Barry kept trying to interrupt me. When I finished, I shoved the handy gadget back into my bag and sat down.

"You're clean, but I needed to be sure."

"I'm glad you're happy, but that was totally unnecessary. I do the same thing every morning. Mitch would have told you so."

"Some things a girl likes to find out for herself. Exactly what do you know about Mitch, Barry? How long has he been with you?"

"DD, he's a junior partner in the company and my numero-uno troubleshooter. The best there is. He came on board six months ago. Wonder now how I managed without him. I hear you two didn't exactly hit it off last night. But I vouch for him. He's smart, just like you. And he's got a sense of humor just like yours. He's really a straight-arrow, just like you, although you don't want anybody to know that."

"Well, somebody is making copies of your stuff. It could be him. Why is he so hot for me not to take this job?"

"Mitch is highly intelligent and a perfectionist. He doesn't know you at all. This situation needs to be looked at from the wrong end of the prism, which is exactly what your friend Harry Marley at the Treasury Department told me you do best."

*I'd been pestering Harry Marley to help me get information on Scotty ever since he'd disappeared, and Harry, I knew, was fed up with me. So I wondered exactly what he'd said to Barry about me. I wondered too if Harry had ever replaced his favorite hundred dollar bill cuff link that had gotten buried in the rubble of the old Consolidated building.*

"Listen DD, forget about Mitch. Now are you gonna take the job?"

"Only if you promise me two things. One, you'll let me set up a micro video camera in your office. I've got one of those teeny wireless systems with a 2.4 GHz color camera that I can install right there" — I pointed to his ceiling — "in that sprinkler head."

"No. I can't agree. I'm certain the copies weren't taken from here. I'm here all the time."

"You can't be certain of anything right now, Barry."

"Look, I don't have surveillance video here in my office because it could backfire and be the cause of a leak. Furthermore DD, you're dead wrong if you still suspect Mitch is involved. He's done the most work on tracing the whereabouts of the pirated copies. I have a duty to be loyal to my people."

"Either I set up the monitoring system in your office here or I don't take the job. Choose A or B." I got up to leave.

Barry scowled. "Why do I feel like I'm being blackmailed."

I unlocked the door, ready to walk out.

"Barry, when I hook up, I won't hook up to any computers. It'll be a stand-alone operation, and I'll come in and review the video myself. Only me. How's that for a compromise?"

"Okay. Have it your way," he said, glowering. "Set it up, but I don't like it."

"And you've got to promise me that you won't tell anyone, even Herman. And certainly not Mitch."

"This is crazy. You might as well suspect your cat."

"I often do. Look Barry, I'm sorry, but it's got to be that way or not at all." I turned on my heel.

"Wait. All right. All right. Be here at ten tonight, and you can install it. What's your second condition?"

"I need to look at your phone records for the last five months. Will you tell Herman to make copies so I can take them with me?"

"All right, but I'm telling you, you're on the wrong track."

"I've got one more question, Barry. It's on another matter."

"Okay. Shoot."

"Have you heard anything about Scotty Stuart from Jerry Frehling's operation?"

"Not a peep. You know, DD, I have a lot of analogues here — er, you know computer test methodologies. Anyway, I ran them all to see if I could track him. Nothing showed up. They're our competitors, by the way. Can I ask if this is business or personal?"

"It's not business," I assured him. "Just curious, that's all."

I left his office feeling sick at heart. I'd never be able to tell him just how personal it was. As I emerged, Mitch approached, scowling. "What's going on?"

"We were discussing terms," I said noncommittally. "Now can you show me that security?"

Mitch eyed me sourly. Without a wasted word, he took me into his office and detailed the intricacies of their state-of-the-art security system. His explanation was clear, concise, and comprehensive. He had a good mind and answered my questions before I asked them. He also provided the confidential list of banks with names of contact people who'd purchased their encryption software. It was a start, which was more than I had going with him personally. And I kept telling myself to keep it that way. One of the reasons I'd taken this job was the off-chance I'd find out something about Scotty. That wasn't going to be the case, but I hoped I still might get a line on him somehow. Mitch might be sexy, intelligent, and downright attractive, but I was after Scotty. Besides, Mitch might be the one responsible for pirating the software. If so, Barry would have him drawn and quartered before we'd ever get to first base.

"And I'm sorry about what happened to you," Mitch said as I walked out of his office. "I mean finding that body. Why didn't you tell me last night? I wouldn't have said what I said."

"Even though you meant it?"

"Can't you see I'd like to help you?"

"Some kind of help," I said and walked away as his door slammed.

Herman's eyes were expressionless as he handed me the phone records with a too-casual attitude. As we said good-bye, I had the distinct feeling he, too, questioned my ability to do this job.

In the parking lot, I quickly scanned the phone records from Herman, jotting down any international and out-of-state numbers. I'd have Barry run a check to see if any weren't his and follow up from there. One thing I hadn't told Barry was that I'd recently installed Cell Spy Pro in my cell phone. This new technology wasn't illegal — yet — but I expected it to be any day. I could target any cell phone and view the calls made and received, see any photos or text messages stored and even have the target phone call me whenever it made or got a call so I could listen live to conversations. Nothing had to be installed on the target phone. The only big hurdle was that in this case, the target phone was Mitch's. I only used Cell Spy if I had to, and in this case, I had to. I bit my lip and set up Mitch's cell number as a target. I also made a note to remind me to install a Keykatcher recording device tonight that would record all keystrokes made on Barry's main computer — the one that held the software. I'd have to do it without his knowledge or consent, of course. Even then they would probably catch it quickly. How soon would give me a good read on how their security functioned on a day-to-day basis. I suspected I was also going to definitely need my mail-order Portable Lie Detector. Thank God for GadgetUniverse.com.

I paid the twenty buck parking fee and sped back to my office. I still had no real plan. Would my involvement help solve Barry's problem or make it worse? Speaking of worse, if Barry ever found out I was using Keykatcher and Cell Spy Pro, he'd never forgive me. I thought I could explain Keykatcher to him — I hoped. At least all this activity was keeping me from brooding about David and Scotty.

# THIRTEEN

A man can be destroyed
but not defeated.
— ERNEST HEMINGWAY

My tiny office is located in the Loop in the Beech Building, not far from my old office in the Consolidated Bank Building, demolished over a year ago. The new Consolidated Bank Building was supposed to be finished soon, but with all the turmoil in the financial sector, I wasn't counting on it. I'll probably be here for some time, renting one of the many small offices that went vacant when the economy collapsed and everybody downsized. At least the rent is reasonable. The bad part of the bargain is putting up with my landlord, George Vogel. As I inserted my key into the lock, he appeared beside me, springing up full-blown like some pesky Djinn.

"DD, I've been looking for you."

I knew that tone of voice. George was a neat-freak. The last thing I needed today was another lecture from him about cleaning up my office.

He leaned against the doorframe like Samson in the temple. He enjoyed standing too close.

"You really look boss today," he said, cuffing my shoulder playfully.

It was difficult talking with George since we never made eye contact.

"George, I . . ."

He pushed my door inward and clicked on the light. "I heard about what happened — you finding that body and all. I wanted to check things out for you. There, now it's safe for you to go in."

"You don't have to . . ."

He peered into my office over my shoulder. "You should tidy things up, DD. I bet the press will be here today to interview you. You know how hot Hemingway is. You could easily . . ."

"George," I said firmly, maneuvering him out of the doorway. "I don't want to see anybody from the press. You better notify security to keep them out. Are we clear on that?"

"Of course," he responded. "Whatever you want. But why don't you want publicity?

You didn't kill the guy, right?"

*Another person in my orbit who apparently thinks I might be capable of murder. How many more were there?*

"I can't talk about that," I told him. "And I've got to get to work now." I stepped back quickly and closed and locked the door to emphasize my point. Hopefully he wouldn't come back, at least for today.

Yesterday's pounding headache was back, accompanied by a sick feeling in the pit of my stomach. Maybe I did have a concussion. I made a note to call and check what that head scan would cost. I unearthed a bottle of Advil at the back of a drawer, swallowed the last three with a gulp of water, then worked up a list of calls I wanted to make before answering the summons to Phil's office.

While I waited for the Advil to kick in, I propped my feet on my desk and checked MapQuest for the best route to City College. It was the logical place to start digging up some information on David, and I planned to stop there later today. I felt sure the cops weren't doing anything except suspecting me. I wondered whether they had a tail on me. Probably one of those GPS tracking devices.

I forced myself to call the dreaded IRS

and spoke to Miss Wang. She informed me that Mr. Poussant was not yet in and no, she didn't know what time he would be. All I could do was leave a message.

Rifling through some papers, I found the number for Chicago Security, Inc. I called and asked for their president, Jimmy Lee Yarborough. Jimmy Lee and I had met at a demonstration on the latest high-tech advances in home and business security. He'd hired me last week to handle what he called "a real tough case" of false alarms. His company had won out in a hotly contested competition to install a state-of-the-art security system at a sprawling, new and very posh assisted living facility called Monarch Care on Chicago's North Side. Jimmie Lee asked me to investigate why the security system's computerized alarm was going haywire and setting off a slew of false alarms. After the first few alarms, Monarch Care began to charge-back the costs to Jimmy Lee's company, so he was anxious to get the problem straightened out before it ruined him. I'd been lucky and solved the case on Saturday before David's murder — although it seemed more like a million years ago.

Finally, he came on the line. "Jimmy Lee? It's DD McGil."

"Miss McGil? What's up? If you need more information on that senior citizen case, you got to get it from Manny. He's got all the particulars. Hold on, and I'll transfer you."

"Wait, Jimmy Lee. I don't need any more information. I'm calling to tell you I solved the case."

"What? Impossible." He belly-laughed. "We just gave you the dang thing a few days ago. Two other agencies were working on it before I gave it to you, and they couldn't find a thing wrong. They checked and rechecked everything, and tell me they can't pinpoint why that fool alarm goes off all the time. So what makes you think you're so good you got it already solved?"

"Jimmy Lee, if I didn't know you better, I might be mad because you called in two other agencies before you called me. As it is, I'm willing to bet I'm right. How's an extra $200 bonus sound?" My headache was getting marginally better.

"If you got this one bagged, DD McGil, two big ones would be well worth it. But the odds are against you. And if you're wrong, I'm gonna tell Aggie to take that $200 right off the top end of your invoice." He chuckled again. "You don't have a prayer."

"Remember what Ernest Hemingway said, Jimmy Lee. 'In addition to prayer, there is effort.' Well, this comes as a direct result of same. Are you sitting down?"

"What the hell does Hemingway have to do with this? Have you got somethin' or not?"

"Do you remember Cap'n Crunch?"

"DD, you been drinkin'?" he asked.

"I'm disgustingly sober," I said, chuckling. "Do you remember a few years back when a bunch of young guys — they called themselves 'Phone Phreques' — used the Cap'n Crunch prize whistle to break into one of the big telephone systems?"

"Oh, yeah. I remember. It was a big deal. So?"

"So, as Sherlock Holmes said, when you have eliminated everything but the improbable, then that must be the answer — or something like that."

"You saying Cap'n Crunch was responsible for all those false alarms?"

"No. I'm saying it was the bird. The bird did it."

"Okay, now I know you been drinking. I heard about you finding some guy's body. Where you calling from? Home? I'll send somebody over to help you."

I laughed. "Honestly, I'm completely

sober. Listen. You know that mean-tempered African grey parrot they keep as a pet at Monarch Care? You must have seen him or at least heard of him. They keep him in a big cage in the recreation room next to the main lobby. I think his name's Hal, and he's mean and loud, but he's clever."

"What does their parrot have to with anything, DD?"

"He's the one that's been setting off all the false alarms. You know, Jimmy Lee, maybe you could get him a TV spot when this is all cleared up."

"You're makin' all this up, DD. I been in the security business over twenty years, and I never heard nothing like this." He paused, thinking it over. "The parrot? You sure?"

"I'm positive."

"Just how does he do it?"

"That's why you pay me the big bucks, Jimmy Lee. And next time, don't go calling me third or fourth. Call me first."

"Okay, I promise. But tell me how the damn bird does it. C'mon. I got a right to know."

"Well, to make it simple, the bird — excuse the pun — 'parrots' the security code for the computer hook-up that runs all the security. He must have been around when your guys were there installing the system and testing it, and he memorized the tonal sequence of the code. Now, whenever he decides to sing out the sequence, he turns on the alarm. He's got one hell of an ear, and he's got the tones down perfect. He's just like a blue box, like those guys used to bilk the telephone system."

"No shit. Wait till I tell everybody," he said. "About that bonus, DD."

I rang off, a little embarrassed at the easy money I'd be getting, but glad to have the case off my plate so I could concentrate on David. As for Barry's problem, I didn't have a clue. Maybe I'd be able to go to sleep with it on my mind and wake up with a miracle solution. They say you can dream solutions to your problems. It hadn't worked when I tried it for the Scotty problem, but right now, that was my best hope.

I quickly scanned the rest of my messages. The only call I needed to return was from Karl Patrick. I know him because we've had lunch together now and then ever since circumstances had thrown us together on the first case I'd done for American Insurance. He'd jumped in headfirst and bailed me out when I was in trouble. Under all his brusque brouhaha was a soft heart, only he doesn't like anybody to know.

His secretary Annette put me on hold, and

a few minutes later, Karl said, "Hello, DD."

"Hi. I'm returning your call."

"I heard what happened," he said. "You doing okay?"

"Well, yes and no. Thanks."

"You got everybody and his brother calling me to represent you. First Lauren Stephenson called and hired me to represent you. Then Morgan Fernandez called wanting the same thing. You might as well put me on retainer."

I was speechless. Lauren had really meant it when she said she thought I needed help, and she'd put her money where her . . . And Morgan had called Karl, too. Maybe things were worse than I thought.

"You still there?" he asked.

"Yes. But I don't think I need a lawyer. Don't get me wrong. If and when I do something, you're the one I'll call."

"Consensus is this, DD. We're all worried. My network of sources tells me that if the cops don't get a break soon and find the real killer, they're going to revisit your involvement. Is it true you spent the night with Barnes?"

"Geez, how'd your people find out so fast? I suppose you even know what color panties I had on."

"I heard you weren't wearing any. Am I

paying my sources for bad information? Look, I've been able to dig up some stuff on the sexual harassment suit against Barnes. It's pretty serious stuff, DD. The cops must have felt there was a good case against him because they handcuffed him and dragged him out of class. Word is he was in a real fight for his academic career."

"The paper didn't give any details. Who filed suit against him? Who was he supposed to have harassed?"

"I couldn't find out all the details, professional ethics and all that. His lawyer isn't saying much, even in confidence. But a lot of it's public record, so I'll tell you what we uncovered. He was charged with making lewd suggestions and touching a student's breast. Her name's Debbie Majors. Seventeen years old, lives with her parents, and is, supposedly, a Vestal Virgin."

"Karl, this doesn't sound like the old David. Everybody knows he was a womanizer, but harassment? I can't see it."

"Did he mention anything about the suit to you?"

"Not a word."

"Well, after he got slapped with criminal, civil, and administrative charges by the victim and the school, he hired one of the top firms to defend him. Just last week, the criminal charges were dismissed for lack of sufficient evidence. It made *Law Digest,* but the papers didn't pick it up. He still had the civil and the administrative proceedings to go through."

"All we talked about was Hemingway," I said, vividly remembering the night.

"From the information I've gathered, your friend wasn't just researching Hemingway, he was trying to emulate him. Drinking a lot, living dangerously, and . . ."

"And what?"

"Being prolific with the ladies," he said gently.

Karl had just filled in the blank I couldn't force myself to face. All David's womanizing escapades might explain why he was at City College instead of a more prestigious institution.

"It seems that a few years ago," Karl continued, "David was named a third party in a high-profile divorce. Then, about a year after that, the IRS decided to investigate his expense accounts.

"He had a full professorship at Boston University. He must have been hot stuff for that to have happened. When he was asked to leave there about a year and a half ago, he came back to Chicago where City College offered him a vice-chair in the English department. Then, a little over two months ago, the sexual harassment suit was filed against him."

"What were his chances of winning the civil suit?"

"From what I gather this morning, he had an excellent chance. But who knows about the administrative hearing? Office politics might have tied up the whole issue for years."

"If they dropped the criminal charges, couldn't David have sued the college for false arrest?"

"His attorney told me they'd discussed filing for wrongful arrest as a counter attack, but they wanted to get through the civil charges first. What did he tell you about the Hemingway manuscripts?" Karl inquired.

"He was worried because the whole question of ownership was up in the air. The next morning, American Insurance hired me to help clear up details on the coverage. I was in Phil Richy's office on the phone with David when he was shot. Now I'm the number one suspect."

"When can you come in, DD? We need to prepare some things in case the cops pick you up."

"I'm hoping they'll find out what's going

on and drop their interest in me."

"Don't count on it. Get yourself over here today. It's best to be prepared. Oh, by the way, my investigator told me David's apartment was ransacked. Did they get the manuscripts?"

"I don't know. David told me that he needed time to get them before our meeting, so I don't think they were in his apartment."

"That's an important detail. Do you have any idea where they are?"

"No. Maybe he's got a safe-deposit in some bank. He told me there were tons of security problems, and that's why he wanted the auction to happen as quickly as possible."

"Do you have any idea how valuable those manuscripts are?"

The figure Karl quoted made me catch my breath.

I said good-bye after promising Karl for the sixth time that I wouldn't talk to the cops without him.

On the way to my meeting with Phil and Matt, the conversation with Karl kept going round and round in my head. Would the cops arrest me, even though they'd found no powder residue? Did I, as Karl insinuated, make a mistake by talking to them without legal advice, even though I was innocent? And if the Hemingway manuscripts were lost again, would their value increase? American Insurance could be in the hopper for a big payoff, and Matt wasn't going to like that one bit.

# FOURTEEN

Always do sober what you said
you'd do drunk. That will teach you
to keep your mouth shut.
— ERNEST HEMINGWAY

I dreaded seeing Matt again. I admit I've made a lot of mistakes in my life. Jumping into bed with Matt after Frank died was one of the big ones. Now Matt was mad because I told the cops he was involved. I was probably going to lose this job — maybe worse. Hopefully Phil would be on my side and help ease the awkward situation. I took a deep breath and opened the door to Phil's office.

Matt stood in the middle of the room. Alone.

"Hello, DD," he said in that sexy voice of his. "Come in." He took my arm and firmly closed the door behind us.

"Where's Phil?"

"Sit down, DD."

He perched on the edge of Phil's desk and leaned toward me, our legs touching. He looked smashing, as usual, and very at ease, even in someone else's office.

"I suppose you're upset because I had to tell the cops I was working for you."

"Quite the contrary, DD. I'll admit I wasn't happy about having to turn around and come right back, but I know you did what you had to do. I want you to know that I corroborated everything you told them. I did my best to discourage the cops from considering you a suspect. Now I hope something positive can come out of all this. You're looking very beautiful today."

*This was not what I expected.* "Sure," I deadpanned.

"It's time we talked things over, DD."

"There's nothing to talk over." I swiveled around, disentangling my legs.

"Oh, yes there is. And since we're working together, we've got to come to some kind of understanding." He touched my shoulder. "We can't leave things like they are."

I wasn't happy about my part in my panties ending up on the floor in *l'affaire* Matt King, but as far as I was concerned it was over, and I said as much.

"No, it's not," he insisted. "I'm still crazy

about you. Turn down the deep freeze for a minute. Let's call a truce."

I lowered my eyes and studied the floor, hoping Phil would return and rescue me.

"It's been a long time, DD. Why haven't you answered any of my calls or letters?" He lifted my chin, forcing me to look into his handsome face.

"You even refused the flowers I've sent. What's going on? I thought we had something special. I told you I'm in love with you. You gave me the impression the feeling was mutual. Was I wrong?"

I turned away. In the history of the world, I knew I wasn't the first and wouldn't be the last to have things turn around and bite me in the ass. Usually I investigate a thing to death before I do it, buy it, or sleep with it. In Matt's case, I was thinking with my hormones instead of my brain. I didn't want any pity, but I didn't want to take up where we'd left off either.

"Let's just leave it that I made a mistake, okay? It *was* a long time ago," I said, sick at heart as I recalled how Matt had made me come alive again after Frank's death.

"It was no one-night stand, DD, and you know it. I still want you."

"And I'm sure that goes for wifey and the kiddies, too," I said wearily.

"So that's the problem." Matt stood up and faced me. "Look, you knew what we were doing as well as I did."

"Did I?"

Matt perched on the edge of the desk, leaning both hands on the arms of my chair, encircling me with his body as well as his aura. "I want you to be my lover. What's so wrong? You had the same arrangement with Frank. You told me so. What's so different?"

"Don't compare yourself to Frank," I said, pushing his arms out of the way.

I stood up and went over to Phil's window, keeping my back to Matt. "Frank and I were engaged to be married. That was entirely different."

Matt came over and gently clasped my shoulders. "After his death, you ended up paying all his bills and everything, didn't you?"

"Only because his stepbrother, Ken, was a son of a bitch."

"I wanted to help you forget," he said softly.

I thought of Scotty, who really had helped me forget. And now Scotty was gone too. I was glad Matt didn't know anything about that whole episode — or did he?

"DD, I still want to be with you. We're good together, and you know it."

I stood immobile, bracing myself against his overwhelming presence. I fought to stay indifferent. They say men think about sex more than women, but I don't believe one word of that.

He spun me around. "DD, take a look at yourself. You're making a living as an insurance investigator, and you're good at it, I'll give you that. But you deserve better. I can put you up in style in a Lake Shore Drive condo and really take care of you. You can go back into academics if you want. You could do anything you want. How about it?"

I turned away. In spite of everything, I wanted to say yes. He was so damned attractive. He made my pheromones bounce off the walls. But I'd never be happy thinking about the kids.

"Matt, it won't work," I finally said. I headed for the door and wrenched it open. Phil was standing on the other side, blocking my exit.

"What happened to you?" I asked gruffly.

"What's going on?" Phil asked sheepishly.

Matt, now at my side, said, "I asked Phil to step out for a few minutes so we could talk privately. He knows I'm angry at you for embroiling me in the David Barnes mess. But since we have to work together on this case, I was sure we could reach some common ground and stay friends. And we have, haven't we?"

They waited in silence for my answer. Matt didn't appear the least bit uncomfortable, but Phil's eyes were begging me to stop the torture.

"What exactly does American Insurance want me to do?" I gave in reluctantly.

"Well, let's sit down and review our situation," Matt suggested, corralling us back into the office like the three of us were best buddies planning a frat party weekend.

"To put it succinctly," Matt said, "we've evolved a three-prong strategy to insulate ourselves from all liability over these supposed Hemingway manuscripts."

Matt had used the royal "we" in referring to American Insurance. Apparently the company was letting him call all the shots. I was going to have to watch my backside.

"My staff has checked out several key facts. Item: David Barnes died intestate. Even more in our favor, he had no close living relatives. He was an only child, and his parents died last year in a car crash. I've got someone checking for distant relatives, but it looks like we'll be off the hook insofar as a claim against the estate is concerned.

"Item Two. Nobody seems to be able to locate the original manuscripts. His lawyer, his friends, his colleagues, his bank, the cops — no one knows where he put them. Or if somebody does know, they're not talking. So, our guess is that nobody will file a claim unless it can be proved that the stuff is really lost. I've put a top national firm on the search job. These guys have been known to find the proverbial needle in the haystack, so it'll turn up. It's just a question of when."

"Matt, you've already hired the big corporate guns. What do you need me for?"

"We need you, DD, to help us in the event both strategies fail. We need to insulate American Insurance from any liability by proving the manuscripts are fakes."

"But you already got opinions that said they were the 'True Gen,' " I countered, using Hemingway's own reporter's slang.

"And how is she supposed to go about proving they're not Hemingway if she can't analyze the originals?" Phil asked.

"First of all, don't worry about the information we already have. We can hold that close, and no one will ever know anything about it. As for your second question, use the same fragments David gave us. You've got the credentials to talk to these academics, DD. You can put a good spin on their computer analysis of the prose. Tell me it's not Papa's work. That's all I'm asking. What

166

are the chances that this guy David Barnes really did get hold of the lost manuscripts? My guess is this was a big fat scam from day one. We went along with it because it meant money for the company, good money and easy money. Now, we need to prove the prose is fake, and I know you can do it for us."

Matt opened his briefcase, pulled out a small sheaf of papers and handed them to me. "I had my office copy two of the story fragments. This should be more than enough for you and your literary friends to prove it's all a big hoax."

Phil rose from his chair, sighing loudly. "Will you take the job, DD?"

"You're the best operative we've got because of your background," Matt said. "Believe me, we checked and you're the only one with the level of university connections to legitimize you with the academics, especially with that one expert the paper mentioned — the one who claims they weren't written by Hemingway. Start with him."

Before I could answer, Matt glanced at his watch. "My schedule's really tight," he said, snapping his briefcase closed. "DD, let's meet for dinner tomorrow night to review your progress. I need to be able to report to

American Insurance every step of the way. Say seven o'clock and I'll leave a message for you where." He swung his briefcase off the desk and opened the door. "I've got to rush. Phil, keep me informed," he ordered as the door slammed shut behind him.

I didn't want this assignment, and I grabbed my briefcase and raced out of Phil's office after Matt to tell him so. "Matt, wait. I . . ."

"He's gone, DD," Phil announced the obvious and shook his head. "What the hell's going on between you and him?"

Phil had been good to me. I knew he deserved an explanation. But not now.

"I gotta go," I said. "I'm sorry. Talk to you later." I headed down the corridor as fast as I could. In the background I could hear Gilda calling him.

In my haste to escape Phil's questions, I squeezed into an already overcrowded elevator, hoping the door would close before he caught up with me. No such luck.

"Wait," Phil called, panting from exertion. He reached in, attempting to pull me out. "We need to talk. You can't just leave."

The massive elevator door slammed against his arm. He retreated, allowing the door to close on his disbelieving face.

"I'll call you later. I promise." Ignoring

168

mutters from fellow passengers, I sank against the wall, wrapped in a dead silence with the curious crowd.

I tried to forget about the scene with Matt and concentrate on the manuscript pages he'd given me to study. Here I was, standing in an elevator with what could turn out to be the literary find of the century tucked into my briefcase. I could hardly wait to get a look. But I was in the midst of a maelstrom. First Matt wanted me to prove the manuscripts weren't fake. Now he wanted me to prove they were. Matt was smart, and I knew he would maneuver heaven and earth so that American Insurance would emerge unscathed from all this. But David had been very smart, too. Had David been clever enough to fake these stories?

# FIFTEEN

The ham on wheat I picked up at Louie's Sandwich Shoppe in the lobby of Phil's building was wrapped in plastic thicker than the ham slice and cost way too much, but I was starving. A glass of wine would have been nice too, but I'd promised myself not to drink until I figured out if the headache was from yesterday's blow on the head or from the Wild Turkey. It's always good to see the path clearly.

Eating the almost-food, I wondered how I was ever going to prove the manuscripts were fake. I remembered I hadn't yet returned Tom Joyce's call. I was still fuming over that ticket he'd pawned off on me — it's what got me into this mess in the first place. But I was sure he'd seen all the TV brouhaha about David and the Hemingway manuscripts. Since his business was rare books and manuscripts, I was sure he could give me some good advice. We'd first met a few years ago when he'd helped me out on a case involving a forged document, and last year he'd given me invaluable advice about the Robert Burns artifacts. Recently he'd mentioned an appraisal he'd handled of the Hemingway books and manuscripts owned by the Oak Park Library, so I knew this would interest him. I punched in his number.

"Hi'ya, DD," Tom answered.

"Don't do that. You know I hate that caller ID."

"I can't believe you don't have it yourself, you being the insurance investigator *et al.*"

"I'm returning your call, but you should be glad I'm still talking to you, considering it's all your fault I'm a suspect in a murder case."

"What?"

"It was that damn ticket you forced on me. As Aristotle would say, that was the root cause."

"Aristotle never said that, DD. What he said was . . ."

"You know what I mean — going to that play started everything. I met David Barnes there that night."

"Wow. He's the guy who got killed. I guess I should say I'm sorry."

"I have a feeling the cosmos was probably

cooking up this mess for me even without that damn ticket. What are the statistical probabilities of jumping into bed with a former boyfriend, who gets shot, and then finding his body."

"With you DD, sometimes I might say the odds are pretty good."

"See, I told you that I shouldn't be talking to you." I paused and asked, "Are you at the bookstore?"

"I've been cataloging a new shipment that just arrived. Is this about finding that body? That's why I called you."

"Tangentially."

"A mystery wrapped in an enigma. Sounds interesting. Are you okay?"

"I wouldn't go that far, but I'm keeping on keeping on. See you there in a bit."

I drove out to the West Town area, about a mile due west of the Merchandise Mart where Tom had moved a few years ago. Just past Oprah's Harpo Studios, I spotted his building, a Californiaesque two story with a sign reading "Joyce And Company."

I parked in a nearby lot, put up the top, and locked the Miata.

A tiny bell tinkled as I opened the door. Tom, wearing black jeans and Rockport walking shoes, emerged from a back room balancing a stack of books. He nodded a greeting.

"That was quick," he said, dumping the books onto a kidney-shaped desk already loaded with piles of paper and computer equipment. "I just picked up this lot in an estate sale." He brushed bits of dust from the front of his brown shirt.

I surveyed all his shelves. "I guess I never told you I was nervous when you moved a few years ago, but this new location suits you well."

"Why were you nervous?" Tom asked as he straightened the pile to keep it from toppling off the desk.

"Don't laugh, but I was afraid that great smell of your old place wouldn't be the same in a new location. But thankfully it is."

"It's the books that do it, not the place. Anyway, I've got more room here."

"True, but in the old place on the 14th floor of the Manhattan Building you were directly across from the federal detention center. Remember how we used to watch the prisoners play basketball on the roof?"

He laughed. "I'm glad to be away from there. Sometimes those prisoners escaped."

"Did any of them ever stop in to browse?"

"Very funny. Sometimes the cops stopped in, but being on the ground floor here does attract more foot traffic."

"Where's Wolfie today?" Tom often baby-sat for a wolf owned by a friend of his in the Upper Peninsula. Despite my initial misgivings, Wolfie and I had become good pals during the problem over the Robbie Burns artifacts.

"He's with his owner in Michigan, and I really miss him. He'll be here again next month when they go on vacation. So what's up? Are you in serious trouble over finding that body?"

"I don't know yet. Tell me what you know about David Barnes."

"I researched him after we talked. I've read some of his academic papers on Hemingway. They were quite good, as a matter of fact. But from what the paper and the TV reported, he supposedly found the Hemingway holy grail — the lost poems and short stories that were stolen from Hadley, his first wife. If true, wow. It would be worth a fortune because of its literary and its historical value."

"I know you're familiar with the Hemingway collection at the Oak Park Library, right?"

"Yeah. I appraised it. A really nice little library. Did I tell you they have a copy of the scarce first edition of Hemingway's second book, *In Our Time?* Only 140 copies were printed in Paris in 1924 at the Three Mountains Press. They've also got an unrecorded variant dust jacket on their copy of *Men Without Women,* 1927."

Tom is a living encyclopedia and his wide range of knowledge is always astounding. I never know just what he's going to say, but I'm always sure it's going to be interesting.

"A little-known Hemingway factoid is that in the two variants of his first edition of *Men Without Women,* the publisher used two different weights of paper, and as a result, you have to literally weigh the books to tell them apart. But I digress. What enigma have you brought today?"

"Would you examine something?" I pulled the copies of the manuscript pages from my briefcase.

Tom grabbed a magnifying glass and carried a page to an empty table against one wall.

I spread out the rest of the pages while he put on a pair of tortoise-shell glasses and rolled up his sleeves. Quiet descended as we both read intently.

**FIRST LEAVES**

The first leaves to fall were

175

off the trees already, and the boy remembered that soon they would slow his passage in the woods and make it dangerous. What things in the woods seemed to be were not always what they were, and he remembered being with his father there, watching a big raccoon scrabbling for crayfish in the shallows.

"Are animals smart?" he asked.

"I guess so. In their ways."

"As smart as people are?"

"Not the way people are. But the smartest man in the world could never be as good as that old raccoon is at being a raccoon."

The boy walked faster, though walking faster could not increase his time in the woods. Soon she would be calling from the house, and then he would go in.

"Have to go," he said, and even in the little time he had been there more leaves had fallen to the ground.

Tom glanced up from the pages. "So I take it this is part of the lost Hemingway works that your David Barnes found. Well, it sure reads like Hemingway."

"This is all I have." I shoved the other pages towards him, and we bent over them.

## COMING HOME

When there was nothing to say he would be quiet, and they did not like that. They thought he should be talking now. His mother had mentioned Irene.

"When are you going to see her?" his mother asked.

"Tomorrow, I guess," he said.

"Your Aunt and Uncle Simms are coming tomorrow."

"Then maybe the day after tomorrow," he said.

He had come back and was with them in the living room, and they thought he should be talking now, since he was back and so many would not be. It must be four o'clock, he thought. The lieutenant had asked him and the corporal

about the girls and the sup-
plies, but neither of them had
said anything. The three girls
had worked in a bakery, and he
and the corporal had caught up
with them as they were leaving
work. The girls would not go
to the hotel in the town, so
he and the corporal took them
to the supply tent. Two of
them had lice all over, so he
and the corporal used only the
other one. He and the corporal
gave presents to all of them
anyway, and the lieutenant
must have seen the five of them
leaving the tent. He asked
about the girls and the sup-
plies for a time, but then he
stopped asking.

He and the corporal had some
good times together, but the
end of them had been strange.
They were lying on their
stomachs side by side, watching for movement in the olive
trees on the opposite hill,
and just one bullet came from
the trees. It hit the corporal
above his right collar bone,

and it must have traveled the length of his body.

"I'm flying," the corporal had said as loudly as he could. "O Jesus, I'm flying," and then he died.

"Do you remember Mrs. Tansy?" his brother asked. "Junior year, Mrs. Tansy?"

"Who? Mrs. Tansy? Yes, that one," he said.

"What an old bitch she was. Sorry, Mother," his brother said. His mother pretended she had not heard.

"Remember when she caught the five of us smoking? Behind the second boiler? All the fuss about that?"

"I didn't know you two smoked in school," his mother said.

"All the fuss about that, and all five of us had to come in early for three days?"

"I remember," he said. The Austrians with two vans in the mud had jumped out of cover as a unit to push at the vans, and then were driven back down by fire, over and over. Up they would pop, like comics in a film, and push and slip and fall in the mud, and sometimes one would be hit and fall and be pulled back down to cover before the rest would pop up again and push and slip and fall in the mud. They were even more comic because a mile and a half up the road the road was cut off, and if they had gotten the vans moving they would have had nowhere to go, but they did not know that.

"It must have been terrible," his mother said.

Goosebumps raced along my spine as I read the crisp prose.

"Well?" I asked.

"Sure reads like Hemingway all right," Tom said. "Lean and mean. Short, clean sentences with clear, action-oriented verbs."

"And loaded with sex, war, and death," I added. "It reminds me in subject a little of *Soldier's Home.*"

He eyed me intently. "I suppose you're going to tell me these pages are part of the lost Hemingway stories I heard about on the news?"

"That's what I'd like to know. Are they real or are they fakes?"

"As Papa himself would say, they sound like the 'true gen.' And they appear to have been typed on an early Corona. If I'm not mistaken, Hemingway used a lot of type-writers in his career, but in the early '20s, he would have used the one that Hadley gave him for his twenty-second birthday. That was in July of 1921, before they left for Paris. I think it was a Corona #3, but I'd consult an expert on that."

"David Barnes told me they did, and it was authenticated."

"Well, next you could run some word tests. There's some fancy academic software on the market that stylistically compares a writing sample to a known author — in this case, Papa."

"That's already been done too," I told him.

"And . . . ?"

"And the analysis concluded they're good enough to be the real thing."

"So what's the problem?" Tom asked.

"When the owner was murdered, the originals went missing."

"Ahh. Short, clean, and loaded with death. I didn't know about them being miss-ing."

"Now the insurance company wants me to prove they're fakes," I explained.

"QED getting them neatly off the hook over any liability." Tom removed his glasses. "That figures. Real or fake, these stories might have been the motive for murder."

"You're the expert. What else could definitively prove they're fakes?"

"I'm coming into this in the middle, and you tell me some tests have already been done. But the first thing to look at is the paper itself."

"The auction house did that, and they concluded it was consistent with what Hemingway would have used. Same thing with the typeface. Hemingway used the same typewriter on all the work that was lost."

"Then the next step would be to examine any watermarks on the paper or the unique imprint residue that would have been left on the page by the fabric of the typewriter ribbon. But to analyze any of these, you've got to have the originals."

"Which we don't."

"Which you don't. Almost every other test requires the originals, so I don't think I can help you, DD. If these weren't done by Hemingway, they're inspired fakes."

"There was a professor on the news who

claimed they were fakes," I told him.

"I saw him too. If I were you, I'd contact him and investigate how he arrived at that conclusion. Without the originals to work with, he's your best resource."

"That's on my to-do list. One thing David told me was that the manuscripts were sent to him at City College."

"Sent to him? That's how he got them? I was going to ask if you knew how he had possession."

"I know. It sounds like something out of a bad novel, but I believed him when he told me the story." I recounted everything David had told me.

"You're going to have to try to find out more about the packaging they came in. Get me something original — anything — and I'll try to help you. The more you find out, the more likely you'll get yourself off the prime suspect list," he said softly. "I heard about that on the news, too.

"Hold it a second," Tom said as he stepped over to another desk to answer his phone.

While I waited, the bell tinkled and a woman customer entered. She was attractive, about five foot four and in her mid-thirties, wearing a pink silk kurti tunic that looked handmade. Tom grinned and beckoned her in. She waved to him and began to browse, obviously at home in the book-shop.

I quickly gathered up the scattered pages of the Hemingway stories and returned them to my briefcase. As I admired her embellished blouse, she narrowed her eyes and stared at me.

"Sorry, I didn't mean to stare. I was admiring your tunic."

"Oh, I bought it on a recent trip to India," she smiled. "But don't I know you?"

"I don't think so. I'm DD McGil."

"Got it. — I saw your picture in today's *Trib*. I've got a kind of photographic memory for faces."

Tom, his conversation finished, walked over. "So, do you two know each other? DD, this is Debra Yates from the Newberry Library. Debra, this is DD McGil, erstwhile academic currently working the insurance fraud beat."

Debra said, "She's the one who found the body. I read all about it."

"Debra's here to pick up *The Real Wizard of Oz,* by Rebecca Loncraine. You'd love it DD." He selected a book from a pile on the corner of one of his tables and wrapped it neatly in brown paper.

"It's all about Frank Baum's widow, Maud. She kept getting loads of fan mail from children for her husband. She couldn't bring herself to tell them he was dead, so instead, she wrote back, posing as him and forging his name. So many letters came, she made a rubber stamp of his signature and carried on the pretense for thirty years."

"That was sweet, don't you think?" Debra said, paying for the book but keeping an eye on me still.

"It was, but today his wife would have a barrage of lawyers telling her she couldn't do that."

Debra Yates nodded and gave me a look I could not decipher as she took the book from Tom and he walked her to the door.

"That wasn't a big sale, but it was a satisfying one," he said, closing the door. "Last time she bought a very expensive book."

"And complained about the price?"

"No. For once I didn't have to persuade someone to pay full price. She said, and I quote, 'The quality lasts long after the sting of the price is forgotten.' "

"So she's your best customer, I take it. Is this getting serious?"

"Don't kid me where book sales are concerned, DD. Anyway, your love life is tumultuous enough for both of us. I'm exhausted just being an observer. Can you stay for dinner? This time we'll do the Casablanca for Mexican."

Last time we'd gone to Furio's. They'd gouged us eight bucks apiece for a glass of Chianti — Rush Street prices. We'd vowed to boycott them.

"Thanks but I'm headed over to City College. I want to see what I can find out from that Hemingway professor." I waved goodbye and wished him *bon appétit.*

# Sixteen

If you have a success you have it
for the wrong reasons. If you become
popular it is always because of the
worst aspects of your work.
— ERNEST HEMINGWAY

Tom hadn't been able to help directly, but he'd confirmed my next move to visit City College. I headed northwest on the Kennedy toward O'Hare Airport, named after Butch O'Hare, a WW II naval aviator hero who was also the son of Al Capone's attorney. Chicago's infamous history is still around, although the City Fathers would like to blot it away.

Rush hour starts early in Chicago but the reversable express lanes were open outbound so I got to the college campus without much delay. The campus was on the northwestern edge of Chicago on land that used to be Dunning Mental Hospital.

People still talked about some of Dunning's inmates like Wolfman, who would scale the eight-foot picket fence when there was a full moon, run over to Mt. Olive Cemetery, and bay like a wolf. And there was the woman who tried to scale the fence but impaled herself on one of the spearhead fence pickets. After Dunning closed, the buildings came down and the new campus opened in the 90s — a six-story glass and chrome building surrounded by acres of asphalt and a kidney shaped retention pond. No hallowed ivy-covered walls in sight on this campus.

The closest parking space was marked "Faculty Only." I pulled in quickly, locked the car, and headed for the main entrance.

I'd stayed away from the academic world since Frank's death and the ensuing row his colleagues had made over my seventeenth-century research. I'd made too many enemies and suffered too much pain. I forced aside the memories and opened the door.

The building's overheated halls exuded an odor like ripe gym clothes. It didn't take a detective to deduce that their air-conditioning system wasn't working during one of the worst heat waves of the summer.

The administration office was locked. I wandered the labyrinthine corridors searching for David's office and finally located the English department on the fifth floor. Anyone who looked like faculty was busy meeting with students or talking on the phone. I spotted a woman alone in a small office and knocked on the open door labeled "Ms. Jeffers / Mr. Cord."

She looked up from her paperwork. "Yes?"

"Are you Mrs. Jeffers?"

"That's Ms. Jeffers," she said in a deep voice. "And I certainly am."

She was a large woman with short reddish hair and a light complexion with no makeup except for her too-red lipstick. She wore ill-fitting jeans and a dress shirt, and her accent was East Coast.

"I'm DD McGil, a friend of David Barnes. I was wondering if you could spare a few minutes to talk to me."

"I've already spent a lot of time with those idiot cops."

"David and I were in grad school together. I'm the one who found his body."

"Oh, yes. I remember your name from this morning's paper." She got up, offered me a chair next to her desk, and shuffled a messy stack of papers. "Here, let me get rid of these."

"Sorry to interrupt."

She smiled thinly. "It's good for my sanity

189

to have a break from these ignoble quizzes. You can't imagine how bad it's gotten. Kids today don't read the classics. They can't tell you if Shakespeare wrote in the same century as Walt Whitman or Walt Disney. The only thing they retain in their little gray brain cells are sports and entertainment factoids. All the dirty little boys care about is getting into the girls' clean little pants, and all the girls think about is . . ." She sighed, her expression somber.

I remembered a recent survey of eighteen-to twenty-year-olds, in which only 32 percent could place the American Civil War in the correct half century. I pointed at the quizzes. "My sympathies. I'm afraid I'd end up strangling the little brats."

"So, you wanted to talk about David." Her tight brown eyes assessed me as she fidgeted with a pair of granny glasses. "How did you come to find his body?"

"I was on the phone with him when he was shot, and I raced over to his apartment. David and I hadn't kept in touch for a lot of years. I found out only two days ago that he was in Chicago. Now I'd like to know something about what his life was like lately."

Ms. Jeffers' face softened. "Seems like we all made good friends in school, then lost touch after we got out into the real world."

We were in a tiny cubicle containing two desks and two chairs. The stuffy air and her White Linen perfume were making me claustrophobic.

"Are you okay?" she asked, touching my arm.

"It's so hot. I feel like the walls are pressing in."

"It is a bit cramped," she said.

"What's wrong with the air-conditioning?" I asked. "This building isn't all that old."

She laughed. "Before they built this campus, we used to be in makeshift trailers, so even without the air conditioning, it's a lot better than it used to be back then. By the way, my first name is Dorothy. Want a Coke?"

I declined. She quickly returned with a regular Coke. "I always load up with extra sugar for that blast I need to deal with the students," she remarked, then paused.

"Poor David," she said finally. "I feel so bad. Beth always felt that he was the brightest of us all. He certainly stood out."

"He was like that in grad school," I agreed, wondering if this was the same Beth who had been quoted in the paper.

"He wasn't just quick, he was truly intelligent. What's more, he was witty. And he chased anything in skirts. His biggest sin was he was never tactful. The rest of the department have settled in as lifers, but David had the talent and the drive to do whatever he wanted."

"Lifers?"

She laughed through her nose. "We'll be here till we're carried out on slabs. But not David. He simply never took teaching seriously, and that charming irreverence allowed him to get away with not giving a damn what anybody else thought."

"Who was he closest to in the department?" I asked.

"He and Martin Sweeney collaborated on the Hemingway presentations." She snorted. "David called them 'dog and phony' shows."

*I bit my lip. If she knew I'd seen the show, maybe she wouldn't tell me her version.*

"They called it 'The Real Hemingway,' " she continued. "David contended people didn't want to read Hemingway, they just wanted to hear about his sex life and his sporting adventures. Unfortunately for Western civilization, he was right. He encouraged Martin to grow a beard and dress and act like Hemingway, and the gimmick was a success. So much so, these days Martin hardly ever comes out of character anymore. Tells everyone to call him Papa."

"Do you think he'd talk to me?"

"He likes talking about Hemingway, but he's been badly hurt by David's death. Earlier today he told me he felt he couldn't go on alone with the rest of the program tour they'd planned."

"Did you hear that David found the lost Hemingway manuscripts?" I asked.

"Oh, we all heard about it, but it's hard to believe," she said. "Personally, I think there was something funny going on. I'm in Women's Studies myself, and I haven't had to read Hemingway since high school. Understandably, I'm not a fan of his. All that macho crap, and of course he didn't have a clue about women."

I didn't agree with her. I liked Lady Brett in *The Sun Also Rises.* But I kept my own counsel.

"I suppose in other circles this find would be significant, and David would have been famous," she said.

"But why wouldn't he have openly announced such an astounding discovery to the faculty?" I asked.

She laughed out loud. "You must never have worked for a bureaucracy. This administration will continue to fight him for the manuscripts even though he's dead."

"Do you think the manuscripts are authentic?" I asked. "And if David and Martin were such good colleagues, why would Martin disagree with David about the manuscripts being genuine?"

"We all wonder that. Ask him yourself. He's taking over David's classes for the remainder of the term, so he'll be around."

I hadn't told Dorothy Jeffers I was with the insurance company, and I didn't want to, so I changed the subject.

"Do you suppose that after the auction and after the news broke, David would have stayed here to teach?"

"Who knows? Beth thought so."

"Did everybody in the department get along well with David?"

"That's what the police were asking us all day yesterday. You're sure you're not with them?"

"No. I told you I'm just trying to find out about David."

"Well," she paused. "He didn't get along with Big Bill. You did know they charged David with sexual harassment?" she asked.

I nodded.

"But do you know how they handled it? The cops barged into his ten o'clock class one morning, handcuffed him in front of his students, and dragged him out to a police car. Can you imagine?"

The David I knew would have gone ballistic. No wonder he hadn't mentioned anything to me about it the other night.

"Sounds horrible," I said. "Why couldn't they have waited? Do you believe he did it?"

"I'm sure that David was guilty of sexual harassment at some time. Most men are. And David behaved sometimes just like his idol, Papa Hemingway. However, with David, it was the women who always seemed to flock to him.

"None of us in the department believed the student," she continued thoughtfully, rubbing the string of tiny pearls around her neck. "She is a girl who can't do enough to attract male attention. But once she made a complaint, the administration had to follow through."

"Do you think David would have won the harassment suit?"

She rose and circled the two small desks. "Beth led the fight for him. We all tried our best to back David, but the administration didn't care what we said. As if I'd go out of my way to defend anyone I thought might be guilty. The administration organized a witch hunt against David, and he decided to fight back. I think that's why he ran for department chair. Beth persuaded him, and

I backed him. Have you met our current chair, Bill Butler?"

"No."

"Everybody calls him Big Bill." She snorted. "Frankly, he's embarrassing. He dresses and acts like a cowboy who's just arrived in the bigs."

"I take it he's not very good?"

"He's ambitious, and he's clever. He jumps into bed with the administration on every issue — larger class size, more paperwork, standardized testing — you know the kind of crap that sells out the faculty a millimeter at a time. There's constant tension around here. Believe me, this college could teach the Borgias a thing or two. Suffice it to say Big Bill's agenda and that of the faculty don't intersect anywhere."

"What did you and Beth think of David's chances of winning?" Dorothy Jeffers had mentioned Beth three or four times with shining eyes, and I wanted to learn something about her, too.

"I don't know what Beth thought. You'll have to ask her. I thought his chances were good. He would have been a tough chairman who kept the department on point. But the sexual harassment suit really hurt him. Surprisingly, a few of the younger women on the faculty turned against him and backed Big Bill. Most of the rest of us remained loyal, including Beth. I don't understand these young women at all. They're so stupid to let themselves be conned by Big Bill. Anybody with a brain can see he's a fake."

She sighed loudly. "Personally, I was hoping David might collect a bundle from this place for harassing him. Now that he's gone, we're stuck with the buffoon," she added bitterly.

"You mentioned Beth several times. Is that the Beth Moyers who was quoted in today's paper?"

"Yes. She and David were . . . good friends."

"Do you mean to imply they were lovers?"

"I didn't say that."

Dorothy Jeffers had become agitated, and I welcomed the sudden interruption of noise in the hallway.

Dorothy went to the door and opened it. In the hallway, a big man wearing a tan suit and cowboy boots had his arm around a pretty young girl. She was sobbing.

"You mustn't blame yourself," the big man said softly, trying to calm her. "It's not your fault."

"Can I do anything to help?" Dorothy offered. "Would you like a glass of water?"

Cowboy boots looked away from the girl, seeing us for the first time. His hair was caught in a long pony tail, and he wore one of those universally unattractive silver tipped string ties. He shifted uncomfortably while the girl continued to sob on his shoulder.

"No. Everything'll be fine, thanks, Dotty," he drawled and quickly shepherded the girl down the corridor.

Ms. Jeffers stiffened when he called her Dotty.

"Was that . . . ?" I asked.

"Our ersatz chairman."

"He's hard to miss," I admitted.

"I told you he's a fake, and I meant it." She leaned toward me and whispered, "I investigated. First of all, he isn't even from The Lone Star state. Probably never even been there. He was born in Brooklyn, top of his class at C.U.N.Y. He makes up the accent and the outfit as he goes along."

"Why the charade?" I asked, wondering how to get back to the subject of David and Beth without wearing out my welcome.

"Good question," she said. "He adopted the persona to ensure he would stand out in the crowd. And as soon as he transformed himself into Big Bill, his career skyrocketed.

It's perverse. Personally, I think he's a little mad."

I remembered the Harvard University grad who'd masqueraded as a street person to help organize one of Chicago's political wards. Maybe it was more common than we suspected. "Who was the girl?" I asked.

"She's Debbie Majors, the student who filed the harassment charges against David. Wonder what that was all about?"

"You wonder what *what* was all about?" asked a strident voice directly behind us.

"Oh, Bette," Dorothy Jeffers said, turning. "You startled me. This is Miss McGil, an old friend of David's."

"Hello. I'm Bette Abramawitz," she said loudly, shaking my hand like she was pumping iron. "We were sorry about David." She turned to Dorothy. "I was looking for Beth."

"Beth? Everybody's looking for her today. But I haven't seen her." Dorothy turned to me. "Bette's in Administration. She wanted David to drop out of the race for chairman. Didn't you, Bette?"

"Why go over it now? He's gone, and it's done. But I won't deny I tried to discourage him. Those charges of harassment stick, even if you're innocent. And with David, who could believe he was completely innocent?" She took a tissue from her purse and wiped perspiration from her brow.

"He wasn't going to drop out, though," she continued, dropping the tissue into a wastebasket adjacent to Dorothy's desk. "He called me last week and said he'd found out about Big Bill not being from Texas, and he was going to make it public."

"Didn't the college verify Big Bill's vita and transcripts?" I asked.

"Well . . ." she hedged. "We now have a new policy in place and everything's scrutinized. Anyway, we do know he lied on the job application," Bette stated emphatically.

Statistically I knew Big Bill was in the majority. Over 72 percent of job applicants lie about something or other, and most get away with it. I didn't think it would be prudent for me to discuss statistics with Bette and Dorothy. Instead I questioned if the lies on his application were that important.

Bette said, "My guess is that if David had exposed Big Bill as a fraud, Big Bill would be dead meat. There's nothing as damaging as lying about oneself in academia. I believe the election would have gone to David, despite the sexual harassment stuff."

She was probably right. Nobody would blackmail somebody for not being from Texas. But if you're caught faking academic credentials, your career would go down the toilet in a heartbeat.

"Look what happened to that Pulitzer Prize–winning history professor at Mount Holyoke College," Dorothy Jeffers interjected. "I can't remember his name now. Even after he apologized for lying about being a Vietnam combat veteran, he was suspended for a year without pay and had to give up his endowed chair."

I told Bette that Dorothy and I had been discussing the lost Hemingway stories. She agreed with Dorothy that David's star would have risen again meteorically with the ensuing scholarly research.

"Why David didn't tell us about the manuscripts being sent to him is something I'll never understand," Bette Abramawitz said. "He'd have gotten a big raise and the manuscripts would have been protected. Now, even though they rightly belong to us, we'll have to go after them in court."

"Why is the college claiming ownership?" I asked.

"Our attorney found out that they were mailed to this address," she explained. "Which clearly shows that whoever sent them knew David only in connection with his work at the college. Just like any research project in private industry, everything he generates while he works for us, we own. It's strictly a legal issue. We'll win on this one, I've no doubt."

"Bette used to teach contract law before she went into administration," Dorothy interjected.

"How well do you think Debbie Majors knows Big Bill?" I asked her.

Bette pursed her lips. "I don't know. I haven't noticed anything unusual. Well, I'm still trying to find Beth." Without saying goodbye, she turned abruptly and trotted off down the corridor.

"Do you think," Dorothy asked, "that the college really might get ownership of the Hemingway manuscripts now that David is . . . ?"

"We were talking about Beth," I interrupted. "I'd like to meet her."

"Her cubicle's just down the hall. Number one-two-five. But Bette said she's not there." Dorothy Jeffers glanced at her watch. "Oh, I've got to get to class." She gathered up papers from her desk and jammed them into a lumpy, already full briefcase.

"Do you know what Beth's schedule is, or where I could leave a message for her?" I asked as she yanked a blocky purse out of the bottom desk drawer.

"Sorry." She locked her desk. "Check with

administration. I've got to go."

Ushering me out of her cubicle, she locked the door and hurried down the hall.

# SEVENTEEN

Wandering the suffocating halls, I spotted a reporter I'd seen on WGN-TV coming toward me, with a cameraman following close behind. I ducked into the closest office and let them pass. I didn't need more publicity. After they were gone, I continued down the corridor and found a plaque reading, "David Barnes, Assistant Chair, English Department." This was probably where the WGN reporter had been coming from. I checked the corridor again, now nearly empty, and knocked, wondering if the new occupant, Martin Sweeney, might already be ensconced. No answer.

I tried the door. Locked. I was sure the police had already checked everything over, but I was nosy and wanted to see for myself. It took me less than a nanosecond to decide to break in. I yanked my trusty Dyno tool lock pick out of the zipper compartment in my purse. Thank heavens the cops had returned it. I twisted it gently in the lock, and the door opened like magic. I entered and closed the door quickly behind me.

My working environment isn't the neatest, as George, my landlord at The Beecham, continually reminds me. However, I immediately realized that the state of David's office overstepped the bounds, even for messy people. Papers were strewn about like the aftermath of a blizzard. Every surface of the desk, floor, bookcases, and computer table was covered. I was sure this hadn't been done during the police search. They leave things messy, but not in shambles.

David's computer was under a mass of student essays. I turned it on and hunched over the monitor until the screen came on, waiting for the prompt. My nerves were on edge, and when I heard a key inserted in the lock, I jumped back from the computer. The office door swung open and a heavy-set man burst in.

"Who are you? What are you doing in here? How'd you get in? Are you a student?"

The burly man sported a trim white beard and was dressed casually in beige shorts and sandals, no socks, and a big belt buckle that read *Gott Mit Uns.* I recognized him immediately as the guy who'd played Hemingway the other night.

"Well?" he barked. "Are you going to tell me, or must I call security?"

I wasn't keen on another hassle with the cops. "I'm DD McGil, and you must be Martin Sweeney." I smiled. "I've been looking all over for you."

He stepped farther into the office and inspected me closely.

"Do I know you?" he asked. Then he noticed the mess. "Say, what's going on in here?"

"Looks like somebody trashed the place," I said, and explained that Dorothy Jeffers had told me he'd be taking David's classes.

"How'd you get in?" he asked, walking around the desk.

"I'm with American Insurance," I told him, hoping he'd forget the last question. "I just got here a moment ago." The truth and nothing but the truth. Just not the whole truth.

"Why do you want to see me?" he asked as he unearthed the telephone under the debris on David's desk. He picked up the receiver and pushed some buttons.

"Security? This is Martin Sweeney. Yeah. Well, now I'm up in David Barnes' office. Yeah, that's the one. Yes, I know the police searched it yesterday. Look, it's been

trashed. Just get up here right away, okay?"
He banged down the receiver. The computer
screen was still showing white snow. Martin
clicked it off and asked me, "Did you see
anybody leaving when you came down the
corridor?"

"No I didn't."

"What's American Insurance got to do
with me?" he asked. A grease spot on the
left leg of his khaki shorts kept catching my
attention.

"I've been hired by American to locate
the Hemingway manuscripts they insured
for David. Naturally, they've got a heavy
financial reason for wanting them found.
Would you, by any chance, know where they
are?"

"Hell, sister, I sure wish I did."

I disliked being called sister when I wasn't,
even though I knew Hemingway often used
the appellation on his female acquaintances.

"And," he continued, "even if they aren't
the 'true gen' as Hemingway himself would
say, they're going to be worth plenty right
now."

"That's what the paper quoted you as saying. How can you be so sure the fragments
weren't written by Hemingway when other
experts believe they were?"

"I've been around a long time, and my

nose can smell crap coming down the pike. David was a good friend, but I couldn't support him on this. I think he was working a con."

"What kind of con?" I asked.

"I think he was salting the find with some unpublished Hemingway fragments and making up all the rest."

"Wow," I said. "That would be a coup. But it would be one hell of a job. Do you think he had the skill to get away with something like that?"

"I don't know. But nobody got to see more than small fragments. Anyway, you'll never convince me that somebody just up and sent him all those manuscripts in the very same valise that was lost in 1922. Who? David and I investigated all over in Michigan and here in Oak Park too. That valise was lost only a year after Hemingway and Hadley were married. There just wasn't any place left to look. My opinion? David was lying, pure and simple."

Martin Sweeney walked to the doorway and asked, "What happens if American Insurance doesn't find the manuscripts?"

"That's what they're worried about, Mr. Sweeney."

"Call me Papa. Everybody does."

"Nobody's made any claims yet. If there

is a claim in the future and if the stuff isn't found, they're going to have to pay out based on the binder coverage."

"It was David who . . . Oh, good, that was fast. Look at this mess," he said to the uniformed campus security guard hurrying down the hall toward us.

"Anything stolen?" the guard inquired, taking everything in with his big eyes as he pulled a notebook out of his pocket. His badge read Ortiz.

"I couldn't tell you what he had in here. I just picked up the key from administration five minutes ago. Didn't the police take inventory yesterday?"

"Who's this?" Ortiz pointed at me and blocked the doorway.

"She was here when I walked in," Martin said.

The guard flipped a page in the notebook. "You better explain," he said to me.

I detailed my meeting with Dorothy Jeffers, said the door was open, and repeated that I'd walked in only a few seconds before Martin Sweeney. Ortiz proceeded to question me, and by the time he was finished, he had more vitals on me than my doctor.

"Okay, you two can go now," Ortiz said, then pulled out his two-way radio and ordered someone on the other end to come seal off the office.

Martin nodded and over the static, I heard him murmur, "Must be done under the circumstances."

As Martin initialed a document for Ortiz, I said, "We need to discuss a few more details. Naturally you can see that if American Insurance fails to locate the manuscripts, they'd want to try to prove them fakes to lower their risk."

"How can I help?"

"By taking me through your analysis of the materials to help me sort out your reasoning. I'm sure I could get American Insurance to pop for some money to pay for your expertise." *Assuming I could convince Matt.*

"Sounds interesting. Unfortunately, I'm tied up right now. Can you come to Oak Park tomorrow? I'm doing a tight schedule of lectures and seminars, but we could meet at the Hemingway Trust. Three o'clock? I'll have a half-hour."

"Thanks. I'll be there."

"What's going on? Why is security here?" asked a slim woman with ash blonde hair who'd approached from behind.

"Oh, Beth," Martin said, putting his arm around her shoulders. "It looks like somebody trashed David's office."

The ash-blonde pointed in my direction. "And you are?"

"DD McGil." I extended my hand.

She didn't take it. "So you're DD McGil."

"Miss McGil was just . . . ," Martin began when Ortiz interrupted.

"I'm leaving now to file my report, Dr. Sweeney. Oh, hello, Dr. Moyers." He smiled at her, then turned and departed down the long hall.

Despite the heat, Beth looked cool in her sleeveless berry colored dress. A cloisonné butterfly pin over her right breast flashed blue and yellow, and her light perfume was pleasant. I took a step toward her. "I'd like to talk to you, Dr. Moyers."

"What about? David?"

"He and I were friends many years ago, and . . ."

"I know all about that," she said coolly, fingering the butterfly pin. "And I also know he was searching for you. Isn't it a coincidence that the day he found you, he turns up dead. Murdered."

"It wasn't like that," I protested as classes let out and the corridor filled with noisy students.

"Can we please talk somewhere private?" I asked her.

"I don't want to talk to you. I don't have

to talk to anybody but the police."

"Well, legally, you . . ."

She brushed me aside and strode quickly away.

I waived to Martin, saying, "Meet you tomorrow." Then I followed Beth and her delightful perfume down the corridor. When I caught up, she turned and yelled, "Stop following me. You have no right to harass me. Why did David have to find you. He . . ." She began to cry and a small crowd of curious students clustered around her, casting condemning stares in my direction.

"I only want to ask a few questions about David. Why are you so angry with me? I didn't kill him."

"That's what you say, but I don't believe you." She turned and hurried toward the side exit door. I followed, hoping that when her tears dried, she'd calm down and we could talk.

# EIGHTEEN

Forget your personal tragedy. We are all
bitched from the start . . .
— ERNEST HEMINGWAY

The campus had settled into that quiet lull
between day and evening classes. The usual
late afternoon breezes off the lake hadn't
materialized, and it was very hot. The
humid air hung in deep silence over the
parking lot.

Many of the cars were now gone. Beth
deftly zigzagged around those remaining
toward her target, a blue Saturn station
wagon. She wasn't exactly running, but it
was clear she was evading me. Nevertheless,
I managed to catch up as she climbed in
and slammed the door.

I rapped on the window, but she turned
the ignition key and barely glanced my way
as the Saturn's motor roared to life.

"Beth," I called, but she gunned the gas

and backed out fast.

I ran after her. "Wait," I shouted.

A loud mechanical clash from her car told me her engine was doing maximum rpm's. When the Saturn backed out to the road, it didn't stop or go into forward gear. Instead it continued to accelerate backward at a high rate of speed and with a lot of engine noise. I wondered if her gears were stuck, and I called out to her again as the Saturn raced across the grassy buffer on the other side of the road.

Still in reverse, her car was churning up the grassy turf, leaving deep ruts in the irrigated green expanse. Through the windshield, I saw Beth. Her eyes and mouth formed three perfect "O's" as the car sped backwards toward a huge weeping willow tree on the bank of the retention pond.

"Beth," I yelled as she crashed into the tree. It sounded like something you'd hear at a downtown Chicago intersection, entirely out of place in this quiet, bucolic setting. The momentum of the crash tossed the Saturn's front end up in the air. The front tires were spinning, and I heard the pitch of the car's motor increase to a scream as the weight came off the wheels. Weeping willow branches had gotten entangled in the door. I watched in horror as the car moved downward in slow motion, the weeping willow branches gently waving, and somersaulted into the murky retention pond. It landed wheels up with a thudding splash, and the screaming engine cut off abruptly.

"Help! Someone help." I didn't wait to see if anyone heard. Dropping my purse, I kicked off my high heels and raced down the embankment, frantically trying to avoid tripping in the deep ruts the Saturn's tires had made.

I smelled gas as I plunged into the spreading iridescence on the pond's surface.

Cars sink rapidly, most in two to three minutes. This one was going even faster into the dark water because it was upside down. I reached out, grabbed a door handle, and was instantly sucked under with the car in a loud belch as the interior gave up its air.

I held on and tried to get enough leverage to wrench open the door. The driver's window was broken, and the door badly damaged from the crash. Sharp branches from the willow stuck out everywhere, cutting my face and arms, preventing me from getting any purchase.

The water was so murky, all I could see inside was the bright outline of Beth's dress. Reaching through the broken window, I pushed her, trying to shove her over to the passenger side. I hadn't seen her put on a seat belt, so maybe she could get out that way. She didn't move.

I had to go up for air. I took three big gulps, still smelling gas. I wasn't going to give up. I dove back down. The water stopped churning, and the sediment began to clear. The car's interior was filled with water now except for some air trapped against the floorboards. I felt like Hamlet's Ophelia, floating with the willow branches, student papers, and empty juice containers.

I lunged into the front seat through the broken window. Beth was lying with one leg over the steering wheel, another tucked under it. Her skirt had drifted up, exposing bloody cuts on her thighs. One arm, wedged between the seats, was covered with spidery scratches that glistened like red tattoos. And her head was a bloody mess.

I grabbed her and tried to back out through the window. Something — one of her shoes — caught on the steering wheel. I tugged again, harder, ripping the dress but not freeing her. Her sharp butterfly pin cut my arm. The branches, the glass, and the metal all grabbed at me. I panicked, letting go of Beth and hoping I could get myself back out the window. I needed air.

I came to the surface, gasping, and got a mouthful of gasoline. Somebody grabbed me by the waist and pulled me to the shore.

"Are you okay?" my savior asked. "An ambulance is on the way."

"She's still in the car," I panted, coughing and feeling sick from the gas. "Couldn't get her out."

"We'll take over," he said, as a curious but quiet crowd encircled us. I overheard someone ask no one in particular, "Was it suicide?"

# NINETEEN

Fire Department paramedics gave me a quick once-over, then left the scene. Without Beth. Which meant the coroner was on his way. *Which meant that I had found body number two in as many days. I tensed up at the thought of what the cops were going to say about this.*

I soon learned that my savior was Ortiz, the security guard. The good news was I was alive. The bad news was Ortiz fingered me as the person Beth fought with just before she died. So now I wasn't just a witness, I was a suspect.

When the cops questioned me, they were interested only in confirming that Beth and I had quarreled and why. They asked me why I'd followed her and why I wanted to harm her. I tried diverting their focus to the unusual clashing noises I had heard Beth's Saturn make when she stepped on the gas. Frustrated, I made a scene, insisting they accompany me to the parking lot. Not ready yet to make an arrest, they reluctantly agreed and followed me outside.

"This is where Beth was parked," I told them, pointing to a pool of liquid on the dark asphalt.

"I saw that puddle there when Beth backed her Saturn out. I'm positive it's not water," I insisted and knelt, dipping a finger into the wet substance that was clear and had a smooth, soapy feel, like hand lotion. I sniffed it. It smelled like solvent. I didn't have to do a taste-test.

"It's brake fluid," I announced. "See for yourselves."

The lead cop followed suit. He did the taste-test and spit. His eyes narrowed as he said, "Maybe I agree, but we can't be sure it came from her car."

"Yeah, well when you guys winch that Saturn up from the pond, check the brake line first thing. My guess is it was slashed. And whoever did it, did it right here." I pointed to the stain on the asphalt. "That ain't no little leak. It's an ocean." *And, I thought but didn't say out loud, as Sherlock Holmes said, "one true inference invariably suggests others." This was no accident.*

When they escorted me to a squad car, I spotted Martin Sweeney, Big Bill, Dorothy

Jeffers, and Bette Abramawitz huddled together at the edge of the crowd that had gathered to watch.

The cops drove away rapidly, chattering about a recent swat team incident. I wasn't listening. Instead, I was trying to figure out what else had been done to Beth's car to make it stay in reverse and rev the engine so high. I had no doubt Beth had been murdered, and her murder and David's were connected. And I had no doubt the police would theorize that I could supply the missing link.

# TWENTY

The nameplate of the officer on duty behind the bulletproof glass at the desk read Sergeant More. His sunken eyes focused on me, and I had the distinct feeling he was memorizing my features to try to match me up with a face from the Most Wanted posters tacked on the wall above his desk.

"Before she gives a formal statement, More, have her fill out a 357. Then Lieutenant Lytle wants to see her, okay?" said the officer who'd driven me over.

"Ten four," Sergeant More said, triple-clicking his ballpoint pen as he gave me a deadpan stare. He took a form from the top right-hand drawer and slid it under the window.

"Fill this out."

After returning the 357 form to him, I waited. I'd had a bellyful of being a good citizen and wondered if I should call Karl Patrick. I was just considering sneaking out past Sergeant More when a door marked "Police Personnel Only" opened.

"Miss McGil? I'm Lieutenant Lytle. This way."

I followed him, marveling at his tiny feet in highly polished black shoes. We snaked through a maze of offices, entering one with his name on the door. He indicated the chair next to his desk, and that was the only preliminary nicety I was accorded.

"Miss McGil, we've got more than a dozen statements from bystanders telling us you had an argument with the victim, and you followed her out to her car."

He paused, letting the facts settle like chickens come home to roost.

"As if that's not enough to hold you as a suspect, I just got off the phone with Detective Brewer over to the eighteenth precinct. He says you came across another dead body only yesterday. A Mr . . ." He put on a pair of glasses and pawed through some papers. "Barnes. David Barnes. Right?"

"Yes, I did find David's body."

"Two days, two bodies. That's quite a record, Miss McGil."

"I had nothing to do with David's death or with Beth's."

"But you were talking to Beth about David's murder, is that right?"

222

The cops had ferreted that out right away, and even to me, I reeked of prime suspect. *I definitely needed to call Karl Patrick. He told me not to talk to the cops under any circumstances about anything because their agenda was going to be different from mine — and maybe different from the truth. But maybe I could talk myself out of this.*

"Then why would I have jumped in and tried to save Beth?" I blurted out. "I almost got killed myself."

"How do we know exactly what you were doing down there? Maybe you were trying to keep her under, not bring her up. Let's see here." He fingered the form I'd filled out then pulled out another form. "We gotta go through channels. I also got a report in just now that says you possibly broke into this David Barnes' office at the college and ransacked it." He peered over his half-glasses. "True?"

"Somebody trashed it before I ever got there," I offered dispiritedly, wondering how Karl was going to get me out of this.

He squinted, studying me carefully. "I'm gonna ask you one more time, how well did you know Miss Moyers?"

"I already told you, I never met her before today. But like I told the cops at the scene, I'm sure it wasn't suicide or an accident. I think somebody cut her brake lines and rigged the car to stay in reverse, but it wasn't me. I want my lawyer."

# Twenty-One

Karl Patrick escorted me out of the police station. He wasn't happy.

"I told you a hundred times DD — never talk to the cops. I had a hell of a time convincing them not to arraign you. They were talking charges ranging from murder to breaking and entering."

"Thanks, Karl."

"Know what I think? What they were really mad about was you ordering them to check the brake line. One cop said you were the lippiest broad they'd ever dragged into the station. The only way I got you sprung was to agree with him."

"Don't worry. I won't leave town." I thanked him again, waved good-bye, and grabbed a cab back to the college to retrieve my car. I was very grateful to be away from the smells and sounds of American Justice.

As soon as I paid the taxi driver, I ducked into the college and found the nearest rest room. A few cops still roamed the building, canvassing and taking photos. I wanted to snoop around on my own, but with the cops still around, now wasn't the time. Anyway, I had to install that surveillance equipment in Barry's office tonight.

The mood I was in when I reached Barry's wasn't chatty. I clenched my teeth and went right to work installing the micro-video camera.

"I still don't like what you're doing," Barry protested.

*I didn't like it either.* "I know, Barry," I agreed, but kept on with the installation.

The camera finally became operational just after eleven. When Barry hit the john, I hurriedly installed watchdog trackers between the keyboards and the computers in all his PCs. This handy monitor would log all the keystrokes on each computer, track Internet sites, outgoing e-mail, chat rooms, and Web sites, and the memory would remain intact, even if the computer got unplugged or zapped during a power loss. I didn't have to use any system resources, and since the hardware was only two inches long, I was praying Barry wouldn't notice this tiny addition to all his other paraphernalia. If he knew I was doing this, Barry would kill me for invading his privacy instead of thanking me for providing a key to potentially vital information.

When I finally left at eleven-forty, Barry was still working.

# TWENTY-TWO

Grace under pressure.
— ERNEST HEMINGWAY

Cavalier is never a happy-camper after being left alone all day, so I didn't expect a hearty welcome. But my trouble sensor went off loud and clear when I saw him on the first-floor landing, roaming the halls. I scooped him up, then saw the reason for his loud meows. My apartment door was ajar.

I kicked it wide open and peered in. Overturned furniture, papers, and junk were everywhere. Cavvy surveyed the damage with me, keeping his tail high and meowing his eyewitness version of what had happened.

By the end of my tour, I was absolutely furious. I pulled my red cell phone from my purse and called Lieutenant Lytle.

"Just who do you cops think you are?" I asked. "I demand to see the search warrant.

And what right do you guys have to terrorize my cat? My place is a shambles. I demand restitution. I'm going to sue the department. I'm going to call the Mayor. I'm going to . . ."

"Wait a minute, Miss McGil," he interrupted. "We didn't search your place. We haven't issued any warrant. Are you telling me you've been burglarized?"

"No warrant? Are you sure your guys didn't do this?"

"I'm sending out a squad to take a report."

So now I was an urban crime statistic, one of the apartments that gets robbed every eighteen seconds. My anger at the cops cooled a little as I realized my vandalized apartment might work in my favor and take me off the top of their suspect list. Then I got scared. This was no random break-in. First David's house, then his office, now this. The connection was obvious. Somebody thought I had the Hemingway manuscripts.

I was afraid, and I didn't like the feeling. I gathered up Cavalier, stroking him, hoping it would generate enough of those good alpha vibes for both of us.

Waiting for the cops, I searched the debris for a bottle of aspirin or Advil or Pamperin, anything to kill the headache. I didn't think the cops would mind if I rummaged through the crime scene. The odds were against them getting whoever did this. They never hold out much hope when you get burgled.

I refilled Cavvy's unbreakable water bowl, which had been tipped over. Then I replaced the shards of his broken food dish with a beautiful gold-tipped Staffordshire plate I unearthed, part of the exquisite set Auntie Elizabeth had given me a couple of years ago on a generous whim. I was glad it had escaped damage, but it didn't bear thinking what she'd say if she saw the cat eat from it.

While Cavalier lapped his water, I cut up a piece of flank steak left untouched in the refrigerator. He sniffed it suspiciously at first, then devoured every morsel. Guarding the house must have expended lots of cat calories.

My nerves were so jangled, I jumped when the pair of uniforms rang my doorbell less than ten minutes later. One was a tall, handsome black cop with a trim mustache and sharp eyes. His name tag read Officer Baylor. The other was an American Indian with a name so long, I couldn't pronounce it. They were both preoccupied checking out my front door.

"No signs of forced entry here," the American Indian, Parmonicotte, said, running his hand along the door.

"All these locks are good. Real good," the black cop, Baylor, said approvingly. "They didn't get in through here."

"I think they came through the window off my back porch," I informed them. They followed me into the kitchen.

"Yep," Parmonicotte agreed, pointing. "Broken glass. Evidence."

"We hear you've been having your troubles lately with crime of all sorts," Baylor said.

"Wait a minute," I interrupted. "You guys are here to investigate a burglary, not to accuse me of anything. I would never do this to myself. And my cat was wandering the halls. I'd never do that to him."

They laughed. "Nothing personal," Baylor said, then addressed the other cop. "Hey Chief, let's get this formally recorded."

"Chief? You're the police chief?" I asked, suddenly scared they'd come to arrest me.

"He's the Chief of the Menominee tribe," Baylor said, still laughing at his own wit. "But don't worry. I won't let him send any smoke signals from your apartment."

"If you're through making jokes now, Shaft," Parmonicotte deadpanned, "let's get on with it and see if we can help this little lady and her cat."

"We're not supposed to help this lady or

her cat," Baylor said, punching Parmonicotte in the shoulder. "We're supposed to help the department." He then produced a pen clipped to a small spiral notebook. "Is this exactly how you found things, Miss, or did you touch stuff?" he asked, flipping a page.

I told them about looking for the aspirin and about the plate to feed Cavalier. The cat, showing perfect timing, chimed in with a meow that startled both the cops and me. Who knows, maybe he did understand English.

"Give us the tour," Parmonicotte ordered.

"Any jewelry gone?" asked Baylor, scribbling notes.

"I don't own much," I told them. "And what I have seems to be here, although it's all over the place."

"Coins or stamps?"

"No."

" 'Lectronics?"

"Just TV and a stereo. One VCR. One computer. One Kindle. Nothing seems to have been taken. I don't have anything hotshot."

"What's this?" Parmonicotte knelt and picked up a three by two by one inch silver box that had been smashed.

I looked over his shoulder as he and Baylor examined it. Stamped on a piece of silver casing was, "Emotion Reader TNF100A." Glancing down, I saw a lithium cell battery that had been crushed too. *Damn. Whoever did this had smashed my expensive hand-held lie detector.*

When they finished their tour, Officer Baylor cleared a place, then they flipped the sofa right side up and sat down.

"Seems we have accumulated a bunch of pertinent facts here," Baylor said, tapping his spiral notebook. "But when we lump 'em all together, we got squat. Not one clue except the broken glass telling us how somebody entered."

"And the fact that nothing seems to be missing and the fact that it don't look like a pro job," Parmonicotte observed wryly.

"What else you got they might be looking for?" Baylor eyed me like I was a frog ready for dissection. "Drugs maybe?"

"The only drugs I have are the aspirin, Advil, and Pamprin I told you about already."

"You sure you didn't do this to yourself?" Parmonicotte and Baylor both eyed me with naked interest. "The way we hear it, you're in a lot of trouble with a lot of people. Maybe something like this could help you out."

I could have told them that the mess in my apartment was exactly like the mess in David's office and his apartment, but I kept my mouth shut. I didn't need another visit to a police station.

"Think it's worth lifting for prints, Chief?" Baylor asked.

"No, but we better do it anyway. Orders is orders." Parmonicotte stood up.

"We might find a print somewhere," Baylor said with a wink in my direction as he snapped shut his notebook.

"If this was a burglar, you're really lucky," Baylor continued, unpacking equipment.

"You mean because they didn't find anything worth taking?"

"No. Because they didn't take the food out of your refrig, have a picnic, then piss and crap over everything," Parmonicotte explained, using a big soft brush to dust surfaces with the silk-gray latent print powder.

"With real B & E's, we see it more and more," Baylor added, applying transparent fingerprint hinge lifters when he saw possibles. "They're animals."

Parmonicotte swept the big brush over the back porch window. "It's like these guys have to mark their territory. It keeps gettin' weirder and weirder out there."

"Jeez, it's hot in here. You need central air." Baylor complained.

"Yeah," Parmonicotte agreed. "This humidity makes it hard to lift for prints."

The heat was the least of my worries. The fact that this was no random act scared me, and the enormity of the mess suddenly hit home.

Baylor put away the lifters while Parmonicotte reached down to pet Cavalier, who'd shown a keen interest in their machinations.

"We're done for now. We're leaving," Parmonicotte said, heading for the door.

"The police report'll be available in two days," Baylor informed me. "If you find anything else missing, call us," he added, winking again.

"Maybe you should stay off the streets and clean this place up. Everybody'd be better off," Parmonicotte advised as I closed the door.

Overwhelmed by the mess, I located my oversize wooden breadboard and inserted it across the broken window, wedging it in with my recycling bin.

I was still queasy from that mouthful of gasoline. On top of that my arms, hands, and face had a lot of minor cuts and my neck and back ached from tension and stress. I was a walking ad for a medical disaster. Cavvy too was restless, still upset about witnessing the destruction of his domain, and neither one of us liked the sour smell that was building in the heat from all the food spilled in the kitchen.

When I finally unearthed the answering machine, I was amazed to find its battery backup had worked. Eight messages were waiting. Six were from reporters, one was from Matt, asking me to call him as soon as possible, and the other was my mother, telling me to call my Aunt Elizabeth at once. She'd had one of her premonitions that I was in some kind of danger. "You know something awful happens when she has these feelings, so you better be careful," my mother added. "Oh, and, if you're dating anyone, bring him along for Sunday's dinner."

I couldn't face a conversation with *ma tante* Elizabeth tonight or for that matter with Matt. Both could wait until tomorrow. Instead, I cleared the messages and hunted in the messy bedroom for a pair of shorts and a tee top. I'd have liked a drink, but couldn't find any unbroken liquor bottles. Anyway, I didn't want another hangover on top of everything else. I found some usable sheets, threw them on the bed and crawled in, exhausted and demoralized.

# Twenty-Three:
## Day 4: Wednesday

For the second day in a row, I awoke with a sore head, a tired mind, and the certain feeling that bad luck or worse was dogging me. The sweltering heat was another replay of the past few days. Even standing directly in front of the air conditioner didn't offer much relief.

I picked up broken glass and other debris that could hurt the cat and cleaned up the smelly garbage. Then I rummaged through the mess for something to wear. The navy skirt and white top I unearthed looked like they'd been sat on by an elephant. Too bad. Any straightening up would have to wait. I was going to be too busy today to do anything except get the glass fixed on the porch window.

I riffled through the Yellow Pages and chose the number for Bob the Glazier. He agreed to come right over, but it would cost a premium. It was an emergency, so I was stuck.

There wasn't anything more to do on Barry's case except wait. That was good, because I needed to investigate two deaths and two break-ins. If I could find out anything solid about any one of them, I might discover who was behind all this. It was the only way to defend myself.

My bell rang. Thinking Bob the Glazier had made record time, I opened the door without checking the peephole.

It was the twins.

"We saw the cops and heard what happened to your apartment yesterday, so here we are to help out," Glendy announced, entering with a steaming glass coffeepot.

Lucille followed, balancing a silver tray with a plate of scrambled eggs and toast, a glass of orange juice and a small dish of salmon. I sincerely hoped the salmon was for Cavvy.

"What a feast. You're wonderful," I said, upending the coffee table so they could set down the coffeepot and tray.

Glendy and Lucille roamed through the apartment, surveying the mess while Cavalier and I dug in. We were both hungry, and my food, at least, was good.

The twins returned from their tour, shaking their heads.

"As soon as Cavvy's done eating, we'll take him to our place," Glendy announced.

"He's been traumatized," Lucille noted. "He'll need reassurance till things get straightened up here."

"And we know you'll be out doing the investigating," Glendy concluded, picking up the cat.

When they left with Cav, I assured them everything would be all right, and I almost convinced myself.

Two minutes later, true to his word, Bob the Glazier arrived.

"You was lucky. I was about to leave for my first appointment, but I fit you in first, seeing as it's urgent."

*Yeah, and seeing as I'm paying you a fortune.*

"What with a home invasion every thirty seconds and a burglary every eighteen," he went on, "I can't keep up with things all by myself anymore. I got ten guys out on the streets now."

Bob took out his tools and began to ply his trowel in confident, artistic motions, handling the repair with dispatch.

"What'd they get from you?" he asked.

"Not much."

"You're real lucky. Most times if they don't find what they like, they torch you or garbage the place. Flash you or trash you. Yep, you was real lucky."

"That's what the cops said."

"Crooks ain't just crooks anymore," he said. "Everybody's into power these days."

While he worked, I phoned Dieter, my auto mechanic. He's a whiz with anything automotive and keeps my Miata in great shape.

"Vat's your problem, DD?"

I told him about yesterday, concluding, "There was enough brake fluid in the parking lot to be sure that's where the brake line was severed."

"Hmm," he said.

"What I can't figure out is why the motor red-lined as soon as she shifted into reverse."

"Hmm. What year vas that car, DD?"

I didn't know the year and hated not to be able to talk car talk. "Does blue help?" I joked, looking for a way out without embarrassing myself too much.

"Hmm. If it vasn't this year's brand-new model, chances are good it vas the TV Cable."

"What are you talking about? Cable TV?"

"Ha, you love to joke me. No, TV Cable is dat throttle valve cable. All dose older GM cars have a cable dat connects the throttle valve on top of da engine to da transmission. See?"

*I didn't.*

"German-made cars don't have dis problem."

"Dieter, explain in more detail please."

"Vell, vhat I mean is dis TV cable tells da transmission when to shift depending on how hard it is you step on the gas. But dis could be rigged so ven you shift in reverse, dat cable controls da throttle opening instead of da throttle controlling the transmission."

"So when she shifted into reverse, it was like stepping on the gas too."

"Yah, Liebchen. You got it now."

"So what the hell are you supposed to do if something like that happens?" I asked.

"You can do nothing wid out brakes," he answered softly. "If maybe she shifted out of reverse, she might haf saved herself. But maybe nicht. In da vay you have described da sound of dat engine, it vas turning so fast it prob'ly would have blown up in her lap."

Feeling numb, I thanked him and hung up.

"All done, Miss," Bob the Glazier announced with a satisfied smile. He ran his fingers along the glass to check for smooth lines. "That'll hold." He collected and neatly repacked his tools. "My advice, though, is you should put Lexan in there 'stead of glass."

I frowned. "Isn't Lexan really expensive?"

"It costs lots more, but they can't break it."

He took his check and asked, "Can I leave the back way? I got my truck parked illegal at the Broadway bus stop."

# TWENTY-FOUR

The Beecham Building had cranked up their air conditioning to Arctic, and my office was wonderfully cool. Even better, I'd gotten in without seeing my landlord, George Vogel. I erased the six messages that had come in from reporters since yesterday and gulped some ice cold Coke I'd bought in the lobby. When I phoned for an appointment to see the chairman of the English department, I was put on hold. Being a multi-tasker, I used the time to unwrap and munch half a Mounds bar that was hiding in my desk.

"Miss McGil? Bill Butler here," he announced garrulously.

"I'd like to make an appointment to see you," I told him, swallowing the last bite of the Mounds. "Today, if possible."

"I'll be perfectly blunt," he drawled. "I don't believe that would be at all prudent. You see, I happen to know your name has come up in the investigations concerning the recent deaths of two members of this department."

"Well, that may be so, but . . ."

"And, on advice of my counsel, I will not meet you or have any further conversation with you."

"But it's very important."

The line buzzed dead. I hung up, wondering why he needed counsel. I supposed the cops were questioning him too, so maybe they were looking into other possibilities. Still, I needed to talk to him about the sexual harassment case. As department chair, he'd know more details about exactly what happened. I was getting tired of being stonewalled by everybody. Maybe I'd just walk into his office unannounced and corner him.

I couldn't put off calling Matt any longer so I punched in the number he'd left on my machine last night.

A pleasant female voice announced, "Whitehall Hotel. How may I help you?"

Matt answered on the third ring. "I was just about to call you, DD. I have to cancel our meeting tonight. Something's come up."

*Was that why he'd called me at home last night? I wasn't going to step into a trap.* "Okay, fine," I said.

"Let's reschedule. Tomorrow night here at the Whitehall restaurant at eight o'clock. Anything to report so far?"

I told him briefly what had happened at City College with Beth Moyers and David's office being ransacked. I left out the little details about my being a primo suspect and my own apartment being trashed.

"And nobody seems to know where the manuscripts are. By the way," I added, "I kind of promised Martin Sweeney that American Insurance would pay him for his expertise to help us prove the manuscripts weren't genuine. I hope you're not going to make a liar out of me."

"We'll fork out a reasonable amount for him, DD. Sounds like the ball is rolling in our direction from what he's got to say. Do *you* think David faked the manuscripts?"

"Honestly, Matt, at this point I don't know. I'd have liked to get a look at the computer in David's office, but didn't have time. Now I don't know if I can, because the cops sealed it off."

"You'll think of something, DD. You're the most resourceful girl I've ever met. Keep me posted. Oh, and have you given any more thought to what we discussed in Phil's office?"

*Sure, I thought. But it always comes out the same.*

"I'll be in touch, Matt," I answered. "See you tomorrow night."

*I rang off and stared into space, thinking about the Whitehall. I loved that restaurant, but it was connected to the hotel, and I suspected that's why Matt made reservations there.*

I finished the Coke and called the inscrutable Miss Wang at the IRS. Mr. Poussant, she informed me, was on field duty today, and I'd have to leave a message.

Before I could pick up the phone again, it rang.

"DD McGil?" a deep, pleasant voice asked.

"Yes?"

"This is Mitch Sinclair."

"Hi."

"How's your investigation coming? Barry asked me to call and touch base. I'm here if you need questions answered or want anything."

I wondered if Barry had broken down and told him about the micro-video camera I'd planted. Or maybe they'd found the Keykatcher I'd installed.

"That was really nice of Barry," I said cautiously.

"Look, DD McGil," Mitch said forcefully. "Let's cut the crap and stop playing games. I'm trying to help you. Don't you get it? Somebody's got to, or we'll never solve this."

"I appreciate what you're saying, but . . ."

"But nothing. I see the papers and watch the news. You're a suspect in a murder case. Just how do you propose to help us solve this piracy? Don't you realize this isn't a game? We've got to get to the bottom of this right now or Barry will be out of business and maybe even in jail."

"Every word you say is true," I answered, trying to ignore the heavy lump in the pit of my stomach. "But give me a chance. If I don't come up with something in the next day or so, I'll tell Barry to call in Gilcrest and Stratton. Okay? Truce?"

"I don't agree, but I guess it'll have to be. I just hope you know what you're doing."

I hung up the phone, unsure of the track I was following. I needed more time — time Barry didn't have to give.

# TWENTY-FIVE

As you get older it is harder to have heroes, but it is sort of necessary.
— ERNEST HEMINGWAY

I left the office early to meet Martin Sweeney. I wondered what I might learn from him. David was dead, and even though I was playing detective, nothing was going to change the fact that I would never see him again. If Martin Sweeney convinced me the manuscripts were fake, American Insurance would come out on top. But what about David's reputation? If they were fake, why had David been killed? And what about Beth Moyers? I was sure both of them had been murdered by the same person or persons who trashed my digs. And if they thought I had the manuscripts or knew something dangerous, what else was I in for?

Road construction, also known as improvements-for-our-own-good, made traffic stop-and-go all the way to Oak Park. Insects, formerly the most successful life form on earth, have been superceded by road contractors.

It was hotter here in the western burbs, away from the cooling effect of Lake Michigan. Parking, however, was the same old nightmare as in the city. I was estimating that my chances of winning the lottery were better than finding a spot when I saw an illegal space next to a bus stop and pulled in.

Oak Park was Hemingway's birthplace, and the village tries to make it look much the same as during his boyhood. Today, however, it skirts Chicago's western ghetto, and you don't need different colored street signs to know you stand on the threshold between two different worlds. On one side of the street, vacant, graffitied buildings gaped loudly, declaring gang turf. On the other side, Frank Lloyd Wright buildings attracted tourists, and residents worked hard to keep their manicured green lawns and freshly painted buildings an oasis of civility.

The Oak Park Hemingway Trust was housed in the village high school, a five-story yellow brick edifice covering several square blocks. Tennis courts and a playing field were tacked on one end near a huge parking lot.

Martin had said there was tight security, but no one asked for an ID as I roamed the halls trying to find the archives office. A loud bell rang, signaling the end of classes, and all the doors along the corridor were thrown open with a collective bang. I didn't have to wonder for whom the bell tolled, and before I could get out of the way, waves of students from all directions pushed me here and there, taking me along like a pebble of sand on the Normandy beach during the invasion. I pulled out of the crowd's flow and waited against a wall until the masses cleared.

"You lost, miss?" A white-haired female security guard approached with a concerned look. I saw she was wearing a gun. As the bell rang again and the corridors quickly emptied, she directed me to the archives office on the second floor.

# TWENTY-SIX

Happiness in intelligent people is the
rarest thing I know.
— ERNEST HEMINGWAY

Once upstairs, I easily located the archives.
Inside it was cool and dark — temperature,
humidity, and light controlled to protect the
valuable materials. Blown-up sepia-toned
scenes of early village life covered the walls.

Martin Sweeney was seated at a table in a
separate room at the back of the archives
area. Special lights illuminated his table,
overflowing with stacks of papers. We appeared to be alone.

"Have a seat." He pointed to an adjacent
chair.

"I see you're very busy," I nodded to the
scattered research materials on the table.
"Thanks for taking time to talk with me."

He took off his glasses and squinted at
me. "I'm not sure I should after what hap-

pened yesterday with Beth. I understand the cops think you might be involved in both deaths. Personally, I feel that finding two bodies is more than just coincidence."

Everybody was telling me that. I agreed but didn't tell him so. Nor did I tell him that when I called the Insurance Institute to find the exact odds on an innocent person finding two bodies, they had no stats to offer. Instead, they told me to contact *America's Most Wanted.*

"You're going to have to take my word for it that I wasn't involved in either death. I'm working for the insurance company. I told you that yesterday, and the cops are checking it out. Say, these photos of the village along the walls are fascinating." I pointed at the sepia shots. "Nothing looks like it used to."

"You wouldn't say that if you lived here," Martin said seriously.

"You don't like Oak Park?"

"I grew up here, just like Hemingway. We both started life as Doopers."

"As what?"

"Doopers. *Dear Old Oak Park-ers.* You were either a Dooper or a Greaser. Luckily we both grew out of it."

"Did you help start the local group that promotes Hemingway?"

"God, no. They tout him as a favorite son now, but during his life, people here didn't like him. And Papa in turn didn't like the 'broad lawns and narrow minds' of Oak Park. He never had any desire to come back. Here's a fact," he said, looking up at the ceiling. "His mother wrote him on his twenty-first birthday to 'not come back until his tongue learned not to insult and shame his mother.' They were estranged from that day on. Who could blame him for going to Paris a year later to escape the religious, narrow-minded provincialism that was at its zenith here in the twenties."

He gathered up pages of research material he'd been working on and stacked them in a neat pile.

"This local Hemingway group doesn't like what I do," he explained. "They can't accept the fact that Hemingway totally rejected the self-satisfied, broom-up-your-ass puritanical manners Oak Parkers think they invented. Damn, don't get me started. Now that things have come full circle, Oak Park finds it needs Hemingway. You wouldn't believe what they concoct to attract publicity. They even stage a running of the bulls down the main commercial drag every year," he snorted.

"You mean like in Pamplona?" I asked.

"Ha. The real story is that in June of 1944, Hemingway and another American writer were gored by a bull in the ring at Pamplona where they went to attend a fiesta. But here, in the Oak Park version, they don't use real bulls. Instead they dress up local businessmen in bull suits and horns and run them down a blocked-off street. Papa would puke.

"See, they're just plain wrong. They should be researching what made Papa macho, and that didn't take place here in Oak Park. That happened up in Michigan where his father took him hunting, fishing, and camping, and helped him cultivate a spirit of adventure and curiosity. His mother tried to dampen that spirit. She was totally domineering. She even tried to dress up Hemingway as a girl."

"I didn't know that."

"No one here in Oak Park wants to face the fact that the years he spent here weren't good ones. It started when his parents moved into his mother's family home, and his mother was the little princess Grace. From then on, the deck was stacked against the Hemingway males. Grace took over and had her way in everything. It's said that she won all the arguments, made everybody sing to her tune."

"That doesn't sound like a lot of fun," I agreed. "Hemingway must have reacted to that his whole life. But then, aren't most families a bit off-kilter? Isn't dysfunctional the norm?"

"That proves my thesis. Like most men, as soon as Hemingway was old enough to be on his own, he took charge of his life. He was eighteen and vowed never again to live according to someone else's dictates. He came back here to Oak Park less than half a dozen times. He did attend his father's funeral, but not his mother's."

I wondered what the natives thought of Martin's theories. Before I could figure out a nice way to ask, he said, "Think about it. If you're forced to live your childhood doing someone else's bidding, you don't turn into an obedient adult. You turn into a spoiled adult who gets everything you were forbidden as a child. I ought to know." He smiled. "I grew up with the same crap."

We both chuckled and he asked, "Why do you think Hemingway wanted to be called Papa? Did you know that when his father killed himself, Ernest's mother mailed him the gun his father used? Nice, huh?"

"But I think I read somewhere that Hemingway asked his mother to send him that gun."

"Well, that's one story, but I don't believe it. I think the record needs to be set straight on all the facts. That's why I'm doing all this research on Ernest's years in school here at Oak Park High and the stories he wrote as a student for the school paper." He pointed at the materials on the table. "But, you mentioned something about hiring me."

"Right," I said. "Your evaluation of the manuscripts indicates that they were fake. American Insurance has, as I told you, a vested interest. If the originals aren't located, they'd like to have proof that the stuff was faked. Are you willing to provide a professional opinion to American detailing the reasoning on which you based your conclusion? We'll pay you $10,000."

"I've done an awful lot of research. It would have to be $25,000 minimum."

Briefly, before I agreed, I wondered whether Matt would consider that a reasonable sum.

"You know, I really wish I was wrong," he went on. "But remember, David refused to show anyone, including me, more than a few fragments of his find. That didn't feel right. I hate to allege fraud, but David is — was — very clever. What about American Insurance? Did they see everything before they wrote the coverage?"

"No. They wrote the binder based on the fragments. I was hired to certify the full find for them, but now they're more interested in proving they were fake."

"I see," Martin said.

"How do you defend your conclusion against the other scholars who came out publicly and acclaimed the find as genuine early Hemingway?"

"They're mistaken. It's understandable because those word studies are suggestive but certainly not definitive. If David did this, he had access to all of the word studies software. He would have written the fakes to fool all of these studies." Martin smiled and continued.

"Furthermore, doesn't it sound a bit too pat that someone — no one knows who — just happened to send a parcel to David with the valise and the manuscripts all nicely indexed? I mean, why David, for God's sake? Where is this supposed to have come from?"

"I understand David tried to investigate who mailed it."

"It's too coincidental, especially in the academic world, that he ends up with the manuscripts. We were together on countless research trips up to Michigan, looking for anything Hemingway-related. We had a theory that the valise Hadley lost might have had identifying name tags at an address in Michigan. After all, they'd been in Paris for only a short time. We suspected the valise had been returned to the lost and found office at the Gare de Lyon and sent back to the States, probably to an address in Michigan. My guess was Petoskey." He paused. "But David getting the stuff in the mail? No. Nobody would give up the manuscripts now. They're way too valuable."

The door opened, and an orange-haired woman in a bright pink outfit entered the room with energy and purpose. She nodded at Martin as her high heels clicked her over to the corner desk.

"She's the curator," Martin whispered. "Her name is Olive."

"Have you uncovered anything significant today, Martin?" Miss Olive inquired.

"Nothing in this stack," he replied, collecting the papers to his right and returning them to her desk. "I've still got some to look through, though."

"Our Martin is quite the scholar," Miss Olive smirked, addressing her remark to me. "He's of the minority opinion that our favorite son, Ernest Hemingway, had a hard time here at the high school. Aren't you, Martin?" Her voice dripped with sarcasm.

Martin's jaw was clenched under his beard, and I quickly deduced these two weren't chums.

Miss Olive gave him no chance to reply. "Martin doesn't understand the concept of happy."

"All I'm trying to do is uncover the facts," Martin said. "As a teen, Hemingway had a rough time here in Oak Park."

Martin winked at me. "Here are the facts. When he started school with his sister, she was half a head taller than him. He was too light and too short to do well at sports — all that's well enough known. He did so miserably in football they called him 'lead-ass.' "

Miss Olive pursed her lips. Her face flushed a deep red, clashing with her orange hair.

"And," Martin continued, sensing he was hitting his target, "Ernest was too near-sighted to do well in the rifle club. And he hated playing the cello, which," Martin looked in my direction, "his mother insisted he take up."

"Really?"

"And," Martin raised his arm to punctuate the importance of this, pursuing Miss Olive like a lion pouncing on an injured impala, "didn't we find out that he had once punched holes with a pencil in his bull's-eye target before he shot?" Martin laughed out loud. "That's not really what you'd call Oak Park fair play, is it?"

Miss Olive's lips clamped tightly, and she turned away, hailing a lean, gaunt man dressed in corduroy slacks and a checked shirt who'd lumbered into the Trust. He called a greeting to her, and when he saw Martin, his natural frown deepened.

"Oh, hello, Hal," Martin nodded cheerily at the approaching newcomer. "Miss McGil, this is Hal Schultz, the head of the Oak Park Hemingway Trust.

"Hal, I was reminding Miss Olive about the time Hemingway's mother had to hire a tutor for him to learn Latin. And how about when he lost the lead in the senior play? And didn't he have to go to the senior prom with his own sister?"

"Martin," Hal Schultz barked, his hands in the pockets of his rust-colored corduroy pants, "as Dorothy Parker said at the time about Hemingway, 'of no other living man has so much tripe been penned or spoken.' You're continuing the tradition with half-truths. How many times do we have to tell you that you're not welcome here? You look for anything negative in the Hemingway–Oak Park connection, and use it for bad publicity."

"The truth. That's all I want," Martin told him. "And so should you."

"Even his harshest critics agree that he was a serious, dedicated craftsman," Hal Schultz replied. "He had enormously compelling personal charisma, which was reflected in his writing."

"There's a lot more to it than that," Martin said. "Why did he mistreat so many who'd helped him up the ladder, like Gertrude Stein, Ezra Pound, and Scott Fitzgerald? His ego grew in proportion to his fame, and my thesis is that the basis for his aggression was the negative things he endured right here in good old Oak Park. His experiences in Michigan brought out his good side. Living in the bosom of goody-goody old Oak Park nurtured his nasty side."

Both Hal and Olive vigorously shook their heads.

"Miss McGil, this is the chap I was telling you about who dreamed up the running of the bulls down the streets of Oak Park. It's a pitiful sight, and I feel sorry for you, Hal, that you have to stoop so low. Why don't you come with me this year to the Hemingway Fest in Key West?"

"That's not real, either, and you know it, Martin. You're always trying to stir up trouble. You know we want those manuscripts. And in the end we'll get them."

I stood up, interrupting the sparring match.

"Look, I have another appointment. I'll get a contract out to you covering your professional testimony, if that's agreed."

"Fine," he said as we walked toward the door. "But I know what this is going to do to David's reputation. I wish it didn't have to go any further."

As I was leaving, a tall, anorexic-looking woman swooped in, nearly knocking me against the wall.

"Hi, Andrea," Martin said genially.

Barely acknowledging Martin, she rushed over to speak in hushed tones to Hal Schultz, eliminating further eavesdropping on his part.

Martin and I checked the corridors for any other news anchors all the way out of the building. He, too, was trying to avoid further interviews.

Visible waves of heat radiated off the parking lot, and I wondered when this weather would break. There was no sign of rain, but in Chicago, weather changes, like us Midwesterners, tend to be abrupt.

I wasn't sure what I believed about Hemingway, but I was glad I didn't have to deal with Hal, Miss Olive, or Andrea on a regular basis. Even an hour raking a Zen Garden wasn't going to help calm those three. Martin, I suspected, was right. Hemingway probably had been unhappy as a teenager. But which of us wasn't, to one degree or another. Good old golden rule days.

# Twenty-Seven

Never confuse movement with action.
— ERNEST HEMINGWAY

Before I left, Martin and I commiserated about Beth's death. The English Department was in a shambles. He invited me to join him at a nearby restaurant. "They make a great Papa Doble — Hemingway's favorite drink. Rum, fresh lime, grapefruit, and maraschino cherry juice shaken and stirred. You'd like it."

I'd thanked him, but took a rain check. Today was my Aikido class, and even though I was sore from yesterday and maybe had a mild concussion, I was nevertheless determined to go. A good workout would clear my mind and maybe stimulate those little gray cells. Anyway, it was better than raking one of those Zen Gardens.

Aikido, developed in the early twentieth century, is the most recent of the martial arts. It means, literally, *the Ki Way,* which is difficult to translate. There's no Western equivalent of Ki. Life Force is probably close. My friend Lauren's always telling me that Aikido is a good thing because it legally channels all my pent-up aggressions.

The changing room had already cleared out as I hurriedly donned my regulation-wear Gi. Sensei, the Master, always began promptly at the appointed hour. Latecomers were not admitted. I rushed to the arena and nearly collided with the Master in the entryway.

I was going for the second black stripe on my orange belt, so I had to perfect nine self-defense escapes with twenty position stances and blocks. All the complex and subtle maneuvers made me feel inscrutable — or at least as inscrutable as any Westerner can.

Sensei always began class with a series of civilized, ritualized maneuvers, then broke into full-fledged combat. Tonight we were practicing the two-handed lapel grab — the escape and setup.

"In Aikido," Sensei emphasized in measured tones, "one must always follow the lead of one's opponent, blending into that opponent, directing the opponent's own flow of force back against him in order to subdue him."

He made it sound so simple.

Cato, our instructor, chose a member of the class to demonstrate.

"You must memorize the sequence of these maneuvers." Cato glared at each of us before beginning. "Kick with double high block." He raised his leg and proceeded to demonstrate in slow motion with the student. "Punch and pin your opponent's arm under your arm." He did so.

"Punch on your opponent's hip with your hip; drive your upper body down hard on your opponent's arm, and take your back leg off the floor. Then kick your opponent's leg out and complete with a throw." Cato easily subdued the student on the floor.

"Now we will have a second demonstration," Cato announced and called on me to play guinea pig. Walking into the circle, I repeated the five maneuvers over and over to myself: kick, punch, block, drop, and throw.

Cato smiled his impersonal smile as we commenced to grapple. Cast as the attacker, I'd be getting the worst of it, and it was in moments like this I almost hated Lauren for encouraging me to enroll.

Cato took pains not to spare me as he kicked, punched, blocked, dropped, and threw me. As he crashed me to the mat, I knew there was no malice in it, just as there is no malice in it when you squash a bug.

When it was my turn to practice on him, I tried to remember to direct his own flow of force back against him. Secretly, I was enjoying putting him onto the mat. On balance, I loved this stuff, and when the demonstration ended, we bowed respectfully to each other — no hard feelings — and the class began practicing.

After an hour, I was exhausted, but at least I wasn't thinking about my problems. The long, cool shower was therapeutic. The concussion was gone for now, and I felt refreshed and in better spirits as I left for home. Most of last night's mess was still there to clean, and I needed a good sleep. I knew it was going to take time to get over David's death and losing Scotty. I was desperately trying not to sink into that same dark pit I'd hibernated in after Frank died.

I jumped into the Miata, jammed the key into the ignition and fired her up. Or tried to. Nothing happened. The key turned, but the ignition didn't ignite. I tried again. No coughs, no wheezes. Nothing.

"Dammit, Dieter," I said out loud. Miata's are generally reliable, and Dieter, my German mechanic, always kept mine in great shape. Feeling crabby and impotent, I got out and raised the hood, hoping I could spot something fixable. I walked around, examining the engine compartment. First I checked the coil wire. That was okay. Everything else looked good until I saw the severed battery cable. The red positive cable was in two separate pieces, and fresh copper glinted on each end. Warning bells went off in my head as I thought of Beth's Saturn, and I silently apologized to Dieter. Like my apartment, I knew this wasn't coincidence. Then I remembered Aunt Elizabeth's phone call. My mother told me to call Auntie because she'd had one of her premonitions. And I hadn't called. I reminded myself to watch my back.

I called Dieter on my cell. He often worked late, and I hoped to catch him. It rang and rang. Just as I was ready to give up, he answered.

"Dis better be good, whoever you are," he snorted. "You got me oud from under a Volvo."

I explained what happened, and he said a few choice words in German that I didn't understand. "Not goot," he said, switching back to his version of English. "Dis maybe is connected to dat lady's accident yesterday, or maybe somebody just vanted to steal your battery. You vatch yourself, DD. Take a taxicab. Leave the key under da mat and I tow her in tonight soon as I can. You pick her up in da morning after ten."

I dumped the phone back in my purse and checked my money. There was enough maybe to have a cabbie drop the flag and take me a mile, but not enough to get me home. I was dead tired, but I was gonna have to take the EL home.

I trudged up the long, baroque iron stairway to the elevated platform to wait for a train. Built in the 1890s, it still served its purpose today, only now its ornate detail was covered over by innumerable coats of industrial green paint and the grime from countless hands. The sound of shuffling footsteps from behind made me turn round. A trim guy in his late twenties continued up the stairs ahead of me, and I was too tired to even admire his butt. More footsteps from behind, and this time I moved to the right to let whoever pass. The move saved my life. I felt a tremendous pain in my left shoulder and fell forward, instinctively clutching my purse.

"Hey. HEY!" someone shouted.

I felt the stairs vibrate beneath me and shut my eyes for a second. When I opened them, I saw a pair of men's loafers and felt strong arms lifting me. It was Mr. Trim-butt.

"You okay?" he asked, supporting me.

"Did you see who hit me?" I asked as I brushed the grime along with a piece of old gum off my knees.

"Not really. All I could see was the back of some guy. He ran down the stairs, but at least he didn't get your purse."

*I didn't think it was the purse the guy was after, but I didn't tell that to Trim-butt.*

My collarbone and neck ached, and my left arm was numb. I flexed it until it started to throb, and at least I knew the blood was again circulating.

"Is there any blood?" I asked, turning my head and getting dizzy.

"None I can see, but you need a doctor. Here, I'll help you down the stairs, and we'll call the cops."

*If the cops saw me again, I'd be locked up for sure.* "No. I'll be fine. I want to go up to the train."

I hung on while he assisted me up the remaining stairs to the wooden platform decorated in equal parts with advertising and graffiti. A street musician leaned against a Doublemint Chewing Gum billboard and played a mournful sax, substituting volume for talent.

"I really think you should call the cops," Trim-butt said as he followed me through the turnstile.

"Honestly, I'll be fine." I saw the lights of an approaching train and said, "I've got to be somewhere."

I watched the motorman seated in the front car twist a large brass handle, and the "A" train squealed to a stop with sparks and an acrid smell.

"This is my train," I told him. "Thanks again for your help."

I jumped aboard, the doors shut, and the train pulled slowly out. My arm stung, but whoever hit me had meant to do more damage than just that. I wondered again who it was. I also wondered about Aunt Elizabeth's canny prediction.

# Twenty-Eight

The dignity of movement of an iceberg
is due to only one-ninth of it being
above water.
— ERNEST HEMINGWAY

I was ready for a wee drink as I climbed the
stairs to my apartment. Tonight I'd have to
clean it all up. I was worn out mentally and
physically, so I wasn't thrilled when I
reached the landing and Glendy and Lucille
called me over.

"DD, we're so glad you're back. How did
today go?" They both smiled brightly.
"Cavvy is fine, but we've been worried
about you."

The twins are spry chicks who are always
on the go. They don't seem to understand
that I work for a living and can't join the
Junior League or be around all day. I love
them dearly so I acted interested, even
though I was dead tired.

"Come in with us," Glendy urged, prodding me gently toward their place.

"We'll get you a drinkey," Lucille added, guiding me by the elbow.

"A little wets is what you need. And we've got a surprise for you, too." Glendy pushed me into their doorway where I collided with Mitch Sinclair.

"What the . . . ?" I stammered.

"Hello," he smiled, his muscular arms slowly unwinding me.

I tried to focus on his face. *What was he doing here?*

"I was passing by," he explained, as if I had uttered my last thought. "I wanted to see you and ask if we could start over."

"I guess you already met the twins, Glendy and Lucille," I said, at a loss for anything else. "Well, ladies, meet Mitch Sinclair."

"We've already met," he said, smiling and bowing. "And it's been a pleasure."

Glendy batted her eyes. "He said he's the one who made that ruckus outside your door the other night."

"He's been here waiting for you a whole hour, DD." Lucille announced, implying it was somehow my fault.

"I didn't mind the wait," Mitch interjected. "I came here to ask you to give me another chance. These two lovelies have been telling me all about you."

I hoped, for his sake, they hadn't regaled him with the wisdom of Deepak Chopra.

"Look, DD." The sisters pointed at a huge bouquet of red roses on a side table. "He even brought flowers."

"He's so good looking," Glendy whispered in my direction. "And such nice manners."

The Quisling Cavalier was curled up on one of the twins' Victorian puffy red pillows. He blinked twice, then settled back into cat sleep.

I grabbed Mitch's elbow and pulled him to the door. "We've got to leave now."

"Good-bye, ladies." He bowed again. "And thanks for the hospitality."

"Can't you stay awhile?" Glendy asked.

"No, but I promise I'll tell you everything later. He's just a business acquaintance."

"You can't fool us, DD," Glendy followed me and stage whispered as I ducked through the doorway.

"Bye, you two," I said, wanting to get Mitch Sinclair out of there. I still couldn't be positive he wasn't ripping off Barry, but seeing as he'd been with Glendy and Lucille for the past hour, I was certain he wasn't the one who'd hit me on the L-train stairs.

We walked down the hall to my door and waited until Glendy and Lucille, reluctantly, closed theirs.

He handed me a small box of Godivas. "The flowers were for you, too, to make up for last night. But I couldn't resist giving them to the twins. They're really pretty special, aren't they?"

"Look, it was nice of you to come and the flowers and chocolates and all," I said, unlocking my door. "And don't get me wrong, I appreciate it."

"Aren't you going to ask me in?"

"I've had another rotten day. I just want to go to bed."

"Do you always go to bed so early? What happened to our truce?" he asked gently, looking into my eyes.

Overtired and despondent, I wanted to agree. Could I take the risk? He was so damn handsome, standing there, trying to be nice. I felt a little like I was betraying Scotty, but in another way he was so much like Scotty, I couldn't help but be attracted to him. I wanted to say yes. But I said nothing, and I said it for much too long.

He shook his head. "Frankly I don't even know why I bother with you. I took time tonight from a big job I'm wrapping up with Barry to see you." He turned and walked away.

"Wait," I called after his handsome back.

He stopped but didn't turn around.

"My apartment got burgled yesterday. That's why I didn't invite you in." I kicked my door wide open. "I think it might have something to do with that murder case I'm working on, and I don't want to get you involved. It could be dangerous. Please try to understand."

Mitch came back. His soft brown eyes were guileless as he surveyed the apartment.

"The girls told me, but I didn't want to pry. How can you be sure this isn't connected to what you're trying to do for Barry. Maybe it's not your other case."

"No. I'm sure the same somebody who did this to me did it to somebody else, too."

"What were they looking for?"

"I think you probably can guess. It's all over the newspapers, TV, and the Internet. The Hemingway papers. Somebody thinks I've got the Hemingway papers."

"Wow." He stepped in and I shut the door. My apartment was still the same mess as when I'd left this morning.

"I'm going to ask you one question, DD. Do you have the Hemingway papers?"

"At least you didn't ask me if I killed David. Almost everyone else has." I sat down and signed deeply.

"About the papers. No, I don't have them.

And I don't know who has them or where they are. David had a lawyer — somebody named Mike Ekins, I think, was his name. One of the attorney firms I'm working for is contacting him. Hopefully David told him where they are, but I'm not sure."

"Why wouldn't his attorney know?"

"David was being really cautious with the original materials. He told me he didn't trust anyone. I thought I might get some answers from a certain computer, but it wouldn't even turn on."

"What computer?"

"David's laptop. I turned it on, but it was just snow."

"Well, today's your lucky day. You know I'm the expert on computers. Let me help you."

"Thanks, but I can't . . ."

"Don't say no, DD. Let me help. I'm being very selfish. The sooner you clear this up, the sooner you can go to work on Barry's problem full time. I can't convince him to drop you from the case, so I figure I better join you."

Maybe Mitch was right. I decided to accept his help. "Okay, if you're really game. I need a look at what's in David's laptop, but my car's laid up. Could you drive me to City College?" *I didn't tell him the computer was in a room sealed off by the police. The truth and nothing but the truth. Just not the whole truth.*

We walked down three flights and out of the lobby into the humid evening air.

"It's hazy, but you can just see the big dipper right there," Mitch pointed as he unlocked a dark green Jaguar, parked right in front of my building.

"Great car," I said, running my fingers along its curvy front fender and admiring its sleek rear end. I wondered if it was true that you are what you drive — like Sanpaku, you are what you eat.

"However did you get this parking space?" I asked him. "I've been here over three years, but the closest I've ever parked is a block away."

"This car's a company vehicle, and it's always lucky about parking spaces." He smiled and turned the air on full blast as we got in. I gave him directions, and he pulled into traffic.

"Give me the lowdown on what you need from this computer, so I can plan what to do when we get there."

He was a good, fast driver, and his clean, masculine scent mixed with that of the car. I decided to tell him everything, and left out only the parts about the "no entry, crime scene" tape across David's door and the fact that we were going to commit not only breaking and entering, but burglary as well. Or was it grand theft? Maybe I should be seriously thinking about a career in criminal law.

When we reached City College, he skillfully guided the Jaguar into a parking space near the entrance.

"See what I mean?" Mitch smiled. "This car always finds a good spot to park."

He held the door open and waited for me to get out. I was having a sudden attack of conscience. I wasn't sure why I'd involved him in this. Even though I suspected he might be ripping off Barry, in my heart I was hoping madly he wasn't the one. In spite of our earlier spats and differences of opinion, I was strongly attracted to him. And Cavalier liked him, and I tend to rely on his cat-stincts. But if this caper went wrong, Mitch could be facing real problems. I saw myself having to tell Barry what happened. Worse yet, telling my Aunt Elizabeth, who would definitely not approve of breaking and entering. "Life's a test, DD," she's always telling me. "And you're failing it." But we were here now, and I did want that laptop.

"Thanks," I said and slid out.

The clock on the first floor read nine p.m.,

consistent with the quiet corridors and the scattered students quietly milling around. Once again there was no security and we entered without challenge. The air conditioning had apparently been fixed, and as we retraced the route to David's office, the halls weren't nearly as uncomfortable.

"It smells awful in here," Mitch said.

"Yeah, they've had problems with the air conditioning," I explained as we approached target. The yellow "Police Line-Do Not Cross" tape was still strung across the door.

"Wait." Mitch grabbed my arm and pointed at the tape. "We can't go in here, DD."

Houdini-like, I unfastened the tape and unlocked the door faster than he could say illegal. I pulled him in and closed the door.

The mass of paper was gone. Everything was now spotless, all traces of David's existence wiped clean from what had once been his domain, neatened no doubt as an act of respect for the dead.

"I don't like this, DD. I might be able to talk my way out of this if we get caught. But with your connections with this case, they'll put you in jail and throw away the key."

"Maybe. Maybe not." I turned on the computer. "I'm sorry you're involved. But

I've got to see what's in here." The laptop beeped loudly as it tried unsuccessfully to boot itself up. Mitch and I looked warily at each other as the screen on the monitor dissolved into a snowy static, just as it had done before.

"See what I mean," I said as Mitch bent over and fiddled with the keyboard.

"I could fix this," Mitch said.

"Really? Then let's go." I turned off the computer and closed it.

"What are you doing?" Mitch asked as I handed him the laptop.

"Just take it." I ordered. "Let's get out of here."

"You can't do this, DD. This is nuts," he insisted. "We'll get caught. They'll throw away the key on both of us."

I pulled him out the door and closed it. Then I refastened the tape. Mitch rolled his eyes and said, "I'm calmly planning what to say in my one phone call after the arrest."

"If we get out of here in under ten seconds, we're definitely going to make it. Don't worry, I've already got a lawyer on retainer that we can both use."

"What about the cameras in the parking lot?"

"They can't identify the computer from those cameras. They're too fuzzy. Anyway, almost everybody who comes in and goes out is carrying one. How are they going to know it's us?"

"Are you a Catholic, DD?" he asked softly as he trudged gamely alongside me down the corridor, carrying the prize.

"I'm not, but what does that have to do with anything?"

"If you were, your penance would be Hail Mary's twenty-four seven from now to the end of your natural life."

We hurried to his car without looking back.

# TWENTY-NINE

The computer sat neatly in the backseat of Mitch's Jaguar on the way back to my place.

"I can't believe I helped you hijack this thing," he said for the second time.

"I'm shocked at your complicity, too."

"I don't know why, DD, but I like you. I like you a lot, and I'm beginning to see why Barry thinks you're so special. But this isn't a joking matter if we get caught. Stealing from a government office is a felony."

"The City College is only quasi-governmental," I corrected him. "So it's only a quasi-felony."

"See what I mean? I suppose you'll wisecrack the Angel Gabriel when your time comes."

Mitch's cell phone rang. As he fished for it, mine rang too. I grabbed it and said hello, only to realize I was hearing Mitch's conversation through the Cell Spy Pro software. All the jostling in my purse must have put my phone on ring. I mumbled a few words, and listened shamelessly in on both sides of the conversation. It was Herman at Barry's office calling. He needed to check a figure with Mitch, who promptly gave him the answer off the top of his head. Herman said thanks, and they hung up. It didn't sound suspicious to me. I mumbled a few things into the dead phone, then said goodbye and hung up too.

I was glad the call hadn't incriminated Mitch. I smiled at him and started to put my cell back into my purse when it rang again. This time it wasn't the Cell Spy Pro doing the calling. It was Karl Patrick. And he told me that David's attorney, Mike Ekins, had just been found dead in his garage of carbon monoxide poisoning.

"I gotta go now," Karl said. "But I want you to promise me you'll be careful. I think you're in danger, too. Do you have someone you can call?"

"I'll be fine. Thanks for letting me know. Bye."

"Who was that?" Mitch asked.

"That was my attorney, Karl Patrick."

"Oh, does he call you every couple of hours to see if you're in jail?" he laughed.

"He said that they found David's attorney dead in his garage."

"Oh, sorry, DD." He frowned. "What was it? Not a heart attack. Suicide? Murder?"

"They don't know yet. Carbon monoxide, and Karl suspects murder. He thinks I'm on the list."

"With all this stuff happening to you, I wouldn't be surprised if you are."

I was going to say something smart-alecky to relieve the tension, but I heard a siren and looked in the rearview mirror. A cop car, mars light flashing, was coming up on us fast.

*I thought of the stolen goods in plain view on the backseat. Surely those rinky cameras didn't pick us up. Or did they? Maybe I was going to need Karl Patrick again today.*

"It can't be us he wants to pull over," I said hoping it was true.

"Is that a statement or a question?"

When I didn't reply, he said, "Don't worry. I'm sure you'll have some quasi-amusing lines for this cop."

Mitch pulled to the side of the road, killed the engine, and stared at me. "Even though you're not Catholic, DD, a prayer might not be out of order right now."

In the rearview mirror, I saw the cop exit his vehicle, put on his hat, square his shoulders, and adjust the billy-club at his belt.

"This could be trouble," Mitch said and rolled down his window at the cop's approach. "Yes, Officer? What's the problem?"

"Show me your license and registration," the officer said, playing a flashlight around the car. His name badge read Weinberg, and he was going by the book.

"Look in the glove compartment for the registration, will you, DD?" Mitch asked while Officer Weinberg was busy illuminating the laptop in the backseat with his high-power beam.

Mitch handed his license to the cop.

Officer Weinberg reattached the flashlight to his belt as he grabbed it.

"Ouch," he yelled, holding up his finger. "I'm bleeding. That damn license cut me." He scowled at Mitch.

Remembering the teeth marks Cavvy had left on the license the first night I met Mitch, I leaned toward the open window and interjected: "Oh, sorry, Officer. My cat did that."

"So her cat drives your car? Probably uses the computer, too. All right sir. Step out of the car."

Mitch glanced at me as Weinberg pulled open the door and motioned him to exit.

"What am I supposed to have done, Officer?" Mitch asked, getting out.

"First of all, you made an illegal left turn back there on Broadway. Second, you got some explaining to do about a few things that don't seem right."

I continued searching frantically for the registration card in the glove compartment, praying Mitch wouldn't say anything about breaking and entering.

"I'm gonna have to ask you to do a field sobriety test. I think maybe you and the cat lady over there's been drinking. Drinking and driving is one big no-no."

"Officer, I didn't —"

"Have you taken this test before?"

"Well, no, but I —"

"Then walk this line, sir."

"Believe me officer, I —"

"Are you refusing to take this test, sir?"

"No. I'll do it," I heard Mitch reply.

"Okay, that's good," Officer Weinberg said, watching Mitch walk the line in perfect order. Meanwhile I located the registration card and jumped out of the car to join them.

The cop was saying, "Now about that laptop in the back seat. Is it yours?"

"Here's the vehicle registration, Officer." I shoved the card into his hands, hoping to divert him before Mitch could answer and say it wasn't his. But I was too late.

"It's really very simple," Mitch began.

"You see, we were . . ."

Mitch grabbed his leg where I'd kicked him and glared at me. I pressed my lips together, signaling him to keep quiet.

"I see this vehicle's registered to a company," Officer Weinberg said. "We don't see many company cars that are luxury Jaguars. What kind of company is it? Computer Solutions, Inc. Never heard of it."

"They do computer repairs," I offered. "They're one of the leaders in the industry."

"Is that right? And this laptop is company equipment?" he asked, shining the flashlight again in the back eat.

"That's correct, Officer."

"Mind if I search the rest of the car?"

Mitch pressed his key fob and popped open the trunk. "Be my guest."

His trunk was loaded with books, printouts, a thick briefcase, and a mass of assorted cables and computer spare parts. My head swam when I saw the title of one of the books: *Nine Aspects of Boolean Algebra.*

Officer Weinberg appeared equally dispirited. "Okay, close it. There's nothing here that doesn't tie in with what you've told me. And you passed the sobriety test. You're not drunk, but you're acting strange, and you did make an illegal left turn back there on Broadway."

"I'm not too familiar with this area, Officer. It's her fault," he pointed at me. "She was giving me directions."

"Wait a minute. I don't remember any No Left Turn sign," I defended myself.

"Well, uh." Officer Weinberg swallowed hard, and I sensed a gaping hole in his case.

"I've lived here all my life," I went on, "and I've never seen a sign there."

"Yeah, well, you've got a point. Those crazy right wing students at Northwestern University are always stealing it. If we put one up, they take it down. Must be some kind of collector's item. But that doesn't excuse what you did. It's real dangerous, and you were driving erratic. That's why I gave you the field sobriety test. You need to watch yourself and not act stupid again."

"Yes, Officer," Mitch said.

"I'm gonna let you off with a warning. But the next time somebody stops you, it could wind up costing you five or six hundred bucks. That is, if you haven't killed somebody by then. Here," he returned the license and registration to Mitch. "And get that license fixed up before it really hurts somebody. You two be careful now."

We went back to the Jaguar, keeping our eyes on Officer Weinberg, afraid he was going to change his mind and haul us away in cuffs. But Weinberg threw his hat into the front seat, jumped in, shut off the mars light, and pulled away before we could say, "that was a close call."

"I sense you have a knack for finding someone's weak spot," Mitch said, his nice brown eyes laughing, at least a little. "Why does that make me worry?" he asked as we buckled up and the Jaguar engine purred into action.

I smiled. "Getting a lecture from that cop definitely beat getting a ticket."

"By a very big margin," he agreed, smiling back.

# THIRTY

The powerful Jaguar eased into a parking spot across from my building. Mitch got out and opened the rear door to remove the computer from the backseat.

I got out and closed the car door. As I turned to step around the car onto the curb, Mitch grabbed me and lifted me off my feet. My blouse ripped loudly, and my purse dropped into the street. I fell on top of Mitch and saw a dark car speed past, running over my purse. It had missed me by millimeters.

"Jeez," Mitch said, as we regained our balance. "That was close. He came out of nowhere. Are you okay?"

I tried to stand on my own, but my legs were rubbery. "What the hell just happened?"

He picked up my purse. "Here, lean against me," he said, tightening his arm. "That damn fool was speeding, and he didn't have his lights on. You're still trembling," he said, holding me gently but firmly.

"You saved my life," I said, looking into his strong face and tingling at his touch. If it hadn't been such a dangerous moment, it might have been fun.

"This is the second time tonight the fates have smiled on me," I said, inspecting my ripped blouse.

"What else happened?" he asked.

"My car wouldn't start, so I took the elevated, and somebody hit me from behind as I was climbing the stairs to the platform. Luckily, another passenger came along."

"My God, DD, you are on somebody's list." He continued to support me with one arm while he reached into the car and pulled out the laptop with his other.

We walked slowly into my building.

"I was wondering if any of what's been happening to you might be related to our case and not Hemingway," he said.

"I don't think so. Things started happening before I agreed to help Barry. And now with David's attorney dead, too, I'm quite sure it's something to do with the Hemingway manuscripts. That's why I needed the information in this computer."

Normally I don't discuss my cases with anybody, but he really reminded me of

Scotty. As we walked up the stairs to my door, I told him everything — the Hemingway manuscripts, finding the bodies of both David and Beth, being a suspect, and how every room I walked into lately seemed to have been ransacked.

"Don't you think we should call the cops about the almost hit and run down there?" he suggested as I unlocked the door. I flipped on the lights and cleaned off a space on my messy coffee table for the laptop.

"No," I said as Mitch set it down gently.

"You're right. This place looks really awful," he said, looking at the shambles.

"I'm definitely not up for another encounter with the cops tonight," I told him. "Anyway, what good would it do? Did you get the license plate? Can you describe who was driving or what kind of car it was?"

"Not really," he said after some thought. "It was a dark two-door, but I'm not even sure of the make. It all happened so fast. I suppose it would be useless. What about letting your attorney know?"

"Oh, it is you," Glendy chirped as she entered the apartment carrying Cavalier.

"We heard voices and came to check things out," Lucille chimed in just behind her.

Meanwhile, Cavalier rushed over, sniffing

Mitch's pant leg, meowing for attention. Mitch picked him up and made a fuss over him, which of course the little brat ate up like catnip.

"You can't be too careful," said Glendy.

"Not after what happened here," Lucille added, seeing Mitch. "Oh, it's the nice man who brought us the roses. You're back. That's good."

"We'll go now," Glendy said, looking at my ripped blouse. She picked up Cavalier and headed for the door.

"Yes, you two are busy," Lucille winked at me as they waved and left.

I closed the door.

"So, they're kind of your guardian angels?" Mitch asked.

"First of all for the record, they . . . Oh, never mind. It's too complicated," I said, turning on the laptop. "But thanks for not telling them about what happened downstairs." I couldn't help noticing his strong jaw line as he looked into my eyes. I kept feeling guilty about Scotty, but was attracted to him nonetheless.

"You're an interesting woman, DD. Very interesting."

I watched him and tugged at my blouse to minimize the tear.

The computer came to life, but it was still

all snow.

"Since you're the expert, can you get it to boot up?"

"Probably needs a low-level format," Mitch said thoughtfully. Then I can reinstall the operating system," he advised, smiling.

"I know a little about computers," I admitted, thinking of Scotty. "A friend of mine once told me that a format would destroy all the data on the hard disk, and I want to read whatever's there."

"Oh, that's a lot more complicated." Our eyes met again, and a warm glow engulfed me.

"Want something to drink?" I asked, breaking the spell. "Coke, wine, a gin and tonic?"

"Make it a G & T. Lots of ice, light on the gin and lime."

"That's how I like mine," I said, and left to prepare the drinks, hunting for ingredients and unbroken glasses in the messy kitchen.

"Thanks," he said, taking a small glass from me.

"Sorry, but this was all I could find that wasn't broken."

He patted the sofa. "Here. Sit down next to me."

I did so. When our knees touched, I felt a

shock of electric warmth.

"I'm worried about you, DD. What happened down there wasn't a random act. Someone is after you. Someone wants to kill you. Doesn't that scare you?"

"It hasn't sunk in yet," I said dully, wanting to be truthful. "I suppose it's true and I suppose I ought to be panicky. Probably I'll get there later tonight."

"Exactly. Now what I want to talk about is this. I'm staying here with you tonight and . . ."

"You don't have to . . ."

"Never mind what I have to do or don't have to do. The decision's been made. I'm not leaving you alone. If you want to call in a private detective, that's fine. I'll leave. But unless you do, I'm not letting you stay alone here tonight. In fact, I'd prefer it if you came to my place."

"No. That's impossible."

"I thought you'd say that. So here I am and here I stay. *Capisce?* Discussion over. Now I need to know a few details about what happened to this computer," he said as he bent over the computer, his remarkably long, tan fingers blurring over the keyboard. I couldn't follow what he was doing, so I spent the time admiring his deft hands and wrists and trying to suppress thoughts I was having about him being naked in my bed. What was wrong with me?

"Do you know any details about what happened to this machine?"

I snapped out of my dream world. "I don't know. I found it like this in David's office. Which, by the way, was also trashed."

"Mmm . . ." he murmured, totally focused on the problem. "This is one sick puppy. This isn't going to be easy."

The next half-hour dragged like the Ice Age while I watched him work in silence. His concentration was complete, and he didn't pause to explain his manipulations.

"The hard disk is still configured," he said finally. "All the sectors and tracks that hold information are still there and functional, but all the files providing access to information have been deleted. Windows — your operating system — has been erased from the machine, and it can't get to them."

"So, where do we go from here?" I asked as our shoulders touched. I was glad he was a software guru, and I hoped to hide my own ignorance. A vision of a talking Barbie doll uttering "Math Is Hard" flashed through the lowest level of my consciousness.

"Well, I can reinstall Windows first of all.

Then we'll take a look at what damage might have been done to the file structure itself. The Windows files may still be there but not be functional. I need my utility kit," he explained with a warm, conspiratorial smile as he got up and went to the door. "Be right back. Luckily I've got all kinds of stuff in the car."

He returned with a bag and drew out some software packets. His face contorted with concentration as he placed a CD into the port and started punching keys.

"Can you really figure out what's wrong here?" I asked, impressed.

"Means a lot to you, huh? I'll play doctor." He smiled and lightly touched my hand. "You know, I feel as if tonight I've met the good twin. You rob, you lie, but it's evident you're doing it all for a good cause. And saving yourself on the elevated train was unbelievable. You're quite a fascinating woman, Miss DD McGil."

"I am?" I asked as he softly traced an indefinable pattern up my left arm. He moved a bit closer as he turned back to the computer. Maybe the old adage was true. In the midst of death, we need life, or something life-affirming like sex. Our knees touched as he began to work again in earnest.

"What happened here? This is bad. Real bad."

"What?" I couldn't understand what he was seeing on the screen. "Tell me, please."

"Computers are another life form, DD," he pronounced as he reached into his bag and pulled out a software package decorated with lightning bolts labeled ZAP.

"What we have here," Mitch explained, his brown eyes reflecting the excitement of the chase, "is no less than the neutron bomb of the computer world." He pointed at the ZAP package.

"Somebody Zapped this computer. This little program will access a file, overwrite it with zeros, and then save the file in its altered state with all the zeros. Then it deletes the file in the usual way, changing the name in the file allocation table so the machine won't display it anymore. There's no information in the files anymore, only zeros. It's like a file doomsday package, guaranteed to ensure that you can't restore the file anytime, anyplace, anywhere." He paused, his eyes now hard and clear.

"All you got left here is a lot of little zeros. Sorry." He blinked and took my hand again.

My heart sunk. "Damn," I muttered. "Whoever erased everything was pretty clever."

Mitch turned to look at me, his mouth serious, his eyes still in the hunt. "I've got an idea. Maybe he wasn't as smart as he thought he was. Let's see here . . ."

We were sitting even closer now so as to both be in on the chase. I inhaled his maleness and watched him work.

"We've got him, the bastard." He turned to face me. His eyes danced, and he smiled triumphantly. "Whoever did this was a real overachiever. See this?" He pointed to the screen with one hand and slipped the other around my waist.

"What?" I asked, putting a hand on his knee.

The monitor displayed a directory of file names. I wasn't sure I understood, and the Barbie vision flashed again. I felt completely confused. I felt comfortable, like I was sitting next to Scotty, but it was Mitch. I didn't need this turmoil. I needed Scotty back again. But since I couldn't have that, I was awfully glad Mitch was here.

He smiled a wicked smile. "Now we know why the machine shut down. Whoever did this planned to nuke the whole system at one fell swoop — like a massive air strike designed to eliminate every living thing in sight."

Mitch paused and lifted my other hand to

his lips, slowly kissing each finger.

"That tastes wonderful," he whispered in my ear. My stomach felt like the biblical fiery furnace. He kissed me behind my ear. "I did save your life, you know."

"That's true," I agreed softly.

"And helping hijack this stuff has already engaged us in mutual criminal activity."

"True again." I smiled.

"Good. That's settled then. Now, let's get back to this problem. Whoever fooled with this was in a big hurry. He stupidly tried to zap the entire hard disc. See, the ZAP program is designed to kill individual files or small blocks of files. That's why the machine shut down. The ZAP program killed all the Windows files first, which made everything stop before any individual files got erased. With me so far?" He smiled and caressed a lock of my hair, like Scotty used to. *God, it felt wonderful. What was I doing? What if Scotty came back? This was awful.*

"So does this mean we can get to the files after all?" I asked.

"In a word, maybe. Let's give it a try. I've reinstalled Windows, so we can get to the directories. Now we have to coax out all these deleted names from the file allocation table to restore the files."

Somewhat anti-climactically I found myself in the hunt. "Just how do you do that?"

"By substituting a letter for the dollar sign the ZAP program used to overwrite the file names. That'll make the files available to us again. You choose the letter," he offered, his eyes sparkling with the possibility of victory on the horizon.

"Make it a D, for David."

"D it is. For DD." Mitch grinned and punched it into the keyboard. "You see," he said, lightly stroking my arm, "you can think of a computer as a big file cabinet with a lot of drawers. All the addresses — that is, the sectors and tracks — where the information resides, are still in there, a little bit stored here and little bit stored there. Think of it as putting Humpty-Dumpty back together again. Ahhh, here we go."

He returned both hands to the keyboard as together we hunted through several directories, none revealing anything of special interest. David had kept extensive records on his students and on his course work, but we found nothing on the harassment case or his problems fighting for the chairmanship of the department.

Finally we entered a directory labeled "BL&NM." Flashing colors and lights took us into a word processing program that popped onto the screen, prompting us for a password. I groaned my disappointment.

Mitch asked, "Can you guess what David's password might be?"

"No idea. What do people usually use?"

"There is no usual. Everybody picks something they won't forget, like their mother's name. Look, don't worry." Mitch flashed a devious smile. "We should be able to get around this pretty easy. All these programs leave a hole a mile wide, a trap door, to cover their asses if somebody forgets a password. It happens all the time." He punched a few keys, waited, then punched a few more.

I had an idea. "Mitch, BL&NM. I think that might refer to Broad Lawns and Narrow Minds. What Hemingway said about Oak Park. Does that help?"

"Not really. That's just the directory. Wait a minute. Here. Got it," he said as the program released its files to us. We leaned forward in synch, scrutinizing the screen together. Our shoulders touched and he moved closer, pressing his leg against mine.

He said, "You're very beautiful. But of course you know that."

"You're not so bad yourself." I grinned.

"Pay dirt, DD," he pointed to the screen. We pulled up a file in which David described the battered valise he'd received in the package. He outlined his failed attempts to trace the package, then detailed his theories about the whereabouts of the manuscripts for the past eighty-nine years. He described the raggedy luggage tag still attached by a slim thread, but noted it was unreadable. In the file were his speculations that since Hadley and Ernest had only recently been married, their return address must have been the Michigan Hemingway residence. Like most young men who returned from the war, Ernest had found it difficult to fit back into normal life, especially in straitlaced, Puritan Oak Park, the Oak Park of Broad Lawns and Narrow Minds. The war had made Ernest a man; yet upon his return, his mother continued to treat him like a boy. His Michigan friends were more tolerant, and undoubtedly that's why he spent his time up in Michigan and got married there instead of in Oak Park before leaving for Europe. By what route, David wondered, had the greatest find of twentieth century American literature taken to travel from Paris to Michigan to him?

There were also records of the research pilgrimages he and Martin Sweeney had made to Michigan. David advanced his belief that they had been absolutely correct in their suspicion that the valise had been returned to the lost and found in Paris, then forwarded to the states. He speculated that the stationmaster at the Seney, Michigan, stop on the railway line had decided to hold on to the valise until he could return it personally to Ernest, especially since it was well known that Hemingway and his family were not on good terms. But Ernest didn't return for many years, not until 1949 for his father's funeral. And by then, he guessed, the old stationmaster must have died or forgotten the valise, long hidden in an attic or basement.

Another file described the papers in the valise. They consisted of eleven Hemingway short stories, the first part of a novel, and twenty poems, one of which, entitled, "Cats Are Good Luck," made me smile.

Of particular interest in this file were David's speculations on who had sent the valise to him and why. He strongly suspected a member of the Hemingway family of sending it, one he'd personally interviewed who didn't get along with other family members, didn't like the Oak Park Hemingway Trust, and wanted to create problems.

I pointed to the screen where David had worked out the anagram "Regacs Ma Fily" to be "Grace's Family."

I looked at Mitch. "If that's true, then

maybe whoever sent it killed David because he was going to auction off the material instead of donating it for research."

We continued searching. Another file of 186,485 bytes came up with a blank screen and a "File Incomplete" message.

The final file in the directory was the largest, and it had a different extension. Calling it up cleared the word processing program from the screen and brought up a hash of words, symbols and numbers. As Mitch scrolled through it, some familiar words caught my eye. They were the same Hemingway fragments that had been printed in the paper.

"You know, Mitch, I've seen something like this before. It looks like it's an analysis of the word patterns, punctuation, word occurrences, and sentence structure in the manuscripts. This is how you can spot a forgery from the real thing."

Our heads were almost touching. Mitch turned to me, breathing huskily, and pulled me close. His touch was exhilarating. I swallowed hard, and as his deft hands moved down my body, I felt lightheaded.

"Remember," he whispered in my ear, "I saved your life tonight."

"Cad," I rejoined, bending closer.

"And you've only got one bed."

"How do you know that?"

"I checked when you got the drinks."

We kissed, first long and tender, then hard and demanding. The computer forgotten, he ran his hands up my legs and under my clothes. I could feel the delicious liberation as various fasteners gave way to his probing fingers. Our breath came in short spurts as we undressed each other with wild abandon. We kissed again, and as his mouth dropped to my breast, I knew it was too late to be cautious. I was glad he was staying. I shivered with a whole body thrill and succumbed to the moment.

# THIRTY-ONE:
# DAY 5: THURSDAY

If two people love each other there can
be no happy end to it.
— ERNEST HEMINGWAY

I woke before dawn, surprised to find a
Prince Charming asleep in my bed. Then I
remembered last night. Muted light from
the street lamp outside my bedroom window
illuminated Mitch's naked body. I watched
as he slept, and the fierce flame he'd ignited
last night rekindled. He reminded me so
much of Scotty. I'm sure a psychiatrist
would call it transference. Whatever it was, I
guessed I was coming to the conclusion I'd
never see Scotty again. I snuggled closer.

The movement woke him. "You are real,"
he whispered. "Come here." Mitch cradled
me tightly, enclosing my universe in his
embrace.

"I was afraid I was dreaming," he said.

He brushed my cheek and lightly kissed

my hair, my ear, my neck. His hands traveled slowly down my back, my waist, my hips. His tight buttocks moved with mine, and one position led to another.

Next time I woke, it was much later. Now it was light, and I was alone in my bed with the delicious afterglow of our torrid lovemaking. I had slept the sleep of the dead, but now my mind was crystal clear. I felt refreshed, like Moses coming down from the mountain.

"Good morning, beautiful," Mitch said, arriving with a cup of tea, two slices of toast and a wicked smile.

He handed me the cup. "All I could find was some milk, so I put in a splash. Hope that's how you like it."

"The English way — exactly how I like it."

He climbed back into bed, still naked, a Greek God handing me a slice of toast.

"Butter and cinnamon," he pointed to the dark concoction on top. "And I had to hunt like hell in that mess out there to find it."

"You're a witch doctor." I sipped the tea and tasted the cinnamon toast, blinking because I was afraid I was going to wake up.

"I could get used to this," I warned him, munching the last of the toast. His wonderful brown eyes were watching my every move. This morning, it felt as if I'd known him forever but it was only a couple of days.

"So could I," he said, moving closer and kissing me softly. "Mmm, love women who taste like cinnamon," he murmured as the cup slipped from my fingers to the carpet with a soft thud.

"Must be some hang-up from your child-hood," I whispered as our arms reached out and our bodies entangled.

Mitch was every girl's dream lover — tender, ardent, demanding, creative, fear-less, humorous, considerate, and athletic. He was so much like Scotty that my heart ached even though I was giddily happy. Afterward, in the shower, we laughed to-gether at absolutely nothing, never taking our eyes off one another.

"I'm glad you stayed last night," I said softly.

"Tell me more about what happened to your friend David," he encouraged as he lathered my back.

I told him everything, as if I were writing a client report, leaving out no details. The more we talked, the clearer things became.

"Unfortunately, whoever did it is coming after you now," he said. "Turn around."

"Beth must have known something," I

said, turning in the cool water. "And that attorney, too. Now somebody thinks I know something or saw something and wants me out of the way like them."

"DD, you're not going to be safe until the cops get some tangible proof and make an arrest."

"I agree. But the trouble is, I don't know how to get tangible proof."

"Big Bill had a motive for killing David. And Debbie Majors certainly had a motive if those harassment charges are true," Mitch observed.

"But I have trouble seeing her as the one who hit me twice and disabled my car," I said, lathering his back.

"You of all people shouldn't be so sexist." Mitch turned and laughed, his hands straying.

"Whoa. Cut that out." I squirmed out of his grasp and attacked him with the soap.

"Okay, okay. I give up. Hey, maybe Big Bill and Debbie Majors were in it together."

"It would explain a lot if Big Bill got Debbie Majors to bring a false charge against David," I agreed thoughtfully.

When I told him about my impressions of Martin Sweeney and Hal Schultz of the Trust, I admitted I could find no motives for either one of them to have killed David.

"And if Martin Sweeney was the one who hit me on the elevated stairs, somebody would have reported that Ernest Hemingway tried to attack me."

Mitch smiled, stepped out of the shower, grabbed a towel and gently dried my back. "From what you've told me," he said, "I'd have to agree. It seems Martin Sweeney will lose a lot of money because of the canceled lecture tour, so what would be his motive? And Hal Schultz and the Trust would be much better off with David and the manuscripts than without them."

"Still, they both might have some reason we don't know yet." I grabbed another towel and dried Mitch's back.

"That feels great," he said. "If you ask me, they both sound like odd ducks. But you find a lot of people in these small fringe groups who are a bit off. To be honest, it's hard to envision academic types like them killing in cold blood."

"Now it's you who's being dogmatic," I challenged, flicking his butt with the towel, thinking back to my own experiences at the university and knowing with dreadful certainty that academics could kill with the best of them. "One thing to remember is that Martin and David were good friends. Maybe Martin knows more than he told me.

I'm not sure I believe everything he said. But then why would he claim the find was a fake?"

"Good point," Mitch said. "Unless he had his own plans."

"And then there's Bette Abramawitz," I mused, folding the towel. "She hated David and wanted those manuscripts for the college. I could see her shooting him and knocking me out with glee. But why were Beth Moyers and Mike Ekins killed? And just where does Matt fit into all of this?"

I sighed as Mitch turned around. "There's still too many unanswered questions. I'll have to watch my back."

"I'll watch your back," he leered. "And don't you forget it."

The phone rang, interrupting another interlude.

"Don't answer," Mitch said.

"It might be urgent," I said and picked it up. I didn't want Matt leaving a message on my answer machine asking when I was going to come live with him for Mitch to overhear.

It was Don, calling to find out if I'd done the job yet at Graue Mill. I'd ducked two of his calls already and was feeling a little guilty.

"It's scheduled for tonight," I assured him.

"Talk to a woman named Priscilla when you get there. She's the Mill's Vice-President and can answer any of your questions. And DD, be sure that report's on my desk early tomorrow morning," he warned before ringing off.

As we dressed, Mitch said he knew of Graue Mill. "It's an interesting place. But I wonder how much security you'll have to add to keep the vandals at bay."

"Don't worry, I'll come up with something," I said as I searched unsuccessfully through the litter for my black appointment book. "The industry's got new devices, like infrared photo equipment that might help finger the little shits. Look at this crap. I can't find the damn thing. All I'm doing is making the mess worse."

"Don't worry, your appointment book will turn up once you straighten out stuff. You know," he said, turning serious, "I came here last night to make you see reason about the job you took for Barry. I never figured on . . ."

"On what? Making me see reason?"

"I never figured on you. Come here," he said, holding me gently. "Look, don't take this wrong, but just what are you doing for Barry?"

I looked up and surveyed his handsome

314

features. "Believe me, I am doing something, even though you might not agree with it. But I do appreciate your help, Mitch. I mean that. I've been rude, and I'm sorry. And I am going to tell you everything, but not right now."

I took out two nickels, a dime, and a quarter from my purse, and asked, "Do you, by chance, have any change?"

"Change?"

"Yeah. Nickels, dimes, quarters kind of thing. They want exact change for the damn bus, and I've only got forty-five cents."

"What bus? Oh, yeah, I forgot about your car. How much do you need? Where are you going, anyway?"

"To Dieter's. My mechanic. He's on Clark Street, north of here."

"C'mon. I'll drop you there."

# THIRTY-TWO

Living so close to Wrigley Field is part blessing, part curse. Mere proximity to the ballpark cheers me up no end, even though I don't get to every game. My job won't ever make me rich, but I can take the afternoon off when I want, and I don't have any boss to tell me he saw me on TV. In my book, that makes up for a lot of the crap I have to go through.

Traffic, however, is impossible when there's a home game. And today the Pittsburgh Pirates were in town for a double header. I blinked and thought about Scotty. We'd been planning to go to a game and sit in the bleachers. Planning to cheer, and swear at the umps, and feed each other hot dogs, and exit the park arm in arm, singing the happy songs of too many ballpark beers. But we'd never gotten to, and we never would.

"Like to go to a game sometime?" Mitch asked.

I told him I'd like that very much as he hit the brakes to avoid the noisy fans, many of them shirtless teens, already pouring out of the Cubbie Lounge, spilling into traffic.

We were comfortable with each other, even though less than twenty-four hours earlier, we'd been at odds. I was content as we inched along in the bumper-to-bumper traffic, which didn't thin until we got a couple miles away from Wrigley Field.

Mitch turned on the radio, and as we pulled into Dieter's immaculate garage, the DJ announced that this morning's low temperature of 93 degrees in the shade had broken the record set in 1995.

"See you tonight," he said, as I got out of the car.

"No, I can't. I've already got a . . ."

"Date?" he asked. "I thought you said you didn't have a boyfriend."

"No. It's not that. I've got a meeting. About the Hemingway stuff." I didn't want to tell him about Matt.

"You don't have to explain."

"I know, but I wanted to."

"What time should I be at your place? Or do you want to come to mine tonight? I'm not leaving you alone until this Hemingway thing is settled, so you might as well agree with good grace. Otherwise I'll have to force

317

myself on you."

"If you come over, we'll have to pick up and clean up. I can't stand the mess."

"I'm game. How about nine o'clock? If you're late, I'll be waiting over at the twins' place."

As Mitch pulled away, I realized I'd be running the check on the micro-video in Barry's office. Oh hell, what was going to happen if Mitch was guilty of pirating the software? I was already in very deep. The motion-activated video had been running intermittently for two nights, and if Mitch was on it, I'd committed a colossal error in going to bed with him. If it turned out to be Herman on the video, Barry would hate me forever. And if nobody was on the video, I didn't have my portable lie detector anymore, so I'd have to start investigating all the banks, and it would get a lot more complicated. I didn't want to admit to Barry that the case was beyond my capabilities. Mitch would undoubtedly have me pilloried for marking time in the investigation and for considering him my number one suspect. And he'd be justified. One way or the other, I had the awful sense that our developing relationship was doomed.

Dieter was busy, as usual, but rushed over and grabbed my arm when I came into the shop. I was fond of Dieter, who was like a brother to me, letting me spend many hours watching him fix cars and drink German beers from his perpetually stocked refrigerator. We always had interesting conversations, and I'd grown to actually kind of like the smell of grease.

Today, he was too upset to offer me a beer.

"Dis battery cable vas cut, DD. Here, look. You see dose marks and how there is no fray. Dis vas no accident."

"I guessed as much," I replied, and told him I was having trouble with a case I was working on.

"You need to quit dat insurance work, DD. You got brains, and you got a body. What do you do it for? And by de vay, who vas dat good-looking guy dropping you off just now in da Jaguar? Sure, it's got good rear-wheel drive and a strong in-line six, but it's nicht a Mercedes. He should buy a nice 420 E dat's made by real craftsmen. Dat would really turn you on, heh?"

I thanked Dieter, paid my bill and explained I had to leave right away for an appointment.

One of his guys pulled the Miata out front for me, helped me put the top down, then held open the door as I slid in.

"Ouch," I said, burning my butt as I sat

down. "Ow," I yelled, touching the steering wheel. The interior was stifling. Heat had settled into every nook and cranny. Even the gear shift, usually as cold as Italian marble, felt like it might melt in my hand. We needed a good storm to break this heat wave, but none was forecast.

I drove to Barry's, thinking dreamily of last night and dreading finding out what the mini spy cam had captured.

# THIRTY-THREE

You can wipe out your opponents. But if you do it unjustly you become eligible for being wiped out yourself.

— ERNEST HEMINGWAY

Herman Marx was on the phone when I arrived. He waived me into Barry's office without even a how-are-you, like he was anxious to get me over with.

Barry was inspecting his phone, checking the high-power debugger device he'd installed to ensure he wasn't being tapped.

"Show time," I said, dumping my purse on the table.

"I expected you earlier," Barry scolded.

I ignored his ill humor and dragged a chair directly under the ceiling tile where I'd secreted the equipment.

"Barry," I questioned him as I climbed onto the chair and reached for the camera, "were any of those phone numbers I gave you not yours?"

"No. They could all be accounted for. No help there at all."

He put his phone back together and tried to assist me as I fumbled around trying to remove the ceiling tile.

"DD, you really shouldn't wear those high heels if you're gonna do this kind of work."

I kept maneuvering the ceiling tile until it finally shifted, then slid it gently out of the way.

If that thing doesn't have anything incriminating yet," Barry said as he held the chair steady, "I don't want to reinstall it again. It makes me nervous."

"I know," I sympathized as I stretched and tried to grab hold of the tiny device.

"Damn," I swore as my fingers scraped against a hard edge and the nail on my index finger ripped.

I stretched again, this time grabbing the thing. The office door opened and closed, but my head was in the ceiling so I couldn't see what was happening.

"What's going on?" Mitch Sinclair asked, appearing around my legs. "Trying to kill yourself, DD McGil?"

I looked down at him and smiled crookedly. I'd wanted to see him again. And soon. But not just now.

"Well, I personally didn't think last night was all that bad," he said softly.

I lowered the micro-cam and twisted around to look directly at Mitch. His devilish smile, so inviting last night, was equally inviting this morning.

"Hi," I greeted him with a brittle smile and looked to Barry for help. I sure didn't want Mitch around when we viewed this video.

"What's this?" Mitch stared up at the displaced ceiling tile, then at the sprinkler head. I was sure he saw the tiny camera I'd attached, and I could almost see the rapid addition taking place in his cerebral cortex.

"One of those spy cams? Barry, did you know she was doing this?" Mitch demanded.

"Well," Barry waffled, his lips pursed. He glared at me, then at Mitch. "Yes and no."

"I think it's a great idea," Mitch said. "I guess she does know what she's doing, after all."

He reached up and took the tiny camera from me. "Here. Let me help." He steadied me with his other hand as I stepped down from the chair.

"Who are you after? Not Herman?"

I gulped hard, and stayed silent.

Barry looked at me and took pity. He grabbed the camera from Mitch. "Here, let me take that."

I'd regained my balance and was wondering how to get rid of Mitch before we viewed the video.

Barry released the thumbnail drive from the camera and inserted it into one of his computers. "We can feed it right into this monitor."

As Barry pulled up the video, Mitch brushed the dirt off the chair I'd stood on and returned it to the conference table. Then, with a flourish, he offered me a seat.

His brown eyes looked me over as he held the chair. I sat down, and he put his hands on my shoulders and bent down, speaking softly in my ear. "Hi, beautiful. I had an extraordinary time last night. How about you?"

After last night, deep down I was positive that Mitch couldn't be involved. Nonetheless, I didn't want him finding out that he had been targeted as my prime suspect. I was going to have to ask him to leave. "Look, what we're doing here . . ."

"Is that in the WMV format for digital?" Mitch asked.

"Yep. Here we go," Barry answered as the video began to play on the monitor, capturing our full attention. The three of us huddled around the monitor, intently watching. The color and clarity were so good I was able to count the number of paper clips in the holder on Barry's desk.

The first mug on the video was instantly recognizable. It was me, snapped the night the camera was installed. The next dozen frames were of Barry and me together, then a few of Barry alone.

"It's motion sensitive. Good thinking," Mitch observed, absorbed in the proceedings.

Barry smiled, seeing himself on the screen. "Look. There I am yesterday morning."

During business hours, Barry never stopped working. People went in and out. I paid particular attention to the fact that neither Mitch nor Herman was ever alone in Barry's office. My innards gave a big sigh of relief. So far, so good.

"This isn't getting us anywhere, DD," Barry lamented. "It's just a waste of time and money. I'm more convinced than ever that the software was passed through one of the banks."

"Security in the banks is too tough, Barry," I explained. "They've had years and lots of resources to develop foolproof security. That's why I'm betting that whatever happened, happened here. At the source."

Barry was downcast. "I don't buy it, DD."

"Let's give her a chance," Mitch said, turning the tables and taking my side. "I think running this video was a good idea."

"What's with the sudden *entente cordiale* between you two? Not that I'm not glad, but it's kind of sudden, isn't it? Where are those tidal waves of animosity I was getting used to?"

Mitch sidestepped the issue and pointed to the monitor. "Look there." A man and a woman had appeared on the screen. "Who the hell are they?"

Barry stared at the screen. "That's just the cleaning crew."

"I thought you told me nobody else was allowed in your office, Barry," I said. "That's not strictly true, is it?"

"Well, I never thought about it. Besides, it's the cleaning people. Hell, they're like the mailman. They don't even speak English, and you're trying to tell me they have the technical skill to pirate sophisticated software? C'mon."

"Barry, we don't have to look any further. Right there. That's your leak," I pronounced *ex cathedra*. "I'm positive."

I knew it sounded crazy, but I also knew what I was talking about.

"It's all circumstantial, DD," Barry said, shaking his head.

I took a deep breath. "You can cancel your cleaning contract right now and release your updated software version later today. You're in the clear."

"But they didn't do anything out of the ordinary," Barry countered. "How can you make that leap? First you suspect Mitch, and now you suspect the cleaning crew."

"What?" Mitch turned to me. "You suspected me?"

"Jeez, DD, maybe Mitch was right from the start. Maybe it's time I call Gilcrest and Stratton in on this."

"DD," Mitch sputtered, hands on hips, waiting for my answer.

Instead, I pointed to the video. One member of the crew was noodling around the computer way too long. As he bent over it, I could see he'd turned it on and was pulling files up onto the screen. "Look at this, Barry."

"The son of a bee," Barry said, replaying the tape again.

I grabbed Barry's phone and pressed the intercom button. "Herman," I said, "come in here right now, will you?"

Herman came in and immediately noticed the video.

"Herman, what's the phone number for the building's management?"

He rattled the phone number off the top of his head like I knew he would. I'd only known him a short time, but it was evident he liked to show off.

I picked up Barry's phone, punched in the number and waited. The three of them were silent, staring at me.

A bored male voice answered, "Building Maintenance. Rickman speaking."

"Hello, Mr. Rickman. This is Mary Spence calling, secretary to Mr. Post. You know, we're moving into that vacant space in your building next week."

"DD, don't . . ." Barry said. I shushed him and continued.

"Yes, that's it, Suite 1702. Right. Well, what I called about was that Mr. Post is extremely particular about office cleaning. He's terribly fussy — won't have a stray paper clip on the carpet, you understand. Everything must be in its place. What cleaning company do you have for the building?

"Yes, I see. You've had them for years and no complaints at all. They're all Bosnian immigrants? Well, I don't know. Do they speak any English? What? Oh, really? That's very true. Yes indeed. Well, thank you so much, Mr. Rickman. We'll see you next week." I hung up.

"What the heck was that all about?" Barry

asked. "Who's this Mary Spence and Mr. Post you were talking about?"

"Never mind. Sometimes I have to make things up. You're paying me to investigate, so I'm investigating."

"DD, do you speak Bosnian?" Mitch inquired.

"I don't have to speak it."

"Well how in hell do you expect to find out anything from these people when you don't speak their language?" Barry challenged. "I understand there's something like three or four national languages all mixed up with the Serbo-Croatian dialect. It's one of the things they fight about."

"I know. The economy in the Balkans has crashed. All that fighting is the reason that a lot of really bright, well-educated people have fled from Bosnia to the U.S. and have had to take work as janitors," I explained while dialing the number Mr. Rickman had given me.

"Cleaning jobs are sometimes the only ones they can get because of the language barrier. I know it's true in my building."

"DD, you've got a real suspicious mind," Mitch observed. "But Barry, think about it. It could be true. They got no business turning on one of our machines. If these guys are well educated and know what they're doing, they could be the ones sending the software out over the Internet. She makes a good inference that it is probably this computer."

I nodded agreement. "Exactly. That's why nothing registered on your phone bill, Barry. They sent whatever they sent over the Internet, then got rid of any evidence of the communication."

A female voice answered cheerily on the third ring. "Kiss Cleaning, where you kiss your dirt good-bye. May I help you?"

"I sure hope so. My boss wants to have daily office cleaning, and your company's been highly recommended by Mr. Rickman."

"Just one moment, please. I'll connect you with Lew, our general manager."

After a moment, a smooth voice came on the line. "Yallo. What can I do for you?"

"Well, I'm not exactly sure."

"Don't worry about a thing. We can do everything. Just tell me what you need."

"I have a big problem. It's my boss. He's really fussy, so whatever company I hire has to have top-notch people. He's fired the last service, and now my job is on the line. Mr. Rickman over at the Kemmer Building says that your best crew works for him, and he hasn't had any problems."

"Yep. That's our top crew, all right."

"But aren't they all Bosnian?"

"Yes, but the supervisor also speaks fluent English."

"Oh, that's what my boss would want, so they could take directions. Could we have the same crew if we signed a contract with you?"

"Absolutely," Lew said enthusiastically. "The leader of that crew is Chris, our top man. Believe it or not, he was a university professor back in Sarajevo. He's a gem. He's gotten together a whole crew of Croats. They all jabber away at each other, but they work like the devil's after them. And Chris is very talented. Plays the piano like a concertmaster. You'll be satisfied, I guarantee it."

"It certainly sounds like it. You've convinced me. I'll talk to my boss and call you for an appointment to come out next week and give us a quote."

"Anytime," Lew said. "Just give me your name and your company . . ."

I hung up and repeated what Lew had said.

"That doesn't mean anything, DD," Barry said. "He could have been a professor of literature or history."

"Barry, you asked me to solve your problem. You said I was the only one who could. And it looks like I've done it. This guy or one of his crew is into computers, and he's illegal and can't get a good job. Believe me, it happens all the time."

"I think we should consider it, Barry. Maybe she's got something," Mitch interjected.

"I don't know, DD. I think you're jumping the gun," Barry said stubbornly.

"I didn't want to do this, but . . ." I pulled out the watchdog tracker I'd installed between Barry's keyboard and the computer.

"You put that tracker on my keyboard?" Barry sputtered.

"You wanted proof. This is it. And as for Gilcrest and Stratton, now's the time to put them on it," I added. "They're the plodders who can dot the i's an cross the t's. Have them get this guy's last name, trace him, and put a tail on him. See what they come up with. I'm betting this is where your problem came from and Occam's razor usually applies, that the simplest explanation tends to be the best one."

"I think we should do it, Barry," Mitch said.

"Meantime, fire this cleaning company right now. Have them return your keys before close of business today. Then get your locks changed and put your new software out on the market. In that order." I smiled what I hoped was a Sphinx smile. "Problem solved."

As they came to a decision, I hoped my show of confidence would carry the day and was not misplaced. The keyboard tracker would convince Barry and Herman, and it seemed that Mitch was already on my side.

Barry finally yielded. "Okay, okay," he said. "I know when I'm outnumbered. We'll do what you say, DD, except that we won't release the revised software for a couple of days until we get something back from Gilcrest and Stratton."

I knew I'd won, but I wasn't sure whether I felt satisfied or miffed at this compromise.

# THIRTY-FOUR

"You know," Mitch said, "I'm getting adjusted to the fact that you may have figured out how that piracy was happening. You're a girl of many surprises."

"I surprise myself a lot, too," I laughed. We kissed good-bye shamelessly in front of Barry's building and reluctantly parted. "See you about nine tonight," he said as he returned to Barry's while I headed for the Beecham Building, careful to see that I wasn't being followed.

When I got off the elevator on my floor, Douglas, the mailman, was slipping today's bills into the slot in my door.

"Howdy," he greeted me with his usual dour smile.

"Hi, Douglas," I smiled cheerily, never giving up hope that one day he'd chuck his bureaucratic absolutism in favor of a toothy smile and a dirty joke.

"Better check your delivery right away."

"What's up?" Somehow, although I was certain he never actually steamed open my mail and read it, he always knew what was going on. "Good news?"

"You got an official notice from the Internal Revenue Service, Miss McGil. I don't see how that can be good news."

Suddenly I didn't feel very well. "Where the IRS is concerned, you're probably right."

"You better take care of it immediately."

"Thanks, Douglas," I closed my door, assured he wasn't going to slip his chains today.

I riffled through the mail. The IRS envelope stood out from the pack and produced an involuntary chill down my spine. Dumping the rest of the mail along with my purse onto my desk, I ripped open the envelope. The letter, dated yesterday, stated that after repeated attempts to contact me and due to repeated appointments I'd missed, they were forced to deem me in default on my taxes and would be forwarding my case to collections. Huge penalties and interest on what I supposedly owed brought the whole bill to a total that was more than I made in a year. Great. Just what I needed.

Enraged, I picked up the phone, ready for another adventure in agony, and dialed the

IRS office. When I got through to Miss Wang, I was sputtering. She surprised me by recognizing my voice. "Oh, Miss McGil," she said, almost friendly. "Yes. He expected your call yesterday." She even got my name right. I was in shock. "Hold on, please," she said.

I waited and I waited. The IRS had no muzak. Instead, I heard a recording on a wheel. "All of our agents are busy. Your concerns are important to us, so please do not hang up until your call can be answered."

I knew God wasn't going to swoop down and fix the IRS just to clear up my little troubles. I realized that the agency had to deal with a lot of problem cases, cases where people did illegal, immoral, and unconscionable things. But why did Mr. Poussant have to be the type of agent who went after the littlest picky things? I might as well have wondered why pigs don't fly.

After what seemed longer than eternity, Miss Wang came back on the line.

"Mr. Poussant will see you tomorrow at ten a.m. sharp. This will be your last appointment. In the event you are not here in person with the documents he requested, your case will be forwarded to collections. Is that understood, Miss McGil?"

I hung up, wondering where she learned to talk like that and trying to convince myself that nothing could go wrong to make me miss this meeting. I'd be there with bells on, even if I had to be carried from a hospital bed.

## THIRTY-FIVE

I handled the remaining messages and was halfway out the door when the phone rang. It was Aunt Elizabeth calling from Scotland.

"DD, why did you not call me back? 'Tis verra important. I had a vision."

"I know, Auntie. It was good of you to call. Mother already told me about it."

" 'Twas not a good one, Daphne."

I realized it must have been bad because Auntie Dragon only calls me Daphne when she's peeved.

" 'Twas to do with stairs and you falling and heavy darkness."

"Don't worry Auntie. It's already happened. Somebody hit me from behind and tried to make me fall down a flight of stairs at the elevated. But I didn't fall. In fact, I'm fine."

"No DD. Harken what I say. 'Tis not yet happened. 'Tis something else. Something worse."

"Auntie, honestly I'm sure it's what already happened. It fit your vision perfectly. And as you see, I'm being very careful."

"DD, attend to me. 'Tis a thing aboot to happen, not a thing already taken place. Mark you, heed my warning. Be sharp on your guard. Would that I were there. A storm is coming for you."

"I'll be fine, Auntie. Really. Love you, darling. And don't worry. How's George doing?" We talked a bit about what was going on with her new husband, George Murray, who was, to my mind, possibly the only person on the face of this earth who could stand up to Auntie Dragon successfully. Before we hung up, she said again, "Mind, watch your back, and be keen on your guard."

I felt somewhat relieved. The last of my Auntie's visions had damn near gotten me killed when I'd been thrown in a closet in the old Consolidated Bank building during demolition. This was obviously much milder and anyway, I'd already survived it.

For a second time, just as I hit the door, the phone rang.

"Hi, DD. Were you able to get to Graue Mill yet?"

"I was just going out the door, Don. You're holding me up, if you must know the truth."

"Sorry. Anne's on my back."

"Tell her not to worry. I agreed to do it, and I'll do it. You'll have everything tonight. Bye."

I hung up and left. I was going to take care of it, but first I had to have something to eat.

There's a small kiosk in the Beecham's lobby, and as I was passing by, Andy, the nice old guy who runs the concession, called me over.

"I saved this specially for you." He held out a giant Hershey bar with almonds. Andy knew my passion for chocolate and had somehow gotten the idea that I liked Hershey's with almonds the best. I don't, but it was too late to tell him.

"Throw in a tuna on white and a can of lemonade, too," I said, pulling some money from my wallet.

"Here you go," he said, putting it all into a brown paper bag along with a napkin. "Thanks. You're a pal." I dumped the money into his open palm with a smile. What I really felt like was a cold beer, but that would have to wait.

Driving west down the Eisenhower Expressway, I hit a bump as I sipped the lemonade and spilled some on my outfit.

With all the trouble I was having in traffic, drinking could be a new Olympic event.

Out of the city now, nature replaced concrete, glass, and bricks. Winter this year had been long and rushed rudely into summer, aborting Chicago's spring. What tulips and daffodils there were had come late, then died mid-bloom from the heat. This was one of the hottest months on record.

The weather reporter on the car radio announced that a storm was due sometime tonight or tomorrow to break the heat wave. After I finished half the tuna sandwich, I reached for the Hershey's bar, but it was a melted mess. That cooling storm couldn't come soon enough for me.

The rest of the drive was spent formulating the report I'd make tonight to Matt. Thus far, my news about the manuscripts wasn't good. I wondered if the cops had found the gun that killed David yet. *Not that I could call and ask them.*

The sun sat low in the sky as I approached the mill. Everything was parked up. *Why couldn't my little Miata always find a convenient space like Mitch's Jaguar, I wondered.* I had to drive all the way over into the unpaved parking lot across the road from Graue Mill. The gravel crackled as I braked to a halt. This lot, too, was crowded as visitors strolled the pretty grounds.

I took the York Road underpass path. It ran parallel to the huge turning mill wheel. The water turning the wheel came from Salt Creek. I stopped to watch the wheel's hypnotic rhythm that seemed to momentarily suspend time. It mirrored my own thoughts about David's murder, going round and round, never stopping, never resting. Despite the intense heat of the summer afternoon, my flesh went clammy. It wasn't only due to the dank creek water running under the little bridge I was crossing. Aunt Elizabeth's warning flashed through my mind again.

As I climbed the worn stone steps up to ground level, the picturesque old mill came into view. It was a beautiful site with the last bits of sun turning the clouds into gray. Off the beaten path, far enough away from traffic and development to remain pristine, Graue Mill was a treasure of yesteryear. It deserved a first-class security system. Dominated by the big, turning mill wheel, the building was three stories, sturdy brick, and clearly made for work. A lower-level basement with tiny windows housed the huge gears to turn the wheels. Somewhere in that basement historians say slaves were hidden on their way farther north, a dank, dreary stop on the Underground Railway to freedom.

Phil and Don both like to give me jobs where I evaluate and recommend security because, they say, I'm into serious risk management for clients. They're always telling me I've gone overboard when I say that if Stonehenge were located in the United States, it would be stolen overnight. Maybe they're right and I'm wrong. But like the Boy Scouts, I believe in being prepared.

I pulled out a pen and notepad and took notes on the exterior perimeter. Most people don't realize that exterior security is as important, if not more important, than interior systems. Properly securing the outside will discourage your average vandal, burglar, or degenerate, and make him, her, or it look elsewhere for easier pickings. I thought about the fact that my own apartment had been broken into and decided to contact the building owner and suggest a few ways to improve exterior security there too.

The mill's old-fashioned paned windows were all fitted with trip tape, the kind that sets off an alarm if it's broken. But there didn't seem to be any security cameras. That was a mistake. Floodlights were positioned on each of the four sides of the building, angled to illuminate the maximum amount of window and brick during the night. These lights helped to provide some deterrence, but I'd probably recommend one of the new microwave proximity sensors for the exterior in addition to what they already had.

Inside the mill on the first floor, a woman dressed in an authentic 1880s costume was concluding a demonstration on grinding corn. Her name-tag identified her as Priscilla, the one Don said I should see. I approached and introduced myself.

"I'm really busy right now with a tour," she said. "I expected you earlier. You'll have to carry on without me." With that, she dismissed me and shepherded her group into the basement area, cautioning them to be careful.

I started my interior evaluation up on the top floor and would work downward. Much of the mill's extensive collection of antiques and late-nineteenth-century memorabilia was housed up here on the third floor. Authentic displays of a blacksmith shop and an apothecary shop made you feel like a visitor to another time. A small window provided a panoramic view of Salt Creek and the outlying area.

As I made some sketches on the locations I'd recommend for installation of motion activated micro-video cameras for both daytime and night security, I heard the first rumbles of thunder off in the distance. *Come on rain, I thought.*

A thorough check of the second floor and the main floor confirmed there were no security cameras there, either, so I identified strategic locations for installing them.

All access and egress was through the main door. It was the only door, and it was wired with an alarm system, but not a state-of-the-art one. I was definitely going to recommend a connected series of infra-red sensors for the entire interior. Also, I made a note to have someone come out to check the Mill's fire-protection measures. I didn't see any safeguards worth mentioning.

By now, Priscilla's big tour was over. There were only a few stragglers left around the spinning wheel. Priscilla was showing them how frontier housewives had done carding. It was a Chinese puzzle to me, and I felt a rush of thankfulness for those pioneer women and their ingenuity.

I interrupted to inform her I was leaving and would file the security report with Don tonight.

Not far from the door, I spied the stairs going down to the lower level, well hidden by a display of handmade wreaths for sale.

*I'd forgotten the basement.*

I skirted the display and descended the old wooden stairs. The basement was approximately forty feet long by fifty feet wide and very dimly lit. Hanging above the stair risers was a collection of ice saws used in frontier winters to cut into the thick ice of Salt Creek. They were huge and ominous looking and reminded me of the instruments of some mutant dentist. Frankly, they gave me the chills.

Along one wall was a mass of big gears and pulleys reminiscent of the intricate inner mechanism of a huge clock. I watched them turn in various directions. Some were ten feet across, going very slowly. Others were only a foot across, speeding faster and faster to pull the larger ones along. Closer examination showed the gears to be all wood, with wicked looking pegs, sharpened by time. These visible gears meshed into dark recesses of still other gears. The ninth circle of hell couldn't be more frightening, and they didn't bear looking at.

I took a few notes. The six windows down here were very small and very high, not large enough for a body to fit through. I was certain that no one could break into the Mill at this sub-level. If blocked off from the first floor, I could easily fathom hidden slaves spending part of a night in their dangerous, awful journey in the underground railway.

I put away my notes. It was time to go. A loud crash of thunder confirmed my decision. The storm must have finally broken. Suddenly I realized the Miata was sitting in the parking lot with her top down. *In the rain. Shit!*

I ran up the old stairs two at a time. As a flash of lightning and another loud clap of thunder shook the old mill, I ran right into Martin Sweeney.

# THIRTY-SIX

There is no hunting like
the hunting of man.
— ERNEST HEMINGWAY

Martin's lips curled as he shoved me down the stairs. A clap of thunder buried my scream. *Was this Auntie's storm warning?*

He jumped down the rest of the stairs and grabbed me, covering my mouth and nose with one big hand. I poked him with an elbow and tried to grab my cell phone from my purse. He knocked the purse from my grip then held down my arms with his other hand. He was big, and strong. I kicked and fought to regain my balance. Sensei would kill me if he knew.

Suddenly the lights went out, and we were in complete darkness.

"Anyone still down there?" Priscilla the Pioneer called from the top of the stairs.

I tried to scream. Martin tightened his

grip and pushed me into a small recess under the stairs. I struggled. His hold got tighter. My vision started to go black. I was afraid I was going to pass out.

"We're closing now," Priscilla called. I could hear her descend the stairs. One, two, three steps down. Everything was so completely black that my eyes hurt searching for some light.

"Is anyone down here?" Bless her little pioneer heart, she had a flashlight and arced the beam back and forth across the gears and along the floor, missing us by inches. I struggled and squirmed, trying to bite and kick but made no headway against Martin's strength.

*Please Priscilla, don't give up.* I had no doubt that if she spotted us, together we could handle Martin.

I got one leg free and tried again to kick, but Martin wrapped a leg around my lower torso and my legs started to cramp.

Priscilla hesitated an instant, then retreated up the stairs. One, two, three steps up. She might as well have been in the next galaxy. When I heard the clang of the big lock on the main door, I knew she'd gone. My heart sank. I stopped struggling. Martin and I were alone in the dank basement. No one was going to hear me, let alone help me.

My body sagged with terror. Martin must have felt it. He unwound his leg and relaxed his hold enough for me to catch a little air up my nose. I almost choked as I tried to swallow.

I tried to regain a foothold. The rhythmic pulse of the turning gears punctuated by lightning flashes made me dizzy. I was suddenly aware of inconsequential things like Martin's offensively sweet aftershave and his gray Nike running shoes. Still no socks, but gone were the loafers.

So it was Martin who'd been after me, and Martin who'd undoubtedly killed David and Beth and Mike Ekins, David's attorney. I knew he was going to kill me, too.

A strong desire for revenge produced a surge of energy. I ground my heel into his Nike and somehow broke his hold. I bolted for the stairs.

Martin was unexpectedly quick for such a big man, and he blocked my way.

"You've caused me no end of trouble, sister," he growled through his beard, looming up over me.

There was no way out of here except up those damn stairs. My heart pounded frantically as I tried to remember the layout down here. The windows were too high and too small, even if I managed to get up there. I was trapped and suddenly knew what the phrase *panic attack* meant. I was having one, and it took all my Scots courage not to whimper.

"I tried to warn you off, but you wouldn't listen," he said in a strange voice I hardly recognized. "You had to keep looking into things, had to take David's computer."

I wondered if finally the real Martin Sweeney had emerged. His nasty, staccato voice made goose bumps rise all over my body.

"I hate nosy broads the worst of all," Martin said, standing over me like the angel of death.

He lunged at me. I stumbled, trying to back away in the pitch black. I could hear him, close to me, breathing. I moved away from the stairs, feeling my way along the wall. In the dark quiet, the harsh sound of the meshing gears was louder than ever.

I was sweating, probably from fear as much as the heat and humidity down here. Did Mother Nature intend sweat to encourage or discourage the stalker? I tried not to think of myself as prey, *a la* Deepak Chopra, but it wasn't working.

"You've been a royal pain from day one when I hit you in David's apartment," Martin said nastily from somewhere in the dark. Without the lightning flashes, it was like Mark Twain's cave, as dark as the grave. "I was almost finished searching his place for anything that might lead the police to me when you arrived. I thought I killed you that day. But you've got nine lives, like some damn cat. Even managed to save yourself on the elevated stairs. Then your boyfriend played Sir Lancelot last night. Well, tonight, your lucky streak is at an end."

Martin's eyes glinted like a wolf 's in the sharp glare of a lightning flash. My eyes were adjusting to the strobic effect, and I thought I spotted a tire iron in his right hand.

"You've been following me," I said.

"Didn't have to. Your little black appointment book had it all in there, neat as a pin."

*My appointment book. I thought it was buried under the mess. I'd never suspected it had been stolen.*

"Now let's get this over with," he said, and in the next flash I saw him lunge at me, his right arm raised.

I spun sideways, narrowly evading the blow. "Martin, please don't kill me."

"I'm not going to kill you," he said, laughing like he was on stage performing. "Ernest Hemingway would never kill anyone. But you could have a nasty accident. You could lose your balance on these old steps and fall down." He rushed me again, but I maneuvered past him. He was close now, too close, and he kept pushing me back toward the stairs.

"Ain't it a shame. They'll find you tomorrow and blame it on the storm and the lights going out."

I thought of Auntie's vision as he pushed me onto the steps. Oh God, she was right again.

"I like to think of what will happen to you more as an act of God. Heavenly risk management to protect Hemingway, you might say."

In the next lightning flash, he was grinning. There was absolutely no way I was going back up those stairs of my own free will. He was going to have to carry me up and then push me down if that's what he wanted. At least I'd give him some grief for all my suffering. I had no plan — only a faint hope that maybe I could stall him and gain a little ground. Trouble was, I didn't know what ground there was to gain until, in another flash of lightning, I saw the horrid ice saws on the wall under the stairs.

"You're getting to be awfully good at murder, aren't you, Martin? Is that part of

Hemingway's macho image or just your own sick self coming out?"

"Shut up," he shouted.

"You're not going to get away with this, Martin."

His laugh reverberated in the heavy air. "I've already gotten away with everything, haven't I? I got away with killing David. I'm not even a suspect. I've got the manuscripts, and —"

"*You've* got them?"

"Surprised at how clever I am? You shouldn't be. They're well hidden. And after I prove to everyone that David faked those fragments, I'll be able to 'find' them myself a few years from now. They'll be worth even more then. David got what was coming to him. Why should they fall into his lap like that? We were partners. We did all the research in Michigan together. But he cut me out, the bastard. I warned him."

I needed to keep him talking to buy a little time to maneuver. I opened my mouth to say something, but blessedly, he continued.

"I didn't want to kill him," he said. "But he was stubborn and selfish. He refused to share with me, the son of a bitch. It was all so easy for him. Always got what he wanted — fame, women, everything."

"Why did you kill Beth?" I asked.

"Had to. I found out David told her he gave me the manuscripts to look over. You have to go, too. That was clear from the start because sooner or later you might remember something from that day in David's apartment."

"Why did you kill David's lawyer?"

"I couldn't let him live because I wasn't sure exactly how much David told him. He was a threat. He had to go, for Hemingway's sake."

A deafening crash of thunder muffled Martin's words as he kept ranting. Another crescendo added fuel to his jealous anger and resentment, and I held out hope he'd grow careless and give me an opening.

"Those manuscripts are worth a king's ransom, and now they're all mine. I won't ever again have to dress up and be what David used to call the side-show dummy. Me, a dummy. He never understood that I was the real star of our show, not him. The audiences loved me. I was Hemingway. He didn't understand that. He shouldn't have tried to cut me out."

Martin kept shouting, repeating himself. Meanwhile, I circled round him, looking for a way to make a break for it.

"It was me they came to see, not him.

Those manuscripts should have come to me."

A searing white light flooded the basement, accompanied by a deafening explosion and a crack of thunder. Hailstones began hitting the small windows. I was certain lightning had struck the Mill itself or somewhere close to it.

"Hemingway wouldn't have killed his best friend," I screamed.

I heard him move, and the next flash of lightning illuminated him poised over me with the tire iron. I tried to duck but wasn't fast enough. It hit me and bounced hard off my left shoulder. I collapsed with pain. For an instant, everything went black.

I struggled to stand but I couldn't. In another flash, I saw Martin grab the tire iron from the floor where it had landed after slamming into my shoulder. *He was coming at me again, only this time I couldn't move.*

I went limp, anticipating what was in store. Suddenly I heard Sensei's voice in my head. "Practice, practice." Somehow my body switched to automatic pilot. I rolled over to my left and heard the tire iron hit the floor where my head had been a millisecond earlier. I crawled to my knees in the darkness and stood up painfully.

Martin came at me again in a fury. I could

hear him babbling. This time I blocked his blow with both my arms and managed to twist and slip out of his grip. I used my Aikido training and did a fly-away pivot and kicked out in the dark.

The blind kick landed in his groin. He groaned loudly.

I heard rustling as he gathered himself to run at me again. I crouched down, getting as close to him as I could estimate, balancing myself with one foot far out in front of the other. I took a deep breath, as Sensei had demonstrated in class.

With a shout, Martin attacked me furiously. I bent my knees and grabbed hold of him with both hands.

"Damn you," I yelled and powered by all my strength, fear, and rage, I leveraged my body and pulled him over my head. What happened was exactly what was supposed to happen. The combined vectors of his attack and my pull catapulted him over the waist-high fence directly into the huge turning wheel's meshing gears.

Martin landed on the sharp wooden spikes with a sickening, pulpy thud. His long, horrible scream crescendoed with the thunder. I covered my ears to escape the sound.

As the lightning continued to flash, I stared up from the floor in horror. Martin's body, sprawled across the turning wheel, was being meshed slowly and painfully into the farther recesses of the gears. After a time, the wheel ground to a sudden, horrid stop.

I sank back against the wall, nearly blacking out from the searing pain in my shoulder and hands. I watched the wheel give a final lurch, then lock up, holding tight its deadly remnants.

Something hit me in the chest and fell to the ground. In the next lightning flash, I bent to retrieve it. It was Martin's bloody *Gott Mit Uns* belt buckle.

# Thirty-Seven:
# Day 6: Friday

The world breaks everyone and afterward
many are strong in the broken places.
But those that will not break it kills.
— ERNEST HEMINGWAY

The heat wave broke last night with the storm. Today was sunny and mild. I was sore as hell from the beating I took last night, but I felt snug and comfortable sitting in the Miata alongside Mitch, who was doing the driving. The car was still soggy in various places from last night's storm, but she was getting air-dried as we drove with the top down. Silently I wondered how long I'd have her after Poussant *et al,* at the IRS got done with me.

"This is a great car," Mitch said, "but I'm not used to this stick shift." He roughly up-shifted into fourth gear, speeding up to keep pace with Lake Shore Drive traffic.

We'd left in a big hurry after I'd explained

everything to Tom Joyce, who'd called several times wondering what was happening. But I made up my mind that I wasn't going to be late for this meeting at the IRS, no matter what happened. Mitch had insisted on coming with me for support and courage, and that was more than okay with me.

He interrupted my reverie. "This is criminal, DD. You've been almost killed half a dozen times in the last couple of days, and this servant of the people, this officious jerk, won't even postpone the inquisition for one day."

I liked my man to be supportive, and Mitch had just gotten an A-plus, but I was nervous and wanted to change the subject.

"At least the check that Matt is sending me will cover some of my IRS payment." I realized I couldn't change the subject. The IRS was all I could think about.

"Boy, you got Matt steamed last night," Mitch remarked. "Those didn't sound like executive words to me."

I had let Mitch listen in to my conversation with Matt last night. I had told Mitch the whole story about Matt, including the worst of it, and he was still gloating over the demise of his rival.

"He was sure pissed that you hadn't

recovered the manuscripts. But I think he was even madder about your statement to the cops that you were sure they were really Hemingway. 'The reserves for this fiasco will kill American's profits for years,' " Mitch falsettoed, paraphrasing Matt. " 'My bonuses are down the tubes. It's what I get for dealing with stupid amateurs like you.' "

"Yeah," I agreed, glad to finally be able to get myself out of the IRS rut. "I thought blood was going to spurt out of his ears when I told him how much he owed me. The bastard was ready to tell me where to put my invoice until I reminded him of the contract that Phil had put together at the start of this whole thing. I'll bet Phil's having some sleepless nights. I'm afraid to call him. Oh well, at least I'll get some money out of the whole awful deal."

"Didn't you talk to Phil last night?" Mitch asked.

"No. I called nine-one-one on my portable, and then later called Matt to cancel our meeting."

"DD, what do you think Martin did with those manuscripts? Do you think anyone will ever find them?"

"I wouldn't bet on it. Martin was a combination of a monomaniac and a miser, with a few other flaws thrown in for good measure. He was also smart. He put those manuscripts where they'd be safe but not easily found. Remember, his plan was to stash them away for a few more years before he rediscovered them. Now his secret's with him in his grave. On the other hand, I'm not sure I'd bet against the firm Matt hired to find them."

"Why was Sweeney after you? Why did he kill Beth and David's lawyer? Why didn't he just lay low?" Mitch asked.

Silently I blessed him for keeping the subject off the IRS. Now I knew how condemned prisoners must feel. "I don't think Martin counted on a couple of things. He had planned on trashing David's computer and removing any information about the manuscripts. He counted on everyone believing him and writing off the manuscripts as fake. No one would look too hard for fakes. But he didn't count on American Insurance being interested, he didn't count on my walking in on him as he was finishing searching David's place, probably for a receipt he'd had to sign when David gave him possession of the manuscripts for safekeeping. And he certainly hadn't counted on us taking David's laptop or on David telling Beth he'd given Martin the manuscripts. And at the last he told me he didn't know exactly what David had told his attorney but he had to kill him because David might have told him something important."

"So David did trust Beth, at least." Mitch said.

"Beth and Dorothy Jeffers had a long-term relationship. David was always a real shit, and I think he wanted what he couldn't have. He put a lot of effort into wooing Beth, and he finally showed her his treasure — the manuscripts — to help convince her. She knew that he gave them to Martin to examine and for safe-keeping, and Martin found out she knew. So Martin had no choice but to get rid of her."

My shoulder was hurting from last night's blow, and it screamed in pain when Mitch jerkily shifted into a hard left turn onto Franklin Street.

"Sorry about that," Mitch apologized.

"Mitch, listen." I reached over and turned up the volume on the radio as a newscaster reported Martin Sweeney's death.

. . . best known for his impersonation of Ernest Hemingway. With three English professors dead, all under mysterious circumstances, officials have canceled graduation ceremonies and announced they are closing the college for the remaining week of the semester. In a related matter, a college student, Debbie Majors, confessed that her sexual harassment suit against one of the dead professors, David Barnes, was a hoax. She said the scheme was cooked up by her lover, Bill Butler, head of the college English department who was jealous of Barnes and worried about losing the chairmanship of the department to him in an upcoming election. Authorities confirm that Butler was arrested yesterday on charges of obstruction of justice and suborning perjury.

"Wow. The entire department's down the tubes. Did you know anything about this?" Mitch asked as we approached our destination.

"No, this is the first I . . ." My explanation was aborted as Mitch jammed on the brakes, and we lurched forward.

"What's going on?" I yelled.

A bunch of police cars, lights flashing, and a squadrol blocked the front of the IRS building. Two bored-looking cops were redirecting traffic.

"Shit," I screamed in frustration. "This is going to make me late."

Mitch took a quick right turn to escape the melee and tried to soothe me. "Some taxpayer probably went postal. There's going to be so much commotion that all of the appointments will be late."

"Pull over right here," I directed.

"DD, that's illegal, but it's your call."

"Just do it," I said.

"Okay," Mitch conceded amiably and parked next to the fireplug. As he killed the engine, I scrambled out, gingerly balancing my purse along with stacks of messy files while struggling to keep the door from hitting the fireplug.

I ran across Franklin Street and felt Mitch hard on my heels.

I reached the building and the door opened in my face. Mr. Poussant appeared.

"Mr. Poussant," I stammered, feeling like a guilty fifth grader. "I can explain. These cops held me up or I would have been on time and . . ."

One of the cops interrupted. "Lady, if you have an appointment with this perp, you'll have to keep it in the lockup. This guy and his secretary had their own little business going, shaking down taxpayers to support their lifestyle."

It took a moment for this news to penetrate my frenzy. Gradually I felt my heart stop racing. As they led Mr. Poussant and Miss Wang away, I stuck my tongue out at them and gave them a great big raspberry.

Mitch and I linked arms and stood in the front of the gathering crowd, watching as first Mr. Poussant and then Miss Wang were led into separate squad cars. When the procession drove out of the lot, I waved good-bye, but the only one who returned my wave was the cop with a mustache riding shotgun.

"So," I said, smiling up at Mitch as we walked arm in arm back to the car. "I probably won't end up any better with another IRS agent, but then again, miracles do happen."

I glanced sideways at him, wondering if this was going to be a long-term relationship or just a torrid affair that would burn out overnight.

"Ha, no parking ticket," I noted with satisfaction as we approached the car. "It must be my lucky day."

"It is your lucky day, but not for that. The cops were too busy arresting Poussant to write out any tickets," Mitch retorted, opening the door for me.

"There. Know what I'd like?" he asked, grinning as he came around and got in the driver's side.

"What?"

"Let's take in a Cubs game on Sunday."

I frowned, remembering my mother's birthday. She'd been a brick, returning all six of Aunt Elizabeth's phone calls for me. "Why do men always have to ask the impossible? I can't. Sunday's my mother's birthday dinner."

"So? Bring her and the twins along." He smiled. "Later, I'll take you all out to dinner. We'll break open a bottle of champagne. Maybe two. I feel like celebrating."

"You mean you're willing to meet her?"

"Absolutely." He raised one arm and flexed his muscles. "Bring on the lions."

We pulled into traffic, and he shifted smoothly into fourth gear. As we purred along, the air felt refreshingly clean after last night's storm.

I breathed deeply, beginning to feel better. Mitch was good for me, and I found I couldn't stop smiling. He couldn't either. I knew I was going to have to tell him all about Scotty, but not today.

All things considered, except for Don's wife, Anne, who blamed me for what happened last night at Graue Mill, and would probably never speak to me again, all was right with the world. Still, somewhere deep inside the happiness, I could hear Auntie Elizabeth warning me to keep a sharp watch over my shoulder for the furies of the fates.

# AUTHOR'S AFTERWORD

All of the information on Ernest Hemingway presented in this novel was gleaned from biographies and from his own writings.

Hemingway was a native son of Oak Park, Illinois. After high school, he went to work as a reporter for the *Kansas City Star.* Six months later, he sailed to Europe on the ship *Chicago* with other Red Cross volunteers. He drove an ambulance and was wounded in Italy in July of 1918. According to some reports, he was where he shouldn't have been, breaking the rules by handing out chocolate and cigarettes to the men in the trenches. He recuperated in the American Red Cross Hospital in Milan and was later awarded the Italian Silver Medal for heroism.

After his discharge, he returned to Oak Park where his old English teacher, Frank Platt, arranged for him to speak to the

Burke Debating Club. On September 3, 1921, he married Hadley Richardson in the Horton Bay country church. She was eight years his senior. They sailed for Paris where the couple could live more inexpensively while Ernest developed his writing career. He was only twenty-two and not yet published. While in Paris, Hemingway worked as a correspondent for the *Toronto Star* and supplemented their income from Hadley's inheritance. He wrote short stories and poems, and associated with other authors such as Gertrude Stein and Ezra Pound, F. Scott Fitzgerald, John Dos Passos, James Joyce, and Ford Maddox Ford.

The incident of the missing valise is accurate. All but one short story had been packed into it when it disappeared from a Paris train station that day in December of 1922. Another story, "My Old Man," had been sent off to *Cosmopolitan*. Hemingway immediately returned from Lausanne, Switzerland, to search for the missing manuscripts. But, despite offering a small reward, nothing was ever recovered. Hemingway and his author friends blamed Hadley for the loss.

Hemingway and Hadley had a son, John Hadley Nicanor Hemingway, nicknamed Bumby, born March 16, 1924. Gertrude

Stein and Alice B. Toklas signed the baptismal certificate as joint godmothers. But Hemingway's marriage to Hadley was never quite the same, and they separated in 1926. Ernest filed for divorce on December 8, 1926. The divorce was final on April 14, 1927. After the divorce, Hemingway married Pauline Pfeiffer, who worked for Paris *Vogue,* on May 10, 1927. Hadley returned to Chicago and married a banker.

Hemingway's novel, *The Sun Also Rises,* was published in September of 1926. It was well received and sold almost 7,000 copies in the first two months. He assigned all the royalties to Hadley.

Hemingway married four times. He committed suicide in Ketchum, Idaho, on July 2, 1961, with a double-barreled Boss shotgun he'd used for shooting pigeons.

# BIBLIOGRAPHY

Baker, Carlos. *Ernest Hemingway, A Life Story.* New York: Charles Scribner's Sons, 1969.

Denis, Brian. *The True Gen: An Intimate Portrait of Ernest Hemingway by Those Who Knew Him.* New York: Grove Press, 1988.

DeVost, Nadine. "Hemingway's Girls: Unnaming and Renaming Hemingway's female characters." *Hemingway Review,* Fall 1994.

Griffin, Peter. *Along With Youth: Hemingway, The Early Years.* New York: Oxford University Press, 1985.

Hemingway, Ernest. *A Moveable Feast.* New York: Charles Scribner's Sons, 1964.

Hemingway's two Love Poems and "Hemingway in Cuba," by Robert Manning. *The Atlantic Monthly,* August, 1965.

Hotchner, A. E. *Papa Hemingway: A Per-*

*sonal Memoir.* New York: Random House, 1965.

Lyttle, Richard B. *Ernest Hemingway: The Life and the Legend.* New York: Atheneum, 1992.

Manning, Robert. "Hemingway in Cuba," and Hemingway's two "Love Poems." *The Atlantic Monthly,* August 1965.

Meyers, Jeffrey. *Hemingway: A Biography.* New York: Harper & Row, 1985.

McLendon, James. *Papa: Hemingway in Key West.* Key West, FL: Langley Press, 1990.

Miller, Linda Patterson, ed. *Letters from the Lost Generation: Gerald and Sara Murphy and Friends.* Piscataway, NJ: Rutgers University Press, 1991.

Murphy, Michael. *Hemingsteen, A Novel Based on the Life of Ernest Hemingway.* Shropshire, UK: Autolycus Press, 1977.

Reynolds, Michael. *Hemingway, The Paris Years.* Oxford, UK: Blackwell, 1989.

Plimpton, George, ed., "Interview with Ernest Hemingway," *Writers At Work: The Paris Review Interviews,* Second Series. New York: Viking Press, 1963.

# PAPA DOBLÉ

### HEMINGWAY'S DAIQUIRI

As served in La Florida, Havana, Cuba
2 1/2 jiggers Bacardi White Label Rum
Juice: 2 Limes
1/2 Grapefruit
6 drops maraschino cherry juice

Place in electric mixer over shaved ice. Whirl
vigorously and serve foaming.

# ABOUT THE AUTHOR

Chicago native **Diane Gilbert Madsen** brings a real feel for the Windy City to her DD McGil Literati Mystery series. Madsen attended the University of Chicago and earned an M.A. in seventeenth-century English literature from Roosevelt University. She was Director of Economic Development for the State of Illinois and oversaw the Tourism and Illinois Film Office during the time *The Blues Brothers* was filmed. She also ran her own consulting business and is listed in *Who's Who in Finance and Industry* and the *World Who's Who of Women.*

Fascinated by crime, history, and business, her interest in writing murder mysteries was sparked when she met the suspect in a murder that occurred near her home. The suspect was convicted, then later exonerated of the crime, and the encounter caused her to rethink how people form their first impressions of murder suspects.

Recently Diane and her husband Tom moved to Florida, where they live at Twin Ponds, a five-acre wildlife sanctuary. Check the latest news at http//www.dianegilbert madsen.com

We hope you have enjoyed this Large Print book. Other Thorndike, Wheeler, Kennebec, and Chivers Press Large Print books are available at your library or directly from the publishers.

For information about current and upcoming titles, please call or write, without obligation, to:

Publisher
Thorndike Press
295 Kennedy Memorial Drive
Waterville, ME 04901
Tel. (800) 223-1244

or visit our Web site at:

http://gale.cengage.com/thorndike

OR

Chivers Large Print
published by AudioGO Ltd
St James House, The Square
Lower Bristol Road
Bath BA2 3SB
England
Tel. +44(0) 800 136919
www.audiogo.co.uk

All our Large Print titles are designed for easy reading, and all our books are made to last.